FRAN

INN FO

Created & Written
by

"Frank Julius" Csenki

www.frankjulius.com

Copyright © JANUARY 2019 Frank Julius Csenki.

Published by

FRANK JULIUS BOOKS

This book is a work of fiction. All the characters,
organizations, and events portrayed in this novel are
either products of the author's imagination or are used
fictitiously

ISBN 978-09959718-0-6

1

FRANK JULIUS BOOKS

BLOOD DICE
(Historical Fiction – Crime Suspense Thriller)

MOSAIC LIFE TILES
(Autobiographic Anthology Series 1)

THE RED JEWEL
(Historical Fiction – Crime Suspense Thriller)

INN FORMATION
(Historical Fiction – Crime Suspense Thriller)

MOSAIC LIFE SQUARES
(Autobiographic Anthology Series 2)

COMING SUMMER 2019

FRANK JULIUS

INN FORMATION

A NOVEL

DEDICATED TO MY BROTHER

JIM

CHAPTER

ONE

M   A   S   A   K   R

Present day – Cairo Egypt.

"Twenty years in all to build The Great Pyramid of Giza," the minister said.

Billy Simpson lifted the Sikorsky chopper off the rooftop helipad of the Jewel of the Pharaohs resort complex. Within five minutes Billy had the helicopter flying above the Giza plateau.

Twenty years in all to build The Great Pyramid of Giza, somehow, I don't think so! Eldon thought as they circled above.

Billy; Eldon and Kimberley's pilot, brought the chopper directly over the Great Pyramid of Giza. It had stood the test of time for the past four thousand years, towering 481 feet high over the Egyptian desert sands,

Accompanying Eldon, Kimberley and Billy was Nasser Agopian; the Egyptian Minister of State for Antiquities Affairs, a most honored position of the highest regard within the government. It not only was a critical ministerial post but one that required a Ph.D. in Egyptology and Nasser was, in fact, that and more.

The site below was in a word; breathtaking. Not just because of the view from seven hundred fifty feet looking down at the majesty of the only remaining seven wonders of the ancient world, but what unfolded in the vista to behold.

Kimberley held onto Eldon's hand as Billy banked the chopper circling the great pyramid. Both Eldon and Kimberley gazed down in awe not finding the words to justify the view. The cloudless afternoon sky and the burning Egyptian sun made for the bright clear skies as far as the eye could see. Humanity's history, coming into view, the endless sprawl of Cairo, the never-ending Nile River flowing through the eternal sands of time. Here, beside the deep Egyptian desert of the Pharaohs is where Eldon and Kimberley built their new hotel. A land where one could look upon four thousand years of history and development.

Eldon gazed out the window, thinking, *it was, in fact, possible for a human to stand with one foot in the 21st century and the other foot firmly planted in the 4th dynasty of 2560 BC. The line was visible, where the city stopped, and the Giza plateau began, now this was fantastic!*

Eldon slid closer in beside Kimberley, wrapping his arm around her shoulder, holding her as the chopper banked.

"Just fantastic, what a sight," Eldon whispered into Kimberley's ear. She reacted, gently squeezing his hand laying in her lap.

"It's amazing hon, just imagine being here when

this was being built, the thousands of workers must have been something!" She turned her head and pecked Eldon on his cheek.

As they looked out of the chopper, Agopian had been providing the running commentary. Naturally, Eldon had not invited the minister along to be their private tour guide. No, it was more of a courtesy extended to Minister Agopian thanking him for all the countless obstacles he had moved out of their way. He had proven invaluable in eliminating lingering barriers concerning construction near antiquities. Agopian got the Egyptian government to modify the proximity threshold laws allowing for their resort's geographical placement. Eldon and Kimberley's resort opened on schedule here in Cairo at the foot of the pyramids. Eldon's invitation for the minister to join him and Kimberley this afternoon was a way of bringing Agopian closer into their world, in forging a friendship for years to come.

Kimberley, with her diplomatic expertise grounded in her former career with the US State Department and with Eldon's ever-growing international hotel footprint, had become a formidable team that any government official would be proud to include in his or her circle of influential friends.

Minister Agopian continued, "Yes the engineering is mind-boggling as you especially, can well appreciate Eldon."

Eldon's hotel and resort empire; Holiday Jewel Hotels and Casinos, was global, from America to Europe and Asia. Now with the recent opening of The Jewel of the Pharaohs Resort and Spa, HJHC was firmly anchored in North Africa, here in the majestic city of Cairo, honoring the legacy of the Pharaohs.

Eldon's building and architectural savvy certainly were not lost upon Nasser. No, Nasser well understood Eldon's appreciation for the complexities in building mega resort properties, even with today's high-tech computer-assisted design capabilities. He believed that Eldon realized, no matter how magnificent his resort properties might be the world over, nothing on earth compared to the wonder and mystery of this ancient marvel below.

Nasser Agopian continued with his informative commentary.

"Our most accurate estimates calculate two million stone blocks, all of various sizes but some weighing several tons, and yet forming perfectly straight edges on all four sides." Eldon took it all in, thinking, *two million stone blocks, each weighing as much as several pickup trucks, right.*

"Interestingly enough," Agopian went on, "There are nine sides to the great pyramid of Giza. You mustn't forget about the base, that is a side as well. Yes, I know most of the world does not know or even think of this, but in fact, it does have nine sides."

Eldon kept listening intently, now it was getting fascinating, he hadn't heard about the nine sides of the five-sided Great Pyramid until just now.

"It first came to light back in the 1930s, and it was a fluke. A photograph taken by a Royal Airforce flyover of the pyramids during the autumnal equinox showed the south side of the great pyramid split into two halves: one half in the dark the other in the light. This revelation happens when the sun reaches a certain angle, and for only a few seconds exposing the two halves of the side. And this will just happen twice a year, during the equinoxial days when the sun rises in the far east. Think of how much more complicated this added geometric design makes the building of the pyramid. Factor in that no two blocks of stone are alike, and it makes the slightly bent two sections of each side an engineering marvel.

Eldon took it all in, calculating in his head while Nasser spoke. Eldon was no Egyptologist, but he had a head for figures and compilation of statistics needing to fit into the reality on the ground. A skeptic to be sure, challenging everything until no stone was left unturned, this was his makeup, helpless to think otherwise. For Eldon to believe in anything, the puzzle had to be complete, or at the very least the missing pieces identified, isolated, and re-associated into the mix.

"Now just imagine this," Agopian said. "To keep this eight-sided edifice on the four sides of the base during construction with an accuracy down to the centimeter or perhaps even the millimeter would be extremely difficult even with modern day architectural engineering software."

Eldon and Kimberley looked at one another as the Minister spoke. Kimberley could tell that Eldon was in his skeptical mood, tightening his forehead muscles, pulling his eyebrows together in a look nothing short of *now that's unbelievable* expression taking over his face.

Kimberley just smiled back at her husband, rolling her eyes, suggesting that he leave this alone for now. Agopian was behind both Kimberley and Eldon, so the look on Eldon's face wasn't something the minister had to concern himself with on this trip, but Eldon would soon enough have a question or two for Nasser when the time was right. She wasn't sure just exactly what portion of Nasser's commentary prompted Eldon's *give me a break* reaction, but she well knew that her husband's computer brain was in gear and something was making those gears grind.

Eldon, in fact, wasn't doubting the fine details concerning the methodology in building the great pyramid of Giza. No, it wasn't any of that. What didn't sit just right with Eldon was the official stance on the timing and duration in building the magnificent structure. In his mind twenty years just wasn't cutting the mustard, and yet the Department of State for Antiquities Affairs officially claimed only twenty years. In Eldon's thinking, to build such a structure in that short amount of time would be impossible, which raised another question, why did the Ministry insist upon just twenty years? That he would need to research.

As Agopian had been speaking, Eldon's mind was taking in the stats and figures, calculating and coming to obviously questionable conclusions, at least in the way Eldon saw things.

Billy brought the chopper around, circling the great structure once again.

Eldon thought, *two million blocks, twenty years. Okay, let's see…ten years is three thousand six hundred fifty days, twenty years would be seven thousand three hundred days.*

He then extrapolated further with a given assumption.

Say the work continued non-stop every day for twenty years. Factoring in an assumption that the workers theoretically did twelve hours each day before the onset of darkness, that would then be seven thousand three hundred days times 12 hours each day. That is then seven hundred twenty minutes daily, times the seven thousand three hundred days for the twenty years would equal five million two hundred fifty-six thousand minutes in all the twenty years of working twelve-hour days.

So, what did that mean? And this was the part where things started going awry.

That meant the two million stones, some weighing several tons, would have to have been placed at a blistering non-stop pace, one stone every two and a half minutes! Not just put down in place, but precisely into space in the exact spot that one stone would occupy for the next four and a half thousand years. Not to mention the several-hundred-mile trip the rock first had to make from the quarry to where the pyramid stood. Oh, and by the way… there were two million blocks that needed quarrying and transportation to the building site."

This was something Eldon was having some difficulty believing. No, he had no problem with the content and wondrous construction, with which Eldon had to be honest about, did boggled his mind, but the insistence of twenty years, well that was too much for Eldon.

He'd let Kimberley in on this later in the day, but he already knew just by the look on her face that she could hardly wait. The events of this day were lining up to make for another one of those lovely discussions over a glass of wine or two this evening at their newly opened mega-resort.

Well, what better place than Cairo was there to discuss the building of the pyramids with his gorgeous wife anyway? This was turning out to be an exciting day." Eldon thought as Billy brought the powerful Sikorsky company chopper around for one more pass over the great pyramid.

"Look hon, here come the school kids from Fort Lauderdale and West Palm Beach," Kimberley said as they circled around for one last pass before heading back to the hotel.

Holiday Jewel Hotels and Casinos' company offices and world headquarters are in Fort Lauderdale Florida. Lately, over the past quarter, there had been a great deal of news and press about the company's expansion into Egypt with the building of their new mega-resort complex; The Cairo Jewel of the Pharaohs Resort and Spa. Both Eldon and Kimberley had been in the public eye back home in Florida over this emerging flap. The move into Egypt was turning out to be a controversial one with some influential people back home questioning the soundness of this new venture.

There were many pundits on both sides of the thinking. Some questioned the financial and political stability of the country due to the recent turmoil over the past few years emanating from the fallout of the Arab Spring, the rise of the Muslim Brotherhood and subsequent banning of the organization, but what of its underpinnings?

Some would ask; a major American hotel and casino company in Egypt? Egypt predominantly Muslim secular, but nevertheless, ninety percent of the population was Sunni Muslim. Many felt that a resort hotel casino operation in an Islamic state would be looked upon as a dangerous business, not one to be amongst the people of Allah.

Eldon, of course, disagreed with those pundits on the left. Egypt already had several well-established hotel-casino operations throughout the country, but none would be as extravagant and opulent as The Jewel of the Pharaohs.

But others on the right, well…times were changing, and Egypt was now stably grounded, with Mubarak long gone, and tourism once again on the rise, Eldon felt the timing was right to expand his global reach. He believed in the power and ability of tourism to bring the world together in an atmosphere of international cooperation and friendship. This was his philosophy.

He had been proven right many a time in his rise to corporate leadership invoking his company's management style and ethics. Holiday Jewel Hotels and Casinos was now an international family destination resort company. Cairo would only enhance his company's stance and reputation. TJOTF (The Jewel of the Pharaohs) could bring the world together like no other hotel resort operation could match in all of Egypt and perhaps in the entire middle east. Even the ultra-luxury resorts in Dubai and Abu Dhabi had taken notice of Eldon and Kimberley's newly opened resort in Cairo.

Since having taken the business over from his late father, Eldon Davis had turned Holiday Jewel Hotels and Casinos into one of the most successful hotel resort operations in the history of the hospitality industry. Eldon now had hotels in most western countries as well as the new Russian Federation in Moscow where HJHC operated three large hotel and casino complexes including the world-famous Red Jewel, the jewel of Moscow in many more ways than what its name alone suggested.

He and Kimberley were now a force within the industry to be sure. Kimberley, with her international former State department connections and diplomatic reach, had opened doors for their company that had remained closed to Eldon before they teamed up to become the predominant global magnates that they now found themselves to be.

Eldon had hoped that his daughter Cathy, and Kimberley's stepdaughter would follow in his footsteps taking over HJHC when the time came. Unfortunately, that flame's light was dimming year after year. Cathy; his loving daughter had chosen a different path. Her passion was medicine. Nevertheless, Eldon was so very proud of his one and only daughter, now a thirtysomething, and well established with her own medical practice in plastic and reconstructive surgery. Cathy Davis had become a surgeon, but Eldon still felt in his heart that when the time came, Cathy would step in and guide Holiday Jewel Hotels and Casinos into the future, at least become its chairperson. Eldon and Kimberley recently considered taking the company public. That was a real possibility and would solve a few problems while allowing their legacy to live on with Cathy being on the board as Chairman and CEO, at arm's length perhaps, but still very much involved.

The press back in Florida over the past year had been for some unknown reason, perhaps just leaning left, the source of some grief over his resort hotel opening. Kimberley and Eldon decided to do something about the negative press they'd been getting. But to put an end to it, Eldon went to the root and the future in one fell swoop. He always thought ahead when taking actionable decisions. He envisioned the outcome regarding future rewards, seeds planted today, grabbing root tomorrow and flowering for many years to come.

They developed an ingenious proactive plan involving the southern Florida community of today and the future. Upon the presentation of their idea, Eldon and Kimberley convinced the local Board of Education to buy in, thereby reducing HJHC's upfront expenses. This move also qualified their sponsorship as an educational contribution making it eligible as a tax write-off.

HJHC launched their primary promotional campaign combining middle school education, industry, and tourism, in the spirit of international cooperation. This building of goodwill was designed to reach across the ocean from Florida to Cairo. Kimberley and Eldon's promotional campaign was time-tested and proven to be successful. Given the right amount of dedication and management expertise, it was designed to take hold in the shaping the American psyche eventually allowing for the buy-in to the expansion of his company into the Egyptian market.

Making an investment with today's dollars resulting in paybacks many times over in the future of his company. Holiday Jewel Hotels and Casinos of Fort Lauderdale embraced both the new world and the ancient world by sponsoring a six-month student exchange program that would have American school children, grades seven through eight traveling to Egypt for a Nile River cruise combined with a visit to the pyramids.

Kimberley set up rotating trips, one every two months seeing American students visiting Egypt, all expenses paid by Eldon and Kimberley's company as an educational and cultural exchange experience. Egyptian children of the same ages would then visit Florida's theme parks and Cape Canaveral while staying at Holiday Jewel Hotels throughout Florida.

Nasser Agopian had gotten wind of this project since it was a cultural exchange and a perfect fit for his bailiwick. Nasser was fully invested personally into this cultural exchange expounding in national print media and television on the generosities of HJHC. The first of these rotating cultural exchange trips was ongoing this very day.

Billy descended a couple hundred feet so that Kimberley, Eldon, and Nasser could get a better view of the buses carrying the children that were soon to disembark and touch the great pyramid of Giza.

Billy hovered the chopper just far enough off at a distance with a clear view of the tour buses carrying the school children making their approach up the road leading to the vast bus parking area. Kimberley was surprised though.

She remarked to Eldon. "Hon look at those buses, there are four of them Eldon, they all seem to be together. There are only supposed to be eighty children on this first trip, that would only require two tour buses, including the minders. I wonder why the need for the extra two buses?"

"Maybe they sent along an extra two in case the buses break down, just as a super safety precaution, not wanting to take a chance on having the kids stranded," Eldon replied, kind of being puzzled himself.

Nasser piped in on Kimberley's question. "I know the reason, for the extra buses Kimberley."

"What is it, Nasser?" Kimberley asked, looking back at Nasser and then quickly glancing back out through the window down into the parking lot as the four tour buses were slowing down.

"We decided it would be nice to pair the children up with same age kids from one of our middle-grade schools in Cairo. Although it was a last-minute decision, we felt it would enhance the American children's outing experience, with a greater appreciation for the cultural exchange aspect. All the Egyptian children paired with the US kids speak English, so we have no language barrier issues, but it is a true cultural exchange and affords an environment of instant friends in the making. So instead of eighty kids, and two buses, we have a total of one hundred sixty kids and four tour buses on this excursion to the pyramids." Nasser finished saying with a huge grin on his face, and sparkling eyes, expressing excitement that he came up with this idea.

Kimberley and Eldon both looked back towards Nasser, expressing their approval.

Suddenly, loud deafening explosions filled the air around the chopper. *What, what was happening?* Everyone thought.

Billy steadied the chopper, then looking down at the parking lot they became horrified. There was the first explosion that sent a shockwave and fireball high up into the air, with flying debris almost reaching the height of the Sikorsky. Billy banked away. Then another explosion causing a huge fireball, filling the sky in front of the chopper, and then another blast.

"Oh my god! Oh my god! Eldon. Eldon! Oh my god, Eldon!" Kimberley was screaming. She started shaking uncontrollably, she couldn't contain herself. Eldon held onto her.

Eldon too was mortified as he looked out the window of the chopper. They had lost count of the number of explosions, perhaps five, maybe six or even more. The carnage that lay below was beyond horrific. All four buses had been demolished, just shards of metal remained. Shattered glass everywhere and body parts were strewn across the parking lot. Everyone in the chopper was in a state of shock. The unthinkable had happened. Or was it? This wasn't the first time.

Kimberley crying out, about to lose control of her mind, "the children, the children!"

"Billy take us down now!" Eldon yelled to Billy. Billy knew what to do instinctively. Billy was Eldon and Kimberley's pilot and bodyguard. Billy was ex-navy. A naval aviator, F14 Tomcat fighter pilot, congressional medal of honor recipient. Billy was their guardian angel, many times over in the past and now.

"Take us down Billy, we need to see who we can help!" Eldon was yelling at Billy, but Billy was just two seconds away from landing the chopper. People around the pyramids ran in all directions. Some to get as far away from the scene as possible and some running in to help, while some just stood off and watched the carnage. There was blood everywhere that one looked. Eldon, Kimberley, and Nasser bolted out of the chopper running to see if they could find survivors. After securing the helicopter, Billy ran to the scene scouring the area for survivors.

Body parts lay scattered for fifty yards in all directions. The tops of the four buses were either blown off or blown to bits with gaping holes in the roofs. Axels and wheels, bus seat cushions and entire rows of seats were thrown about. There were severed heads on the ground as well. The carnage was beyond, beyond.

The children who survived, some crying out in agony, others just stunned, immobilized and shell-shocked not knowing what had happened or even if they were alive or dead. Some had missing limbs, arms blown off, others blinded and laying on the ground yelling out in pain, while others still trapped in their seats with shrapnel having cut through them.

They scattered covering as much area as they could, running through the debris, searching for survivors. As far as Kimberley could tell, with so many body parts covering the ground, most everyone on the buses was killed.

"Kimberley, over here," Eldon yelled, help me with this child.

Eldon was holding a little girl who had half her face blown in, her jaw partially hanging by face skin, but breathing. She was also missing her left arm from the elbow down. She looked to be one of the Egyptian children. Holding onto the girl, cradling her in his lap, the bus from where she was thrown erupted with a second explosion sending another shockwave and shrapnel flying. The situation was pure mayhem.

"Eldon, I found another one alive," Nasser cried

out.

A Caucasian boy, most likely one of the American children, looked to have a severe head injury from where he was bleeding profusely. He also suffered a leg wound, with what looked like part of a bus-seat armrest sticking through his thigh, and left hand was missing fingers, but he was alive, just barely.

Billy came running over to Nasser to help him with his survivor. Eldon was already looking after the girl he found clinging onto life. Confusion was everywhere. Everyone was asking everyone for help. "Let's get them both into the chopper and to a trauma unit," Billy yelled as secondary fuel explosions went off around them.

There was no time to waste, moving as fast as humanly possible picking up three more children, altogether one boy and four girls. They had no stretchers, Eldon, Billy, Kimberley, and Nasser were all now covered in blood after carrying the children in their arms, making their way to the chopper. Billy lifted the Sikorsky off the ground as soon as he could, heading for Cairo General Hospital. His fighter pilot instincts kicked in, flying the chopper with military awareness and evasive tactics. He wasn't sure what was coming next, soon they could all be under attack by RPGs (rocket-propelled grenades) or even stinger anti-aircraft missiles!

"This is private Helo, HJHC 01, requesting emergency air clearance vector to Cairo General Hospital Air Ambulance priority protocol. We are inbounding with five, repeat five, critically injured bomb trauma cases ages twelve to fourteen. Requesting immediate access. ETA five minutes,"

Billy called in on Cairo air ambulance emergency channel.

"This is Cairo General Hospital air ambulance dispatch control, you are cleared to land on helipad number 1, trauma teams being readied to assist on your landing."

Kimberley held onto her unconscious child, alive, another girl, her right leg mangled, with her right foot wholly blown off her leg. Kimberley had applied a tourniquet to the child's leg to arrest the bleeding, but time was of the essence, she was just barely breathing, not to mention the piece of shrapnel still sticking out of her right eye.

Kimberley trembled, she stared at her husband Eldon, her eyes wide open but seeing only oblivion.

"Eldon, what is happening?" Kimberley asked, with terror filling her eyes looking at her husband. Eldon choked back his tears looking at his wife, holding onto a child. Who knows whose child it was, at this moment in time, the child was his and still breathing. Eldon's eyes flushed with tears, his vision blurred.

Nasser and Eldon looked at one another, both men cried openly, tears mixed in with blood streaming down their faces. Nasser held onto the American boy, bleeding badly from his head. The boy was unconscious, still clinging to life, the armrest lodged in his thigh, and hand bleeding badly having lost three fingers.

The next few minutes seemed to be taking forever. When urgency is needed, time itself has a way of stretching just out of reach. Cairo General finally came into view. Billy keyed in on the helipad.

Neither Kimberley or Eldon looked out, they just held onto their children as did Agopian, waiting to feel the chopper touch down.

A huge sigh of relief came over Billy to see that the hospital had dispatched several trauma teams already waiting for his arrival by the helipad. Billy's bloody hands guided the chopper onto the rooftop helipad, and the teams got into action.

Eldon and Kimberley were not about to part with their kids, they followed the trauma teams to hospital emergency. They were now involved, and nothing in this world was going to separate them from these children. Agopian too snapped into action using his ministerial powers arranging for additional emergency response units to the bomb scene.

Billy didn't even think twice, he knew what had to be done. His mission in life on this day was to save more lives. More children needed immediate care. Billy would be there to save as many lives as God would allow him to over the next several hours. He lifted off and was flying back to the scene not ten seconds after he was cleared to go by the trauma team.

As they had been inbound holding onto the bloodied children, some clinging on to their dear lives by just a thread, Eldon, Kimberley, and Agopian had stared at each other, not saying a word but communicating crystal clearly. There were no words needed, they all knew what had happened, and it had happened again, but this time they were right in the middle of the carnage.

The events that darkened this day were reminiscent of the November 17, 1997, Luxor Massacre at Deir el-Bahari. On that day in this country's history, sixty-two tourists were slaughtered. That was pure terrorism with four Egyptians and fifty-eight foreigners, all tourists, meeting their deaths at the hands of six Islamic gunmen who stormed the Mortuary Temple of Hatshepsut killing all.

Many victims were disemboweled having been chopped up with machetes, with notes stuck inside the mutilated bodies praising Islam and demanding the release of Omar Abdel Rahman; *The Blind Sheikh*. The US imprisoned the Sheikh, for his involvement in the 1993 bombing of the world trade center in New York City.

It had happened again, but this time it was mainly children, Egyptian and American kids. Eldon and Kimberley were lost for words. *These precious kids, did Eldon and Kimberley bring this about?* They sat silently staring at one another, both thinking how they had convinced the local school board to buy into this cultural exchange program, for it to end like this, the world had to be spinning out of control. They both sobbed holding onto the precious torn and mutilated children.

But that wasn't all of it. Not so long ago on May 26th of 2017, another bus attack happened. It was on a group of Coptic Christians on their way to a Minya Monastery, when their bus was blocked and surrounded by a large group of Islamic ISIS terrorists bent on killing Christians. The gunmen, all dressed in military uniforms and masks, opened, firing on the bus, killing twenty-eight people including children. And why did that happen? Only because they were

Christians. ISIS after claiming ownership for the slaughter stated that under Sharia law, protection for Christians was not given.

"Eldon, what are we going to do? Eldon, Eldon, what is happening to our world Eldon! Kimberley cried grasping for anything, anything at all from her husband. "What in god's name are we to do Eldon…what?"

Eldon wasn't a religious man but found himself through life sitting on the fence. There were days when he thought he was a believer and there were days when god was impossible. He was raised Christian Presbyterian as was Kimberley, but Eldon hadn't set foot inside a church to pray since he was nine.

Today, he could find no words to express his grief and sorrow. The situation was just too overwhelming. For the first time in his life, Eldon was at a loss finding the words in response to his wife to make things right.

He reached out his blood-soaked hand towards Kimberley. She took his hand into hers. They held onto the children, laying limply in their laps. She squeezed her husband's hand, holding it tightly, finding the strength and reassurance she needed.

Both knew, when the fog cleared, there would be time to sort things out. Right now, nothing needed to be said.

Lost in the rotating thumping sound of the chopper-blades filling the still open fuselage, Eldon thought, *perhaps the Florida news media did have a point to make, and he should have listened. Maybe that point was made today.*

INN FORMATION

He could not escape thinking, *the lives lost today was because of his and Kimberley's desire to bring cultures together, but mainly because of his drive to grow his company's expansion into Egypt. He intended to build trust and cooperation. Instead, death and despair shattered their lives...* his greatest challenge yet.

What Kimberley and Eldon could not have known was that all the answers to all their questions were destined to come through the lives of the two Egyptian girls they held onto so desperately, as Billy brought the chopper gently down onto the rooftop helipad of Cairo General Hospital.

MASAKR

***

CHAPTER

TWO

RETRVL

2002 – Baghdad Iraq

The Franciscan Private School for Boys is nestled along the southern slope of the plateau leading to the shores of Lake Geneva. It offers a majestic panoramic view of the lake and the surrounding Alps. The grandeur of this setting is complemented with an equally broad philosophy to applied education built into an environment of strictly structured learning that is The Franciscan mantra for academic achievement.

Over centuries, several of humanity's greatest thinkers and philosophers, among them Voltaire and Rousseau had made their way to Lausanne. This Swiss city situated in the French-speaking region of the country laid claim to some of the most exclusive and respected private schools, boarding schools, and colleges in Europe.

Deep thinkers throughout European history left their marks of wisdom on the shores of Lake Geneva for future generations to ponder and opine upon the ways of the world.

Of the one hundred twenty-five thousand

residents calling Lausanne home, six percent were Muslim, approximately, seventy-five hundred. Zara Ahmed, age fifteen and his brother Arish Ahmed, age sixteen were two of the six percent, but they were resident students of the private school for boys.

Faaz Ahmed, father to the boys Zara and Arish had decided to allow his sons an educational environment unlike anything offered or available in Saddam Hussein's Iraq of the year 1998. It wasn't due to lack of quality, no, Iraqi schools and universities were of the finest since Saddam had become the president of Iraq. Faaz's reasoning for his boys to experience European life was so they possessed the ability to blend in with western society. To be fully versed in their customs and try understanding the thinking of European and American psyche.

Faaz carefully studied the choices in exposing his sons to western style education but looked for an institution and environment without the trappings of religious overlords.

The school choices in Switzerland seemed most appropriate in providing this secular learning atmosphere for Zara and Arish, while still allowing their core beliefs to remain firmly anchored in the teachings of Muhammed and the Sunni Muslim faith. Here in Lausanne the Sunni Imam of the local Mosque would personally ensure his sons' minds focused on the teachings of Islam while learning the ways of the world, God willing.

Faaz Ahmed; an Iraqi lawyer-businessman was well established in Saddam's Iraq. Faaz and his family enjoyed the lavish generosities Saddam had bestowed upon his family ever since Saddam came to power as the head of the Ba'ath party.

Faaz, became a man of means in Baghdad, lacking for nothing. He was a Sunni and a devoted follower of Saddam Hussein's philosophy in governing Iraq and its people, no matter how brutal Saddam's rule over his people became.

When Saddam fully acquired leadership of The Ba'ath party in 1979 and became the President of Iraq, Saddam took notice of fellow Sunni Muslim; Faaz Ahmed, a member of the Ba'ath party and Saddam's supporter. Saddam invited Faaz under his umbrella as his personal lawyer, thereby both men prospering over the coming years with Saddam issuing the directives, and Faaz approving the legalities as Saddam saw fit to govern.

Saddam held a special appreciation for lawyers in general. The main reason being he too aspired in becoming a lawyer while attending school in Egypt. Those were the scholastically challenging years between 1960 and 1963 where Saddam finished high school but was unsuccessful in pursuing a law degree.

Saddam had a special appreciation for peers who became authorities of the law, and thus a personal admirer of Faaz's abilities in justifying almost anything that Saddam decided to decree. To some extent Faaz enjoyed an element of immunity because he was not officially a government civil servant, acting only as legal counsel and adviser to Saddam while addressing the decrees of the Ba'ath party governing Iraq.

Ironically, Faaz's loyalty and fealty to Saddam would be tested in 1991 during "Desert Storm." This was a time in Iraq's history when Faaz was convinced Saddam's reign would end, but much to Faaz's surprise and to the world's astonishment, the

Americans did not remove Saddam from power. Even to this day, Faaz couldn't understand why the American Coalition led armies commanded by General Schwarzkopf, signed the cease-fire agreement on March 3rd, 1991. It had been almost ten years ago, under that green army tent just south of Basra in the Iraqi desert, that Iraq agreed to a complete unconditional surrender, but by the will of Allah, did not include the removal of Saddam Hussein.

Saddam remained the ruler of Iraq, and Faaz's relationship to Saddam Hussein grew in both loyalty and devotion along with his growing overall admiration for the president. Faaz Ahmed prospered immensely. Faaz was one of Saddam's chosen to live a life of luxury and extravagance, in Saddam's Iraq.

Faaz, decided in January of 1998, to enroll his two sons Zara and Arish to private boarding school in Switzerland. But in four years, the changing times had brought about new predictions in the future of Iraq. He decided to continue shaping the lives of his sons by the will of Allah, bring them home, and groom both boys as centerpieces of destiny, the likes of which the world has never known, God willing.

With having spent four years learning in Switzerland, both boys now speaking fluent English, French, and Mesopotamian Arabic; their mother tongue, equipped them both with a certain comfort level and competence required for their worldly duties as Faaz saw fit.

The brothers' devotion to their father and to honor his wishes grew ever stronger over the years, preparing them both in accepting their father's prescribed directions in life to be bestowed upon them and followed as it was Allah's will.

Faaz Ahmed acted. From his home in Baghdad, he would call his sons' school in Switzerland. He reached for his phone and dialed the number to The Franciscan Private School for Boys in Lausanne.

"Good morning, The Franciscan School for Boys, Michael speaking, how may I help you?" the male voice answered.

"Yes, peace be upon you, Michael and good morning, I am calling from Baghdad. This is Faaz Ahmed, my sons are students at your school, I will need to speak with the headmaster/school administrator," Faaz replied.

"Mr. Ahmed, please hold the line for one moment while I see if Doctor Bern is available to take your call."

"Thank you, Michael, I will hold for a moment," replied Faaz.

"I'm putting you through right away Mr. Ahmed, good day and peace be upon you," replied Michael in courteous customary fashion to Faaz.

"Doctor. Bern speaking, good morning Mr. Ahmed, and peace be upon you, how can I be of service?" Bern said.

"Doctor Bern, peace be upon you. Thank you for taking my call since I am calling on an urgent matter concerning my two boys at The Franciscan under your fine school's tutelage. I am afraid I will have to curtail my sons' ongoing attendance in Lausanne and bring them home, *tout de suite* as they say in French."

"Mr. Ahmed, we at The Franciscan can certainly understand the developing critical situation unfolding on the world stage concerning Iraq and the international community. Whatever your wishes may be in doing what you feel is best for your sons is what we will mirror and put forth as your wishes," replied Bern.

"How would you like us to proceed with your wishes, sir?" Bern further asked of Faaz Ahmed.

"I will speak in private with my two boys. Please arrange to facilitate a private video conferencing session in one of your secure rooms for my boys to receive my call at 4:00 PM your time today. Is this something you can arrange Doctor Bern?" Ahmed asked.

"Consider it done Mr. Ahmed, I will have Zara and Arish ready to receive your video conferencing call in private at exactly 4:00 PM this afternoon."

"I appreciate your immediate concern and cooperation, Doctor Bern, and may I add how pleased I have been with your school's academic program over the past number of years. Yes indeed, the excellence in education and character development you have so lovingly administered to Zara, and Arish has been exemplary. God be with you and peace be upon you, Doctor Bern. I will call promptly at 4:00 PM Lausanne time. Good Day," and with that, the call ended.

Faaz Ahmed, being both a scholar and lawyer having himself received his schooling in London England was a man not to be underestimated as time would prove. He returned home after graduation from the London Academy and went on to earn his law degree from the University of Baghdad.

He was already a young lawyer, working for the

Ba'ath party shortly after Saddam took over leadership and became President of Iraq in 1979. He gained Saddam's attention for the hard-pounding non-stop investigative work into the forces that would seek to undermine Saddam's wishes.

Faaz Ahmed uncovered poorly written adopted legislation that potentially placed Saddam's authority into question and quickly reworded the language to indemnify the President, leading to Saddam taking Faaz under his wings for the many years to come.

Faaz Ahmed worshiped Saddam Hussein and would give his life for Saddam should the need ever arise. Since his rise to the Presidency of Iraq in 1979 Saddam had cleared Iraq of internal enemies, wiped out virtual poverty, built schools throughout Iraq and provided his people with the finest hospitalization and health care known in Mesopotamia past or present. It indeed was the finest, in all the region stretching from Syria to Israel, Persia, and Saudi, none had better care for its people than did Saddam. With the nationalization of the oil companies, Saddam was able to develop a comfortable middle-class society for all Iraqis.

The truth be known, Saddam accomplished this by ruling with an iron fist, dissent was not tolerated, and those who did found themselves hanging by their necks in public view. Iraq was thriving, even after the long bloody war with their arch enemy; Iran. But now there was trouble brewing with the United States of America once again, and all his great achievements were quickly facing jeopardy.

Faaz was convinced already in 2001 that America was looking to find weapons of mass destruction, specifically nuclear weapons and was hell-bent on either finding them or making sure Saddam would never be able to ever consider possessing such weapons.

Faaz was a visionary. He sensed the coming turmoil and toppling of Saddam. Because of this, Faaz had been preparing with his select group of like-minded Saddam supporters. His group had sworn to make it their mission in avenging American injustice that was sure to be unleashed upon the Iraqi people.

Faaz and his group; ISIF (Islam Saddam Iraq Forever) had a plan to be put into place, with the centerpiece hub being his sons Zara and Arish, God willing.

It was now January 2002. For the past decade, Iraq had been engaged in nothing short of a cat and mouse game regarding the United Nations security council Special Commissions (UNSCOM) resolution 687, to verify Iraq's elimination of all biological, chemical and designated missile programs. This resolution of April 03, 1991 also included the IAEA (International Atomic Energy Agency) doing the same in requiring the further elimination of all nuclear weapons capabilities, with full access to all designated sites in Iraq by UN inspection teams. But by this time President George W. Bush, had declared Iraq, Iran and North Korea as the "axis of evil."

Faaz and his ISIF group believed that this declaration by the US president was a message to the world, that the overthrow of Saddam was to be the only solution in meeting the UN resolution.

Faaz Ahmed and his ISIF group saw this as a call to action. The seeds needed to deal with this inevitable US aggression required planting now, to give its roots time to take hold. For the flowers to grow, seeing the desert winds blow its spores across the Atlantic into the heart of America. The ISIF seeds of death will lay dormant until once again given the water of life, to rain down death upon America and its co-conspirators. Saddam's downfall and the destruction of Iraq will not go unpunished.

The ISIF flowers of death seeds, were now to be recalled from Lausanne, Faaz would bring his boys home.

3:50 PM – Lausanne Switzerland time.

Zara and Arish Ahmed had just finished their afternoon prayers and were planning to enjoy the balance of their free time pursuing their hobbies. Both boys were so academically inclined that even their hobbies focused on learning new things.

For Arish, the older boy, his passion for weapons of war grew stronger with every new book on modern guns, firearms or explosive device he came across. He was not of a violent nature. For Arish, it was much more of a fascination of how things worked, specifically how weapons of war had evolved over the centuries. It was evident to Arish that there had never been a weapon of war invented or made that had not been used. Arish devoured every book he could get his hands on that dealt with the topic of munitions and weapons.

He eventually exhausted the school library on the subject and was forced to undertaking weekly visits to the city's central library. There, much to his pleasure, he found more books on the subject than he could ever expect to go through. Arish had chuckled to himself upon his first visit to the public library. He thought, *okay, so there apparently was much more to Swiss armament than just the Swiss Army Knife.*

He was especially pleased and even proud when he read that Saddam Hussein's Republican Guard was in possession and deployed some of the most sophisticated and modern weapons available, of which a good number were manufactured in Iraq. Today was one of those afternoons when he decided to make another trip to the Lausanne public library.

His brother; Zara, well he was more of an admirer of Saddam Hussein than Arish but for a good reason. Zara, already at this young age, took after his father. Zara had more of an interest in history and things he found to be complicated, especially law and order.

He well knew and understood that his father had very close working ties to the president and held his father in the highest regard. Zara appreciated the loyalty his father had for Saddam and his accomplishments for the people of Iraq.

Zara held leaders in high regard who had the power to change history, to command legions and to rule nations. This then fitted very nicely when Zara delved into Saddam Hussein's life and his rise to power.

Saddam had studied in Egypt, finished his schooling there and then returned to Iraq to later become president and leader of the Ba'ath party. The Sunni, party as otherwise known in Iraq.

What stood out to Zara, being purely

serendipitous was his fascination for leadership dovetailing into Saddam's life in Egypt between 1960 and 1963. That reading led him to almost total obsessive learning about the most significant leaders to ever live in the history of the ancient world, and those were The Pharaohs of Egypt and of course the living history of the pyramids.

Zara couldn't get enough of Egyptology, from the early dynastic period of 3150 BCE to 185 BCE of the Ptolemaic Kingdom and all the seventy-five plus Pharaohs in between, including the rule of Alexander the Great, Zara ate it all up.

There was one very specialized area of his Egyptian hobby that he found most fascinating of all, and that related back to the discovery of the Rosetta Stone in the year of 1799 that eventually led to the breaking of the code, and the deciphering of the hieroglyphics. Zara was so fascinated and intrigued by Egyptian hieroglyphics that he kept a daily diary written exclusively in hieroglyphs. It was his way of keeping his journal a secret.

As Zara was about to settle in for the day, and add another entry into his diary, and Arish putting on his coat to head down to the library, a school usher knocked on their door. Arish, who already was standing by the door opened it.

The school usher informed both Arish and Zara that they were to immediately make their way to the private interview chambers, Headmaster Bern was waiting for them. Zara and Arish complied. Arish removed his coat, and Zara put his diary away. The usher escorted the boys to see Dr. Bern.

The two brothers approached the door and

knocked. They waited for a moment or two, but the expected response to their knock; enter, did not come. Instead; they could hear footsteps approaching from the other side, and the two boys stepped back. When the door opened, the Headmaster himself was inviting the two boys into the room.

"Boys come on in, there is an urgent matter that needs addressing," their Headmaster said.

Zara and Arish were coming close to completing their education at The Franciscan and over the past, almost four years had earned high marks and standings in scholastic attainments and with fellow classmates. The two boys were in fact model students, their father Faaz would have it no other way.

The brothers could enjoy the free-thinking Swiss environment but always framed within the parameters of Islam and above all, obedience to their father; Faaz Ahmed. Honoring their father's wishes and the teachings of Muhammed was of highest priority in their lives second to none.

Walking into the room, Zara watched his older brother take the lead as he always did when the two were together following Arish in a respectful manner. Having made two steps into the room, Arish stopped, and the two boys replied to the Headmaster.

"Peace be upon you Headmaster Bern," the boys said in unison, two voices speaking as one.

"Yes, right, please take a seat," Bern motioned for them to proceed.

The room had hardwood flooring, oak walls and was furnished comfortably with dark-colored leather sofas, and chairs. Classically framed oil paintings of the founders of The Franciscan School for Boys, and framed photographs of past School Administrators and Headmasters adorned on the three walls. The view from the room looked out over Lake Geneva, through panoramic windows fitted with blinds. Placed close to the window side of the room were a large boardroom table and several boardroom chairs around it. In the center section of the table, the two middle chairs with the backs to the view were equipped with microphones positioned directly in front of the two chairs.

Bern motioned for the boys to take their positions at the chairs with the microphones. They did.

Headmaster Bern then went to a wall panel pressing a button partially closing the blinds on the panoramic windows, darkening the room to suit better viewing for the video conference call soon to come and viewed on the large projection screen that dropped from the ceiling.

"Boys, your father will be calling in a few minutes. After your call is complete, you may leave the room. Peace be upon you," with that Dr. Bern left the room.

The two brothers sat motionless in their chairs. Then Zara, looked at his brother Arish and asked, "what's going on Arish?"

Arish was smart, so was Zara, but Zara, honoring his older brother always deferred to Arish, expecting him and letting him lead the way. Most times it was the right way. Today, Arish had a concerned somber look upon his face, and answered, "Zara, you've seen the news, you know what is going on with our country…I think father will tell us that we will soon be at war again with the Americans."

Zara looked back at his brother, not flinching, taking a deep breath, sighed, looking down at nothing, but lost in deep thought, replied to his older brother, "yes, I believe you are right Arish."

Suddenly the projector mounted in the ceiling came to life and the screen was filled with their father's face. His image coming in live from Baghdad. Both boys immediately stood up out of their chairs, seeing their father's face live on the screen.

The video conferencing cameras in the boardroom were ceiling mounted as well. Faaz could see his boys almost jumping out of their chairs to stand and greet him. He was pleased.

"Peace be upon you father," the two boys said in unison once again, their voices speaking as one.

Their father replied, "and peace be upon you boys, my sons Zara and Arish, it is with Allah's blessings my heart is filled with joy to see you both well."

With those words spoken, Faaz put his boys at ease. He could tell by the look on their faces that his sons relaxed.

"Boys, I have urgent news," Faaz said.

"Yes, father we are listening," Arish replied.

"Boys, your education will be completed here in Baghdad, God willing," Faaz paused and let that sink in for a few seconds. He saw that Zara and Arish both looked at one another for a moment and then both turned back to focus on Faaz.

"You are to come home, immediately. I will be sending my personal assistant Omar Bakr to bring you back home to Baghdad. That will take place tomorrow."

Although both Zara and Arish were more-less prepared for just about anything regarding news from their father, neither of the boys expected such a sudden, immediate departure. But they knew how to act and what to say. Honoring their father remained and always would be paramount in their lives.

"Yes father," replied Arish, Arish always when speaking spoke both for Zara and himself. This was the way they were raised.

"Bring nothing with you back from Lausanne. Expect Omar's arrival tomorrow morning at 11:00 AM at The Franciscan.

Boys…only bring with you the clothes on your backs and the continued love for your mother who is waiting to see her loving boys back home. Your belongings and scholastic records from The Franciscan will be collected and will follow later. Your immediate departure is not to be delayed. You will be flown back to Iraq by my private jet. You are to follow Omar's instructions in getting you back to Baghdad.

Boys… be aware, Iraqi airspace is about to be closed at any moment. Your arrival back in Iraq is of the greatest urgency. God willing you will touch Iraqi ground tomorrow afternoon. Peace be upon you, my sons."

"Peace be upon you father," the boys replied in unison once again.

The video call ended.

Zara and Arish returned to their room that they shared at The Franciscan and both instinctively unrolled their prayer rugs, placed it down to face Mecca and prayed for the second time this afternoon.

Destiny had called.

***

CHAPTER
III
O N I N G I T

"Just the five we were able to carry back to the hospital with us, that's it Kimberley, just these five kids!" Eldon could hardly get the words out. His eyes tearing up again, his throat tightening to the point of almost unbearable pain as he spoke those words to his wife.

Eldon did not often show his emotions openly but today had taken its toll on Eldon, and he once again started to sob openly. Billy, standing beside Eldon, placed his arms around his friend and boss, bowing his head in mourning the death of all they could not save.

"Eldon, no, that's not possible!" Eldon, there were one hundred sixty children plus another four minders on the buses plus the drivers, Eldon, there have to be more survivors!" Kimberley shouted in disbelief.

Kimberley stood in front of her husband and started beating on Eldon's chest, finally falling into his arms, lying up against his blood-soaked shirt. She collapsed into him, barely able to stand. Eldon hugged her and held her up as she gradually lost all her strength, she buried her head into his chest crying as Eldon led her gingerly towards the hospital chairs along the wall and sat her down, still holding onto his wife.

Eldon sat next to Kimberley, wrapping his arm around her, bringing her closer into his side, and steadying his wife until she slowly started to regain her composure. Gradually Kimberley recovered herself and looked up at her husband and Billy who was still standing.

Billy having stood over Eldon and Kimberley for the past few minutes, took a deep breath, bringing his open palms up to cover his face and then let out a huge sigh. As he breathed out, he lowered his arms, uncovering his face showing a great sadness in his blue eyes. He spoke to Kimberley and Eldon. Both could see that Billy too was visibly shaken.

"Kimberley, I flew back to the parking lot expecting to medivac more children back here to Cairo General, but we only found bodies. Kimberley, there are no other survivors. Egyptian authorities have been on the scene for the past two hours. There is nothing left there but the carnage of body parts. I've already released the chopper's steady-cam video recording from this afternoon's flight, so the authorities have the live footage of what transpired."

He was an ex-naval aviator, a man of steel, who'd been to hell and back during his service career but nothing in his military career came even close to the carnage of the children they witnessed today.

Kimberley listened and looked up at Billy as the big man spoke. Indeed, no words of comfort but only despair came from Billy's mouth. Kimberley wiped her eyes with the tear-soaked towel she'd been holding onto for the past three hours. Kimberley stood from her chair and hugged Billy, saying; "thank you, Billy, thank you for going back looking for more children."

Calmness returned to Kimberley. She reached out for Eldon, and the three of them hugged one another in a tight circle.

"I cannot imagine what tomorrow will bring," Eldon said as the three stood holding onto each other.

"We need to check on the kids we brought in," Eldon said.

By now the emergency medical staff and hospital security cleared Eldon, Kimberley, and Billy with day pass privileges. This enabled the three of them to enter the emergency treatment areas without security checks. They desperately wanted updates on the condition of the children.

Of the five children they flew back with to Cairo General, only one child turned out to be American; Robbie Fox from Fort Lauderdale Florida; age thirteen. All other seventy-nine American kids on this first cultural exchange program, initiated and set up by Kimberley and Eldon had perished, including their adult chaperones along with the four Egyptian tour bus drivers.

The complete devastation of the bus caravan; seeing the fireballs and exploding buses taking place in real time with a bird's eye view had shaken the three of them watching from the chopper like never in their lives. At this moment in time, they drew what little strength remained from one another.

The four other children had been identified; all being Egyptian kids. Four Egyptian girls, Halima Ellithy age thirteen, Sabiha Boutros age fourteen and two girls who turned out to be sisters; Talia Ahmed aged twelve and her older sister Afraa Ahmed age thirteen. The two sisters were the daughters of Zara and Nawar Ahmed of Cairo Egypt. All parents of the surviving children were notified and on route to Cairo General.

Eldon and Kimberley Davis would soon have the honor and great sadness of meeting Zara and Nawar Ahmed in person, parents of the sisters; Talia and Afraa. And yet somehow, even after having saved these unfortunate children's lives, it gave them no comfort, they were still numb to the events having taken place at the Great Pyramid of Giza. Eldon and Kimberley both felt sick their stomachs now knowing that soon they will be face to face with the parents of these children.

The Cairo press corps had now gathered underneath the porte-cochere to the hospital. Thankfully, Cairo General had a great team of public relations professionals and spokespersons who were currently handling the news media. This event had made international news, and the world's media was converging on Cairo. Tomorrow would see hordes of reporters wanting answers.

The Egyptian police and authorities would have their hands more than full. Eldon and Kimberley would be sought out as well for commentary. Eldon had already contacted Felix Balon. Felix was like Billy, not family but nevertheless family. Felix had been with Eldon since Eldon founded his company and trudged through the tough times and good times, and later with Kimberley and Eldon over the years.

Felix was his PR man and company spokesman. Felix if necessary, knew how to deal with the devil himself should the need arise. He was flying in from Moscow tomorrow afternoon.

The wall-mounted television in the emergency waiting room sector tuned to the local station had its reporters already on the scene at the hospital as well as the bomb site. Nasser Agopian was on screen being interviewed by the Cairo news channel reporter.

Kimberley, Eldon, and Billy watched as Nasser tried doing his best in describing what had happened. They appreciated Nasser's efforts and decorum in leaving Kimberley and Eldon's name out of his recollection of the day's events. The fact that the excursion to the pyramids by the school children was a sponsored cultural event was clear, but Holiday Jewel Hotels and Casinos' name, for now, was being kept off the fact sheet.

Eldon stood watching the monitor, watching Agopian addressing the questions from the press, but Eldon wasn't really paying much attention. He looked inward actually. Eldon began drawing on his inner strength. His mind raced, reaching back in time when death paid a personal visit in his life. His mind taking him back to finding Linda's bloody body on the marble floor of his foyer. Linda, his loving wife, murdered in cold blood and the loss of his unborn child. He knew firsthand what it was like to lose a loved one, the love of his life to the evils of the world. And now he would be faced with making his best effort in providing comfort to the victims of his and Kimberley's bright idea; cultural exchange, that ended up in killing these lovely children.

He and Kimberley would have hell to pay when they returned to Florida. Yet, Eldon found peace and strength in Kimberley. She came into his life and saved him from himself after Linda's death, he would have been lost without her. Kimberley here for him now, as she'd always been. Together they would find a way.

Eldon, standing there, watching and not watching Agopian on the screen, lost in thought, he suddenly said, "come on let's go see the kids, I want us to be ready for the parents, we need to deal with this and do what we can. The parents will need us to be strong when facing them."

Eldon would need to deal with the scores of other parents and the entire incident in much more significant ways than he and Kimberley ever considered. This was now a new dimension in their company's future and perhaps its ongoing viability and existence. A lot of things swirled around in Eldon's head this afternoon. He'd have to sort out everything, clearly and soon. Eldon well knew that the events of this day could bring about the total meltdown of his mind and company. He was not about to let that happen.

ONINGIT

***

CHAPTER

FOUR

DAWYTHWS

"Yes Mr. President, it just came in not five minutes ago," Pete Jericho, the president's chief of staff said.

The American president couldn't believe his ears. He looked up from what he was doing, looking straight at Jericho and shouted.

"What the fuck! Eighty-one Americans killed and seventy-nine are kids twelve to fourteen, all blown to bits?" The president stood up out of his chair, spread his arms placing his fists onto his desk, and leaned forward looking directly at Pete Jericho and shouted again as if it was Jericho's fault.

"Who the fuck is it this time? President Trenten demanded.

Within ten seconds The President became as unhinged and livid as Jericho had ever seen him be.

Is it al-Qaeda? Is it ISIS? Is that…that... ah… Muslim Brotherhood? Is it fucking Hamas? God dammit, I swear I'm going to fucking nuke those mother-fuckers along with their pyra-fucking-mids once and for all. I've had it with this! And for that matter, the American people have had enough of this horseshit!" Trenten had really blown his top on receiving this news.

Jericho responded again, "Mr. President, only one American child survived, a thirteen-year-old, all other seventy-nine kids died in the bombing along with the two teachers on the excursion acting as their chaperones. All the Americans killed were from south Florida. Mr. President, from the Egyptian side of things, seventy-six Egyptian kids were killed along with their minders and all the bus drivers on all four buses. An act of terrorism, perhaps the gravest in Egyptian history Mr. President." Jericho finished saying.

"Well, do you have an answer for me? Who's responsible for this?" Jericho wasn't about to anger Trenten even further by suggesting that Egypt had nothing to do with this. The Egyptians were scrambling just as much as the American intelligence community was.

Pete well knew that Trenten had little understanding or appreciation for the factions making up the various terrorist organizations in the middle east. Trenten didn't have the first clue as to the differences between Sunnis and Shia, or Kurds or Turks or even Afghans and Pakistanis, to him they were all towel-heads. Such was the intelligence of Trenten. But someone had to watch the President, and he was it.

Trenten wanted answers, not tomorrow but right now. Jericho had still not gotten comfortable with having to be the president's personal verbal punching bag every time he brought him negative news. This new act of terrorism was of a different level that will hit the reactionary nerve of the American people. The nation will demand administrative action, thought Jericho.

Trenten well knew the immediate implications, even as Jericho delivered the news, but Trenten had no grasp of how he would handle things.

Jericho watched him become totally unhinged and flying blind in this new storm of desert winds blowing down on American power from the Egyptian sands.

"Mr. President, we are on it, sir. None of the known terrorist organizations have come forward to lay claim yet, but we are working on it. We are in close consultation and cooperation with Egyptian authorities. Our State Department and CIA operatives in Egypt have made this their priority Mr. President.

"Yes, yes, the same old bullshit I've heard for the past twenty years. When I was in private life, it was the same thing from past administrations; we are working on it with our allies. This is the last… I don't give a rat's ass what it's going to take or what we have to do, but this has to stop," Trenten went on.

Jericho stood watching and listening to President Trenten dishing out a temper tantrum venting his anger. Jericho well anticipated Trenten's reaction to being nothing short of lashing out, so he just took it as he had countless times before. The president's constant use of profanity was now a commonly accepted normality amongst all white house staff although some people were still having personal difficulties in dealing with his crassness.

Jericho accepted the position as chief of staff in the Trenten administration for one reason and one reason only. That was to serve the country, and not so much the president. Jericho along with most of Trenten's cabinet was on board mainly for the same reason, that being patriotism. Jericho felt it a duty to serve and thereby enjoying the unique position and opportunity to reel in the president before his temper tantrums led to rash decisions that may end up putting the country in peril.

This president and administration had turned out to be the most controversial in recent memory with the most disturbing issue being that President Trenten seemed utterly uneducated in world history and remarkably ignorant in dealing with global problems.

Jericho and his team were in place to curtail and guide the president as best they could in maintaining much needed universal normalcy in running the country and keeping the American people safe. Today's events would test Jericho, his team, the NSA, CIA and DND along with the State Department like never.

"Pete, get me my secretary of defense, the NSA director as well, make that the CIA director too, I want all of them in my office. Where the hell is my secretary of state today, is he off somewhere in Asia or down at foggy bottom? I want them all here in my office in the next two hours!" Trenten shouted at Jericho.

"Yes, Mr. President, they are all in Washington today, remember you have a scheduled meeting this afternoon in the situation room with all of them to address the North Korean situation," Jericho reminded Trenten.

"All right then, I want some answers! What are

we doing to get to the bottom of this? Pete, get in touch with them now and tell them if they don't have answers for me when they get here, they may as well not come. They're all useless to me, understand?" Trenten was fuming, his face turning red almost matching the color of his tie.

"I suppose I have a gallery of reporters already clambering in the press briefing room for me to say something." Trenten mused.

Trenten didn't wait for Pete's response. Instead, he continued with his rant, "you, yes you, not my press secretary, I want you to go to the podium and tell the reporters that I will address the nation this evening at 8:00 PM. That ought to shut them up for a while. All I need from you are the details of what happened, how many killed, etcetera-etcetera in Egypt today, got it? I don't need to know who was responsible, I will make something up and calm the nation."

That is precisely what Jericho was afraid of. He was powerless to do anything about Trenten's way of handling things, but he'd try.

"Mr. President, your speech writers have been made aware of this tragedy and immediately got working on a statement from you sir. Please give their efforts some consideration, I'm sure you will find their crafted wordings very helpful." Jericho was pulling at straws hoping the president would come to his senses.

"All right, get out and get on with things as I said." The president was his usual endearing self.

Jericho headed down to the white house press briefing room. He would face the barrage.

Better him than the president, He thought, *damn those poor kids, what a tragedy, this is going to be some turning point in everything we do from now on, no doubt about it."*

Jericho walked into the press room, taking his place behind the podium. The briefing room was filled, perhaps beyond full. Every reporter had their hands up.

"I'm not here to take questions, I will make a brief statement," Jericho announced.

All the raised hands, lowered.

DAWYTHWS

***

CHAPTER

FIVE

SEDS

January 2002 – Baghdad Iraq

"Peace be upon you father, peace be upon you, father," said greeting their father one after another as they entered their childhood home located on the outskirts of Baghdad on the banks of the Tigris river. The house was almost palatial. Nothing like the palaces Saddam had been building throughout Iraq ever since the end of Desert Storm, but spacious and opulent, nevertheless.

Their mother, Saama, was standing behind her husband Faaz, waiting to hug her boys. She could not hide the proud smile filling her face in welcoming her sons back home under her roof. She stood there with open arms, waiting for her boys to come to her. Allah had brought them safely home, back into her loving arms once again.

"Boys, your mother missed you as the desert flower misses the rain, now go and greet your mother," Faaz motioned to his boys.

"Come, boys, come and pray, we shall pray together as a family once again."

Zara and Arish greeted their mother, they hugged and gave thanks to Allah for the safe journey and followed their father into the house prayer room. They took their places on their prayer rugs, facing Mecca, they knelt and bowed and prayed together. The Ahmed family was whole once again. Praise to Allah.

After evening prayers, Faaz brought his boys into his den where he proceeded to prepare Zara and his brother for the upcoming events to take place tomorrow.

"Boys, I want you both to sleep well tonight. I want you to have clear heads when you wake. Tomorrow will be a crossroads in both your lives. That is enough for tonight. Now go and sleep well and deep, tomorrow brings change," Faaz gazed upon his sons as he smoked on his waterpipe while the boys listened intently. Now, go…and may Allah bring peace to your dreams as you slumber."

And with that, Zara and Arish went to their rooms, both in wonder as to what the new day would bring.

The next day morning came, and morning turned into afternoon. Arish and Zara had not talked much during the day, both anticipating the major events forecasted to come. They waited, but nothing was happening. It was now well past 5:00 PM, afternoon prayers were over with, and the boys waited. Finally, Zara's impatience grew unbearable, and he asked Arish, "I wonder what is going on, when will father call us?"

Arish replied with authority and reassurance, "brother the day is not yet over, relax."

Dinner time came, the boys ate, and they waited.

They watched the local news on Baghdad television. The talk was about weapons of mass destruction. How the international community, arms and weapons inspectors were seeking evidence of Saddam's hidden WMD.

The boys already knew that the inspectors would never find any WMD's anywhere in Iraq. They knew this because Saddam had clearly stated to the world, that all were destroyed many years ago and the inspectors were wasting their time. Zara and Arish looked at one another as Saddam's claim to no weapons of mass destruction aired again in the broadcast. Arish, looking at Zara then said, "American fools. They aren't finding what they are looking for, and never will! Zara, I am of the mind that the Americans and their stupid friends are starting their saber rattling all over again. Remember what I said to you back in Lausanne Zara? War is coming Zara, war is coming, I can feel it in my bones brother, prepare!"

Arish's declaration of things to come was not exactly a surprise to Zara, but it did hit deeply within his heart. Signs of war to begin again was evident. The atmosphere in the city was electric, even just being home for one day, Zara could sense it. Baghdad was on edge. This time it could end everything they ever worked for, the country Saddam and his father had built. Zara shuddered.

The time was now late evening, darkness had fallen over Baghdad, and the night was upon the city.

Their father entered the room and said, "boys get your coats; the time is here. You will come with me."

Zara and Arish, jumped up like springs from the

sofa, almost running for their coats, and followed Faaz out the door and into their SUV.

Faaz drove with his boys on the highway leading out of Baghdad far into the desert sands.

"Father where are we going?" Zara, the inquisitive one asked with the greatest respect and curiosity.

"We, my dear sons, are going into the desert, where only Allah has ears," Faaz said to his boys, not looking at them, but knowing they both stared at him as he drove farther into the desert.

Zara repeated his father's words, "where only Allah has ears."

Zara looked at his brother, bewildered. Arish smiled back at him, saying, "the desert holds many secrets and plans Zara, I think father has one to tell us tonight."

Zara replied, "and I think you are right Arish.

Faaz smiled. His sons were proving to be smarter than even he believed them to be.

Faaz and the boys drove another half hour when Faaz suddenly veered off the highway and onto the desert. It was a moonless pitch-black night. Both boys were keyed up with adrenaline. The moonless sky gave way to the starlit heavens as the boys looked out the window trying to figure out how their father knew where to turn off the highway. Far ahead was only sand and more sand.

The boys looked at one another, puzzled but intrigued. This surely was an adventure!

The SUV climbed a high sand dune, perhaps a hill and started down the other side. At the base was a large open canopy; a tent came into sight set next to a natural stone wall forming the bottom of the hill.

Faaz drove the SUV directly inside the opening of the enormous tent. There were several other vehicles parked already underneath. The boys figured it out; the shelter was there to hide the cars. The top of the tent no doubt was covered with spread sand, perhaps to blind the infra-red prying eyes high in the sky. The vehicles were camouflaged, heat shielded and thus hidden in the desert.

Faaz shut the vehicle off.

"We're here," he said, turning and smiling at his sons before the interior lights dimmed, "Let's go."

The boys jumped out of the vehicle, waiting for their father who they followed walking underneath the canopy leading to the stone wall. They stopped when reaching the wall, and looking back behind them, both boys noticed that the tent and the cars inside had virtually disappeared into the darkness of the desert. If they hadn't known that the shelter was there, they surely would have walked into it. The cars were far off the highway and hidden deep in the dip of the valley. The desert winds would soon cover the tire tracks, they were invisible.

Reaching the wall, forming the side of the hill, the boys realized they had come to the entrance of a natural cave. They followed their father inside a few more meters. The cave grew more prominent and the farther in they went voices could be heard, faint but growing clearer with every step they took.

They arrived. A large open natural rock chamber,

with a ceiling at least ten meters high. Inside the room, the light came from low burning oil lamps, giving off a yellowish glow, placed standing height around the cave. There was enough light but not bright; subdued. Rugs covered the hard sand floor.

At least two dozen men sat in a semi-circle fashion against the back wall. Above them in the center of the group mounted on the wall was something that looked like a flag. Both Zara and Arish keyed in on the flag's design. It was something they were very familiar with, and it spoke to them both. Above the flag was a framed picture of their leader and hero; Saddam Hussein. But first things first. The boys looked at each other as they entered the chamber. Both remained quiet and deferred to their father.

Faaz spoke first since he was the one arriving, "peace be upon you brothers."

"Peace be upon you, brother Faaz," the men all said in unison returning Faaz's greeting.

Then Arish and Zara spoke at once to greet them all, "peace be upon you brothers."

The men responded in kind, "peace be upon you brothers."

Faaz, stepped forward to take his place. Faaz walked to the center of the semi-circle and sat down as the two men moved slightly in opposing directions making room for Faaz. The boys just stood in place. Apparently, there were no spots left for them to sit. This puzzled the boys for a moment, but their curiosity was quickly answered.

Their father motioned for the two boys to sit on the two rugs placed side by side directly in front and center of their father but set back about two meters so that they were center situated in front of all the men.

The boys took their position, sitting down with legs crossed, their eyes moving side to side looking momentarily at the elders facing them, and then settling in and focusing on their father. They both thought *something big, very big was happening*.

Faaz spoke, "before we begin, we give thanks to Allah for his guidance, we will pray."

The men sitting with their backs against the wall were already facing Mecca, the boys were not. They turned around one hundred eighty degrees, knelt and everyone bowed and prayed all speaking quietly, "glory be to god the greatest," three times. After the prayer, each turned first to the right and then to the left saying, "peace be upon you, and the mercy and blessings of Allah."

With prayers being completed, the boys turned around and resumed their position in front of their father.

SEDS

***

CHAPTER

SIX

KRASNGS

The atmosphere in the emergency ward of Cairo General was subdued with a heaviness in the air that lingered and permeated the hearts of the physicians, surgeons, nurses and all who answered the call to save lives.

Nasser Agopian had finished addressing the press for now and rejoined Kimberley, Eldon, and Billy, making their way through ICU and to the beds of the kids they brought in just hours ago.

Kimberley noticed the nurses and some of the doctors, being as human as anyone else occasionally wiping tears from their eyes. Their usual capability to look beyond the injuries no matter how severe and tend to the needs of the patient was outweighed by the immense cruelty and suffering these children were forced to endure, a few of the staff broke down. The totality of the incident at the pyramids, the loss of more than a hundred and sixty, being blown to pieces dominated the thinking of every caregiver and doctor who attended to the needs of the survivors. For some of the emergency room staff, it was too much to deal with.

Eldon and Kimberly walked to Talia Ahmed's bedside. She was the darling little twelve-year-old Egyptian girl to whom Eldon first ran and held in his arms while the bus she was blown from kept exploding behind while Eldon and Kimberley held onto Talia. Her face was partially destroyed, with the left side of her jaw ripped apart. But that wasn't all of it. Talia, bless her heart was severely injured also having lost the lower part of her left arm from below the elbow. She was unconscious, pumped full of drugs.

Kimberley had her arm wrapped around Eldon's as they stood by Talia's bed. Agopian and Billy came over to be with them. The emergency department attending surgeon; Doctor Nabel approached the four.

"Peace be upon you all for the work you did this afternoon," Doctor Nabel greeted everyone standing by Talia's bed.

"Peace be upon you as well Doctor Nabel," replied Eldon, with everyone else saying the same under their breath, all shaking hands with the general surgeon.

"Would you please give us an update on this little girl, Talia is her name I believe," Kimberley said.

"Yes, well, for this young child, the going will be difficult and a long one. Perhaps several years, but with good medical care and the fact that she is young, well that is in her favor for a recovery of sorts," doctor Nabel said in a very unconvincing way.

That last part hit a nerve with Eldon. *Of sorts, what did that mean, of sorts? It meant not good, that's what it meant,* Eldon kept quiet.

Eldon listened while looking at Talia. She was in

a drugged-induced coma. Her head was wrapped entirely with only her eyes visible and an opening for her nose and mouth, but nothing more extensive than a slit.

Nabel continued, "both Talia and her sister Afraa across from us in the bed beside her, she too will have a difficult time, but Talia, well she will require extra special care. You see, she suffered severe facial and head injury. She has sustained a massive injury to the coronoid process of the mandible. The ramus has fractured, and a smaller piece of the mandibular notch has broken off, with the mandibular condyle sustaining further damage. This will require specialized reconstructive surgery, and quite honestly, I don't know if we have the surgeons here in Cairo to do this type of specialized reconstruction. What does this mean in layman's terms? She is suffering from significant damage to the jaw bone that connects the jaw to the zygomatic process of the temporal bone, meaning the skull."

Kimberley held onto Eldon as Doctor Nabel spoke. She started tearing up again, squeezing Eldon's left arm. Eldon reached around with his right arm, covering Kimberley's hand, now holding onto her as she held onto him. It was all too devastating. Billy and Agopian, stood in silence, listening to the doctor.

"We will keep her in this induced coma for some days. Many additional x-rays will be required over the next few weeks. She will not be able to consume food in the normal way, she will have to receive nourishment intravenously or feeding tube. She should have the ability to swallow, but even that will be extremely painful. With drugs, we should be able to manage that pain. Then, of course, there is the matter of her left arm being severed from the elbow down. Hopefully, she is right-handed. Luckily, she suffered no damage to the elbow or above. She should have mobility in the elbow once she is fitted with prosthetics replacing her lower arm and hand, but this too will take much therapy."

Eldon's mind was already miles ahead, perhaps years ahead. He turned his head towards Kimberley, looking her in the eye, and she knew exactly what her husband was thinking. Then they both turned to look at Billy, and Billy knew, Billy nodded. The same would hold true of Talia's sister; Afraa in the bed next to Talia's. Her right leg was bandaged completely and tragically she had lost her right foot. Her head was also dressed. She too was unconscious for the time being.

Doctor Nabel filled them in on the condition of the other two Egyptian girls who were in ICU but expected to make full recoveries as was Robbie Fox, the American student who sustained severe but not life-threatening injuries. Eldon and Kimberley were advised that Robbie's parents were to fly in to see their son the first available flight they could find. Upon hearing that, Eldon contacted Felix, his senior VP of public relations and instructed Felix to have a private jet pick Robbie's parents up in Ft. Lauderdale and fly them to Cairo immediately. Robbie's parents would be landing at Cairo International Airport in the morning.

They visited the bedside of all five children. Robbie was awake but groggy.

"He should be able to speak with his mother and father come tomorrow," Dr. Nabel said.

The other two Egyptian girls' parent were on their way to Cairo General as well, and soon Kimberley and Eldon would get to meet them all.

Zara and Nawar Ahmed were the first two parents to arrive at the hospital, desperate to see their daughters Talia and Afraa. The Cairo police department had taken over the security needs for the hospital. Two city police officers escorted Zara and his wife through to ICU where they met with Doctor Nabel who had the arduous task of listing their daughters' injuries and the hard-difficult road ahead in their young lives.

Nawar and Zara, listened with disbelief as Nabel talked, explaining the situation and current condition of the two girls. The parents were devastated, but neither one cried. Both were sitting down, as was Doctor Nabel, facing them, talking directly and with great compassion in his delivery. It did not help, Nawar finally collapsed in her chair, fainting.

Kimberley, Billy, Eldon, and Agopian stood off at a distance, watching the scene unfold. It was hard to watch. Kimberley couldn't hold it, she started crying again as she saw Nawar collapsing in her chair and falling to the concrete floor. Doctor Nabel and Zara, helped her back onto her chair, regaining consciousness. After a few moments, they stood and followed Doctor Nabel into ICU. They were on their way to see their daughters.

The girls were unrecognizable, heads totally bandaged, faces hidden. They weren't even allowed to hug or touch the girls, risking any further injuries at such a crucial time in their recovery. Zara put his arms out, holding onto the raised railing of the bed, steadying himself, looking at his daughter. He bent his head, and started to cry, then sob openly. He turned around and reached for the other bed, staring at Afraa and cried again. Nawar, she held onto Zara, holding onto his arm, and wiping tears from her eyes.

After a few minutes, Doctor Nabel walked up to the parents and said, "I'd like you to meet the people who saved your daughters."

Zara and Nawar looked up at the doctor. Zara asked, "saved our daughters?"

"Yes, if it weren't for them, your daughters would have perished with the other children," Nabel replied.

The doctor motioned to Eldon, Kimberley, Billy, and Nasser to come over. They had been standing, waiting for Dr. Nabel to call on them when the parents were ready.

Dr. Nabel, making his best attempt in deferring to the honorable Egyptian Minister, first introduced Nasser Agopian; Minister of Antiquities Affairs to Zara and Nawar, and after that allowed the minister to cordially take over introducing Eldon, Kimberley, and Billy.

KRASNGS

***

CHAPTER

SEVEN

PLNTNG

The two boys sitting beside each other with legs crossed and motionless had their eyes trained on their father. The flickering oil lamp flames cast a chorus of dancing shadows onto the walls, making for an attention-catching yet comforting atmosphere.

Arish and Zara had now realized that their uncles, all nine of them, four from their mother's side and five from their father's side of the family formed part of the semi-circle of men facing them. The other men, neither Zara or Arish recognized.

The boys sat, respectfully waiting and waiting for something to happen. The man at the far-right end of the group, whom they did not recognize, stood up and walked three steps, to a table next to the stone wall and picked up what looked to be a folded cloth, turned around, and carried it back to his spot on the floor and sat back down. He then opened the fold, so that the fabric now lay on the top of his upturned palms.

The boys now realized it was the flag, the same flag displayed above their father's head. The design became clear. It was foreboding of things to come, but at this point, neither Zara or Arish could be specific as to what was taking place. The design was troubling yet conveyed an element of avengement and vengeance for Iraq. They were very familiar with the central part of the flag; the *Swords of Qādisīyah, Hands of Victory or the Crossed Swords*. The arched monument was built to commemorate the Iraq-Iran war. That long-lasting conflict was led by Saddam Hussein himself. The base of the arch sculpted directly from molds of Saddam's hands and arms emerging from the ground with each massive hand holding swords over forty meters long, crossing at the tips towering forty meters above the ground. The flag's colors were the red, white and black underneath the shredded stars and stripes, with the crossed swords in green signifying the three stars of the original flag unifying Iraq, Syria, and Egypt.

Both Zara and Arish had visited the monuments many times leading to the Grand Festivities Square in Baghdad. It surely was the most iconic symbol of Iraq, it was the victory arch.

But now it became apparent that the symbol had evolved and taken on a new life, a purpose far beyond that of the Iraq-Iran war. The symbol of the crossed swords, the tips of the two swords ripping and tearing through the middle of the American stars and stripes. The two swords, held by the arms and hands of Saddam had cut deep into the heart of America, and underneath the arch of the swords were the letters: ISIF. And underneath in English to their amazement, were the words; Islam Saddam Iraq Forever.

The man holding the ISIF flag on his open palms bent his head down and kissed the swords on the flag. He then turned to his left, passing the flag with open palms to the man beside him. He too kissed the sword design and passed it on. This followed suit with each man down the line until it came to their father. Faaz also bent to kiss the flag. The ISIF flag made its way to the end, kissed by the last man who then passed it back along the line, until the flag was in their father's hand once again.

Faaz sat with crossed legs, his hands resting on his knees, the flag laying on top of his upturned open palms, and he looked at his sons, then slightly but ever so slightly bowed his head.

The boys looked at one another for a second when suddenly, one of the men they also did not know, spoke.

"We are ISIF, he pronounced the four initials of the flag as if it was a word, saying, "eye-sif."

Yes, the man was speaking English, not Mesopotamic Arabic, it was English. Zara found this unusual since everyone in the room was Iraqi. But then Zara was thinking as the man was even speaking, *the ISIF flag has English words on it, there has to be a reason.* Then it hit him! *The flag was meant for Americans, writing in Arabic wouldn't get the message across, and he was sure whatever that message was, well he and Arish would know before the night was over.*

Then their father spoke, continuing in English, "Islam, Saddam, Iraq, Forever, eye-sif."

Immediately after saying those four words, everyone else in unison repeated, "Islam, Saddam, Iraq, Forever, eye-sif."

There was a pause with an ensuing calm filling the stone chamber afterward. The flickering shadows of the lamp flames danced on the walls. Faaz looking at his two boys stood up and walked three steps forward, sat down and presented the ISIF flag to his firstborn son; Arish. Arish had been watching the events like an Iraqi bird of prey, missing nothing.

Arish, holding his hands out, open palms up, accepted the ISIF flag from his father. Sitting cross-legged he raised the flag towards his face, bent down and kissed the swords. Upon Arish's kissing of the flag, his father said, "the will of Allah will be done, my son."

Arish then held out the flag towards his father. Faaz slipped his open palms underneath the flag and took it from Arish. He then went through the same process with his second born Zara, and upon Zara kissing the swords on the flag, said, "the will of Allah will be done, my son."

Arish and Zara had become part of Faaz's secret Islamic Jihad organization ISIF. The boys had never in their lives felt such a sense of belonging and a reason to be alive as they did this night.

Arish and Zara had arrived. Both boys believed this was a gift from Allah of the highest order.

Faaz Ahmed, his five brothers and four brothers in law comprised the group of ten men who made up the council of ISIF. Faaz was the founder of ISIF, he created the organization just after the Iraqi surrender to the Americans, south of Basra in 1991 marking the end of "Desert Storm." These ten men were all of the same mind, devout Sunni Muslims and dedicated to the preservation of Iraq. The other men who were in attendance for the welcoming of Arish and Zara into the organization were also devout, loyal and idealistic Sunni Muslims with unquestionable honor and fealty to Faaz and the council of ten. If ever ordered to take their own lives, by any one member of the Council of Ten, they would do so without hesitation or question. They too were committed to the preservation of Iraq as they had all known it to be under Saddam, no matter what the future held.

ISIF remained dormant throughout the period following Desert Storm, and well into the years after the start of Shock and Awe, marking the beginning of the US invasion of Iraq in March of 2003. ISIF was formed to be in position and place should Saddam ever fall, and Iraq turned into a failed state leaving its people without a stable government and their daily existence bombed back into the stone age.

ISIF was to act only if those conditions had come to pass. The council well knew that if Great Britain and the USA ever decided to wage war, with all of America's might against Iraq, Saddam and Iraq would fall. There was no military might more powerful than America with their B2 bombers, submarine-launched cruise missiles, and tanks that can move at forty miles per hour bouncing in the desert sands picking off targets two miles in the distance. Not to mention the sheer amount of their armaments. Iraq stood no chance.

By mid-2001 Faaz already felt the international rumblings led by the US, aggravating and rattling Saddam demanding access to Saddam's military sites. By January 2002, Faaz and the Council of Ten had come to realize that war was inevitable. America wasn't having any luck in finding weapons of mass destruction, so the Americans with their oil greedy friends would invade Iraq and look for themselves. Faaz was convinced they'd destroy much of Baghdad and its infrastructure, leaving the country without electricity or fresh drinking water, and then depose Saddam. This was how they saw the future to be, and their prediction of things to come couldn't have been more accurate.

The council decided to act, and in January of 2002, Faaz called his boys home from Switzerland. Twelve months later, "shock and awe," the American invasion of Iraq and the fall of Saddam. ISIF's hatred for America grew with each day. Faaz and the Council worked methodically, ensuring that their will and plan would do a thousand times to America what America did to Iraq.

Faaz went to bed every night, thinking to himself, "the Saudis attacked America on 9-11, not Iraqis, but George Bush retaliated and attacked Iraq, for no good reason. Time had come for America to pay for the destruction of his nation. ISIF will bring America to its knees. As the first Bush president had said, there will be a new world order. Now America will see an even more modern world order, where it will surely be at the bottom of the world's economic garbage heap of despair. With that ISIF quietly engaged for the next sixteen years. From 2003 to the present time, carefully and methodically putting their plan into place and now ready, his boys Zara and Arish just waiting for the call to pull the trigger.

Yes indeed, the planted flowers of death in Egypt had time to take root and grow. The spores of the flowers over the years blew across the Atlantic to every major city in America. The spores would soon be watered, and the flowers of death will rain on America.

ISIF and the Council planed deep and well. After the fall of Iraq, the nation had turned into a failed state, a basket-case. American soldiers were stationed for the next seven years in their fallen country and the religious jihadi groups formed. Iraqi Islamic terrorists were continually attacking the Americans. The jihadists were a constant pain and irritant.

Arish was groomed by ISIF to become a munitions expert and IED (improvised explosives device), technician. This made Arish very happy since he was a fanatic about weapons of war and explosives. But there was a method to Arish's IED war with Americans, a methodology unlike any and nothing like anyone would have ever guessed. ISIF and Arish, were not out to kill Americans, but they were actively involved in protecting Americans and eventually endearing the US commanders to take note of Arish with gratitude and a healthy level of indebtedness. Same thing with Zara, who also helped the American army working as a translator for the US commanders. Iraq had fallen, there was no sense in fighting these Americans who destroyed their country.

ISIF's philosophy was simple. Killing Americans and their coalition friends here in Iraq served no purpose whatsoever. Iraq had fallen, it was a failed state. No number of American GI killings would bring back their country to its once glorious condition. No, the death of Americans would need to happen in America, in the heart of the "*heartland*" that is what needed to be done. There was time.

Now was the time needed to endear them and then take advantage of their gratitude. IEDs in Iraq were the number one cause of American soldier deaths. By 2007, IED's had accounted for sixty-three percent of all US deaths in Iraq. Locating, disarming or destroying IED's was the number one priority for American GI's while engaged in Iraq. Arish was to become a hero and trusted Iraqi in the eyes of the US military. US military commanders figured for every one IED disarmed, ten GI's lives were saved. How wrong they were. Arish was now in his twenties, an agile, bilingual intelligent Iraqi who spoke English, French, and Arabic. He had been quietly working the ISIF plan, and working it was!

Arish's mission during these times was to build IED's, all types. Explosives, directionally focused charges, chemical, biological, incendiary and radiological devices. Arish became an expert in triggering mechanisms as well. He could arm a bomb and set it to trigger by wire, radio, mobile phone or infra-red.

Arish planted the IED's himself. Set up the detonator to fire by remote control, but Arish would never activate one. From time to time he would tell the Americans that it was his daily mission to keep his eyes wide open and ears to the ground, learning where the IED's might be planted. This went on for several years, with Arish claiming to find a dozen IED's which he had secretly planted himself, then showed the Americans where they were. The Yanks were either too stupid to ever catch on or just plain grateful to have a dedicated alliance with an Iraqi national willing to work with the US for possible rewards in the future. Just before the US Military finally pulled out of Iraq in 2011, Arish's hopes were answered.

The US commander recognized Arish's and Zara's contribution to the American effort and offered both boys asylum and immigration to the United States. ISIF, Zara and Arish were on a roll. Zara instead immigrated to Egypt where the second part of his plan was to unfold, and Arish accepted the offer of immigration to the USA where he married, started a family and opened a business.

With funding from his father Faaz, Arish opened Confederated Building Demolition Industries in Las Vegas Nevada. He'd have all the explosives; dynamite, TNT, RDX, and C4 he and ISIF would ever need in bringing America to its knees.

Zara, he immigrated to Egypt; the Sunni haven that Iraq once used to be and Saddam's former home. Zara couldn't be happier, he was now living in the land of the Pharaohs, he was ecstatic. Here he could study what he loved; Egyptology and the hieroglyphics. Zara lived the life of a lawyer in Egypt, as his hero Saddam once aspired to. He married Nawar, the love of his life and the year later his first-born daughter Afraa was born. Talia came the next year. The two girls were the loves of their lives, gifts from Allah.

Zara's destiny was to facilitate a pathway for the death flower seeds into to Egypt from Iraq; Iraqi ISIF refugees, hand-picked by the council of ten. Once successfully in Egypt, nurture the seeds, and ensure the transfer of the flowers to America as new immigrants. Their mission once settled in America… to lay dormant until the time for a call to action came.

Zara oversaw setting up the ISIF "*sleeper cells*" throughout the USA. Most would lead normal, inconspicuous middle-class typical American lives. Some would excel into local politics, becoming pillars of the community, but all… lying in wait.

Ironically and much to Zara's surprise, the American State Department was only too happy to help. Such was the way of Americans. Zara's task in negotiating Iraqi refugees into Egypt was his specialty being an immigration lawyer. With Zara fluent in English, he breezed through the legalities required to further speed things up for Iraqi refugees seeking immigration into the USA through Egypt…and this is where things became much more straightforward than he ever imagined. During the first extraction of US troops from Iraq in 2007, the US Citizen and Immigration Services created the US Refugees and Admissions Program. (USRAP) It stated that Special Immigrant Visas (SIV) would be granted to Iraqi nationals who acted in cooperation with the US Government as translators or interpreters, as of March 20, 2003, for not less than one year. Special consideration was to be given to Iraqi refugees who were seeking immigration to the US through Egypt, Syria or Lebanon. Those who cooperated with the US Army were also eligible for (SIV) status application. Naturally considering this offering by the US Government, ISIF and the Council of Ten made sure that all their organization's refugee members would be seeking US immigration status through Egypt, as Iraqis who had cooperated with the Americans for at least one year after "shock and awe" of March 2003.

Zara was only too happy to facilitate the ISIF refugees transfer to the USA. His father Faaz, back home in Baghdad had been fully engaged in sending his son just the right number of refugees who were sure to make it through the US Immigration interview process and granted refugee status making America their new home.

The time was almost 5:00 PM. Nawar Ahmed was at home by herself. The Ahmeds excelled in their professions with Nawar a professor at the University of Cairo, teaching philosophy, and Zara an established well-respected attorney with his own law firm specializing in immigration services. The Ahmeds with their two daughters enjoyed the benefits that came with upper-class lifestyles available to the well to do of Egypt. Their contemporary style modern home was in The Garden City section of Cairo, located south of Maydan Tahrir, a district encompassing upscale homes, a good number of embassies and dominated by a medieval citadel fortress. Zara favored this section of the city when searching to purchase his young family's forever home. It was in the heart of this region he would make his fortune as an immigration lawyer, he would be surrounded by embassies.

Nawar had already made dinner, she was keeping it warm for her girls and Zara to come home. Her husband arrived, the girls were late, or *was it another one of those after-school special studies days?* Nawar gave it no more thought and expected her girls to come through the door any moment.

Zara came into the kitchen and watched as Nawar covered the plate of pastries she had just baked with plastic wrap to keep fresh.

"Where are the girls?" Zara asked his wife.

"Oh, they should be home any second Zara, probably one of those after-school study sessions," she replied.

Zara's cell phone suddenly rang. He didn't recognize the number, it displayed, *"Private Number,"* he ignored it.

His cell rang again, same caller I.D. displayed, *"Private Number,"* he answered.

Zara listened. The caller was an officer of the Cairo City Police Department calling from Cairo General Hospital. It was Afraa and Talia, they were in emergency. Zara's heart skipped a beat as he dropped the phone.

PLNTNG

***

CHAPTER
EIGHT
TRNTN

The president's men and women gathered in the White House situation room. Not one member of the POTUS' cabinet was absent from this afternoon's meeting. The upcoming situation-room meeting had already been classified; urgent, due to the CIA's new satellite imagery of the hermit regime; North Korea, it was at it again.

Trenten trudged into the situation room like a Texas longhorn bull and was already taking his seat while members of his cabinet were starting to stand. He launched right into a diatribe while some people were still getting ready to stand up. They began to rise then sat back down, looking at one another foolishly.

"I don't give a flying fuck about the situation in North Korea. If I need to, I'll just nuke all those fish-head motherfuckers and be done with the whole North Korea problem once and for all. Whatever they're up to, I don't care. Far as I'm concerned, they're already a wasteland.

What I want answers to right this minute, is who the responsible parties are or whatever Muslim fuckers carried out the bombings in Egypt earlier today. That's what I want to know!" the President almost shouted his demands to the group now cowering around the table.

CIA (Central Intelligence Agency) Director Web Moss responded, "Mr. President we have our people on it now sir."

Trenten cut him off before Director Moss could get another word out.

"So, you don't fucking know, do you Web? And nobody, not one of you with all the intelligence gathering capabilities we have all over this fucking planet, the planes, the drones, the spy satellites in orbit above us… looking at our fucking pubic hairs, you don't fucking know anything!" Trenten was livid and pissed.

"All of you, get the fuck out, and don't call another god-damn situation room meeting until you have something concrete for me."

As people were starting to stand and about to leave, Greg Armstrong; his national security adviser tried responding and said, "Mr. President, we still have the North Korea issue on the table. Everyone paused for a moment and waited for Trenten to react, he did.

"Fuck off Greg, you heard what I said," and with that, the President got up and started leaving the room. On his way out he yelled for his chief of staff, "Pete, have you received the drafts from my speechwriters yet? I want to go over what those geniuses came up with before I address the nation this evening."

Pete Jericho answered the president, "yes, Mr. President, I have them right here." Jericho handed a copy to Trenten as the two walked back together to the west wing and the oval office.

TRNTN

***

CHAPTER
NINE
AWHSPR

Minister Agopian continued with the introduction of Eldon, Kimberley, and Billy to Zara and Nawar. He started in speaking to Zara and Nawar in Arabic at which point, Zara raised his hand slightly making a soft gesture in the air signaling a momentary pause.

Zara spoke in English, saying to the minister, "please both my wife and me are fluent in English minister Agopian if that is more convenient." At this point, Agopian understood, switching to English.

"Zara and Nawar Ahmed, I am honored to introduce you to Mr. Eldon Davis, Mrs. Kimberley Ashton-Davis, and Mr. Billy Simpson."

Nawar and Zara, turned towards Kimberley, Eldon, and Billy, who was now also standing between Talia and Afraa's bedside, then both bowed their heads. After a moment passed, Zara raised his head and looking each in the eye said in English, "peace be upon you and may Allah bless you for all the days of your lives."

Zara delivered his statement of eternal gratitude,

with a calm and humbleness in his voice that sent shivers through all of them, including Agopian who was now watching Zara. Zara then reached out and shook hands with Eldon, Kimberley, and Billy. After Zara shook hands, Nawar did the same, offering her gratitude for saving her daughters.

"Mr. and Mrs. Ahmed, peace be upon you. My wife Kimberley, Mr. Simpson and I are heartbroken this day. It is surely only with the grace of God, we were able to get your daughters into Doctor Nabel's care," Eldon said addressing Zara and Nawar.

Zara reached out and put his arm around his wife. Nawar, wiping her eyes, her head bent down, then looked up at Kimberley, taking a step towards her, hugging Kimberley with an embrace that melted Kimberley's heart. Kimberley teared up again, wiping away more sadness that overcame her. She hugged Nawar back, at which point the two women, made an unbreakable bond that would last for the rest of their lives.

Zara, then reached out to Eldon and Billy, shaking their hands again, and saying, "thank you Mr. Davis and Mr. Simpson for saving our daughters, we are indebted to you forever." There was a pause for longer than normal, almost a *now what?* moment. He then stepped in towards Eldon, almost embracing him leaning in close to Eldon's ear, holding his position for what seemed longer than necessary time and whispered directly into Eldon's ear the words, "thank you, you shall not be forgotten, Eldon Davis."

Having released Eldon, Eldon focused his attention onto Nawar trying his best to comfort her, while Zara then turned towards Billy and did the exact same thing, whispering into Billy's ear, "thank you,

you shall not be forgotten, Billy Simpson."

Billy glanced at Eldon, with a *what was that all about look* on his face, but Eldon was facing the other direction. Both men, found this up- close man to man connection unusual, almost haunting, like there was an attached message to Zara's thank you, you shall not be forgotten. This last move would stay with both Eldon and Billy for a very long time, that neither man could soon forget.

As the introductions had finished, they said their goodbyes and the Ahmeds went on with their hospital related needs. Walking back out of the emergency ICU care area, they were asked to meet with the city police department. Eldon asked Billy to tend to the questions from the authorities for now.

Doctor Nabel had gotten a temporary day-room at Cairo General for Eldon, Billy and Kimberley's use. Kimberley had called the Jewel of the Pharaohs earlier, arranging for her assistant to bring a change of clothes for the three of them. They couldn't be seen in public with blood-soaked or stained clothing. The last thing Eldon wanted was any notoriety for being at the bomb scene, even if it was to save lives. Neither he nor Kimberley were ones for heroic spotlighting.

It was one thing, being able to step forward funding a cultural exchange program, but an entirely different thing being in the limelight after having saved bomb survivors. But tragedy was not a time for notoriety, the less fanfare, the better for everyone at this point. Before leaving for the hotel, they all freshened up, looking like they'd never been involved.

A car from The Jewel of the Pharaoh's Resort and

INN FORMATION

Spa came to collect Kimberley and Eldon from the hospital. Billy would fly the chopper back to the resort when he was done with the authorities for today. Kimberley and Eldon were sure there would be more follow up questions, but for today, they'd had enough.

Arriving back at the hotel, darkness had already fallen on Cairo. It was 8:20 PM as their driver drove up to the grand entrance of the resort marked by two long rows of royal palms wrapped in strings of LED lights running up the length of the tree trunks. Eldon and Kimberley looked straight ahead from the rear seat of the Jaguar limo and could see commotion ahead as they drove closer to the porte-cochere.

"I knew it! I figured some of them would be here by now," Eldon said turning to Kimberley.

"Well, hon it's not like we weren't expecting it after what happened this afternoon," Kimberley added, finding Eldon's hand and taking it into hers.

"Nadia, no problem, just drive right up to the main entrance, Eldon and I will deal with the media, it's okay hon, we'll handle it. No need to turn around and go to the back entrance, besides, I wouldn't be surprised if some of them were waiting for us there too." Kimberley said to the driver.

Nadia eased the Jaguar up to the front entrance. The reporters tried rushing the car, but thankfully the resort's chief of security had cordoned off a section anticipating Eldon and Kimberley's arrival.

"Okay here we go," Eldon said to his wife as they both exited the limo.

"Yeah, I know honey, I just wish Felix could have been here by now, but he won't make it in from

Moscow until the morning," Kimberley replied as they both walked up to face the reporters.

The resort's security's efforts in place did the trick, keeping the throng of reporters at bay.

The international gallery had already gathered but Cairo Today was up front and center with their English-Channel reporter shouting a question. Other news journalists from the big players were also present; BBC, WINN, RT, Al Jazeera, AP, Reuters, even Hong Kong Daily managed to wangle themselves into the fray.

Both Eldon and Kimberley had to find the right words. The way they responded tonight to these reporters would be around the world in the next few minutes. Every letter and syllable forming each word they spoke, and facial expression would matter and could have lasting significance or misinterpretation, they would have to choose their words carefully.

They walked up to the Cairo Today reporter, after all, this tragedy happened in their city, so it was only proper for Kimberley and Eldon to respect the local press first.

All members of the press who gathered this evening knew Eldon and Kimberley with most having interviewed one or the other at some point over the years. There was no need for introductions, so the reporters just dove in.

Their producers and editing teams back in the studios would run the streaming banners underneath their television broadcasts informing their viewers just exactly who Eldon and Kimberley were; owner-operators of The Jewel of the Pharaohs Resort and Spa, and heads of Holiday Jewel Hotels and Casinos of Fort Lauderdale Florida. That background information would scroll along the bottom banners of the all the news broadcasts.

"Mr. Davis, can you tell us what you saw this afternoon?" shouted the Cairo Today reporter.

Eldon took Kimberley's hand, walking up to the newsman. He was about to answer when his mind flashed back in time for a second or two.

Eldon learned a valuable lesson over the years. A lesson he learned from his late father Len before Eldon had taken over Holiday Jewel Hotels upon his dad's passing.

Eldon clearly remembered his father telling him, *son, always be honest with the news media. If they suspect you of shortchanging them, they will dig relentlessly until they uncover the real and full story. It is their profession, bread, and butter, to get the whole story and often more than you bargained on. It was always best to be truthful, that way you will have their respect because you will have earned their trust. They can prove to be your worst enemy or your greatest ally.*

Len, his father, had learned this lesson during the Arab Oil embargo of 1973. Back then, Len's string of hotels strategically built in the sixties and seventies at the city limits on the newly expanding interstate highways of America suffered a tremendous financial impact.

The traveling American public had no choice but to cut back dramatically on their road trips due to nationwide gasoline shortages. That embargo had almost brought about the complete collapse of Len's roadside hotels and inns, faced with days on end zero room occupancy. Some of his hotels were forced to close, adding to Len almost losing his company. When questioned by the news media as to the solvency of his properties, Len tried sugar coating his company's financial stress. This misdirection only led to making the situation worse when days later he began laying off his employees in mass. From that point on, Len always told the truth, and it served him well in the years to come when he needed a positive press for his expanding company once the Arab oil embargo eased.

But Eldon believed that today was not the day to get into details. Today instead, was a day to delve in human emotion. And with that in mind, Eldon responded to the Cairo Today reporter.

"My wife Kimberley and I wish to express our deepest and most sorrowful condolences to all the parents who lost their children today. We cannot begin to express how terribly devastating this day has been for all Egyptians and the shocked and stunned parents of the children back in the United States. As I'm sure, it's been for all people of this good earth."

While Eldon was speaking, not a sound came from the gallery of reporters. The somberness of the moment and the day had accumulated and bottlenecked to hang on every one of Eldon Davis's words. By now this late in the day, all reporters knew that Eldon and Kimberley were eyewitnesses to the explosions, having watched from their helicopter.

The world had seen for perhaps the first time, the video recorded by the HJHC Sikorsky chopper. Some of the reporters were privy to being shown the entire recording, not just the recorded section from the air, but also the balance of the video. The Sikorsky's gimble mounted steady-cams continued recording after the chopper's landing, capturing their heroic efforts saving the children while running around the blast area looking for others. The video showed how they willingly placed themselves in danger, searching for survivors while secondary explosions thundered around them. The camera captured every blood-soaked life-saving attempt as well as the Cairo General trauma teams' quick responsive action in receiving and treating the children upon their landing at the hospital's air ambulance helipad.

The reporters who were in the know and had seen the entire recording knew that Eldon, Kimberley, and Billy were all heroes today, some would write about that in their columns. Their story was already written in their minds, Kimberley, Eldon, Billy and Nasser Agopian would be celebrated in the news, as Americans and Egyptian who went into battle today, to save children from the evils of the world, emerging from the cauldron with five lives. Unfortunately for the world, over one hundred sixty other lives were lost.

All reporters' satellite video hookups were focused on Eldon and Kimberley as they stood in the glare of the video cameras' lights.

Eldon, holding Kimberley around the waist continued, "we are all in shock. For the four of us in that chopper today, and on the ground by the Great Pyramid of Giza…for us, the events of this day have been burned into our lives forever as I'm certain it has been in yours." At this point, both Kimberley and Eldon almost lost it again, the tears came, he turned his head to look at Kimberley. She moved in closer to Eldon, holding onto his arm. Eldon choked up with emotion wiping his eyes, it was genuine and a compelling moment. He went on, "I can only hope that somehow, we will all find a way to continue living our lives, grasping on to the goodness we may find in this world while coping with the evil that surrounds us with every breath we take, no matter where on God's earth we may live. God-Allah is with us all. Thank you for coming."

Eldon and Kimberley turned and walked away, being escorted by hotel security into the foyer of the Jewel of the Pharaohs. Not one reporter even tried asking another question. Most stood with tears in their eyes, now faced with filing follow up reports.

Back inside their residence at the hotel, Eldon turned on the wall-mounted big screen television. It was by default tuned to the local Cairo English language channel, and sure enough, live coverage was still taking place from the bomb scene. Within minutes of having left the scene with the reporters at the hotel's entrance, the local channel was already broadcasting Eldon and Kimberley's arrival at the hotel, playing Eldon's statement to the press. Eldon stood and watched himself giving his condolences, and thoughts of the day. Kimberley walked up beside him, grabbed onto his arm again and they both watched standing in silence when the broadcast switched to the video captured by their chopper, documenting the entire event. Eldon and Kimberley stood watching in horror, reliving their ordeal, watching themselves, Billy and Nasser Agopian running through the carnage looking for survivors. The video was horrific, but neither Kimberley or Eldon could take their eyes off the television screen. Then Eldon's cell phone came to life and rang. Eldon and Kimberley recognized the personal ringtone, it was Cathy, Eldon's daughter back home in Florida.

Eldon retrieved his cell phone, answered it saying, "Hello Cathy."

Before Eldon was able to get another word out, Cathy cut in, "dad, oh dad, what is going on over there? You must be horrified. You and Kimberley must be devasted. Dad, I'm watching you and Kimberley right now on WINN, they've been looping your press statement almost non-stop."

Eldon replied to his daughter's emotionally charged concern for him and Kimberley saying, "Cathy, Kimberley and I are pretty shaken up, no doubt about that. I don't really know what to say, it's just too much sweetheart, it's tough. But Cathy, Kimberley and I need to come home, the parents of those kids will want answers.

"Dad, what is it that you can do? No one can do anything about what's already happened. You intended to provide those children the trip of a lifetime," Cathy spoke passionately to her father.

"Yes Cathy, but their trip of a lifetime turned into their final days. Some parents I'm sure will try to lay the blame at our feet, we'll face them. Neither Kimberley or I will shy away. It's the least we can do, face the anguish of the parents back home who entrusted us in taking care of their children," Eldon replied.

"But Cathy, we're going to need your help with something here. Two of the surviving kids will require the sort of expertise that only a few surgeons possess, and sweetheart, you're one of them." Eldon said, invoking a deep father to daughter connection.

"Dad, you know I'm always there for you. I love

you and Kimberley, just get back here safely for now. When are you leaving?" Cathy asked.

"Billy will be flying us home in the morning sweetheart, I love you, see you in a couple of days, Cathy," Eldon said goodbye to his daughter.

"Cathy sends her love Kimberley," Eldon said to his wife, who was still holding onto Eldon's arm leaning onto him for support.

There was no time with the events of the day and now into the night for Kimberley or Eldon to have dinner or even a bite to eat, but neither one was hungry.

Kimberley then said, "you know hon, I don't know what I want or need, but maybe a drink will settle me, I have to get a grip on things."

"Well, if you're going to have something, I think I'll join you," Eldon replied.

"Wine, or something stronger?" Kimberley asked softly.

"Jack on the rocks, the warmth will relax me."

Kimberley prepared the drinks, Eldon walked up to the counter, took his whiskey in hand, had a sip and then paused a moment, enough time for Kimberley to detect that he had something on his mind he wanted to tell her. Kimberley was right.

She took her wine glass, holding it in front, not having a sip yet and waited with bated breath, raising an eyebrow for her husband to say something.

"A strange thing happened concerning Mr. Ahmed and me at the hospital today, not sure if you caught it, and not just with me, with Billy as well,"

Eldon said matter-of-factly.

"What do you mean Eldon, what happened?" Kimberley asked, now very intrigued with an element of concern.

"Well, just before we said our goodbyes, Zara, sort of hugged me. It was more like he leaned into me, then coming in close to my ear, he whispered, you will not be forgotten, Eldon Davis."

"Really?" Kimberley responded with surprise in her voice.

"The thing is that although it was a reassuring statement of sorts, it also came across kind of haunting, almost foreboding.

I thought it might be something Muslims say to one another, but I'm not Muslim. Strangely I found it both soothing and unnerving if you can follow that." Eldon said, trying to explain the best he could.

"Wow, and you say that Zara did the same with Billy?" Kimberley asked.

"Yeah, as we were leaving Billy told me about Zara whispering into his ear, you will not be forgotten Billy Simpson," Eldon responded.

"It's probably nothing, but it felt peculiar. I guess I'm just not used to this culture and how things go here," Eldon said.

"You could call Nasser tomorrow before we leave or even now and ask him, maybe Zara did the same with Nasser," his wife replied.

"Yeah, maybe so, but Nasser is Coptic Christian, so he might not even know of this up close sort of in your ear statements, perhaps I'll run it by him some other time.

We've all had enough for today. Like I say, I don't know, but right now I'm looking forward to you and me flying back home tomorrow and seeing Cathy. You know what I'm going to talk to her about don't you hon? Eldon asked.

"I sure do Eldon," his wife answered.

AWHSPR

***

CHAPTER

TEN

ZARA-ELDN

Zara was troubled about the events of the day. This attack at the site of The Great Pyramid was something entirely unexpected and yet nothing more than backward thinking by whichever Jihadi group would lay claim to this thoughtless act. Zara well knew it was an attempt to hurt the economy of Egypt by targeting tourists. Tourism accounted for the 20/20/20 factor of the Egyptian economic picture. As of 2018 twenty percent of Egypt's gross national product was derived from tourism. Twenty million tourists visited annually that kept twenty million Egyptians employed in the tourism and related industries, making up the 20/20/20-sided triangular portion of the overall economic pie. This act of aggression although killing Americans and Egyptians was not aimed at the USA. It was meant to further disrupt the current Egyptian government in power by halting travel to Egypt.

Zara figured it had something to do with the now defunct Muslim Brotherhood organization. After the Cairo Arab Spring riots, the organization became the ruling party but shortly afterward things went awry.

The party was ousted, by the military, its president removed, and the organization banned. Recently there had been rumblings of its intention to return. Zara believed these bombings weren't about to accomplish anything, just more chaos in the streets.

Zara's organization; ISIF considered itself an independent Islamic organization not associated with any other groups seeking revenge upon the USA, or the western world. ISIF wanted nothing to do with any Islamic organizations in the Mideast, Saudi, Iran, or Iraq. ISIF was independent, tied to no one other than the legacy of Saddam Hussein and Iraq. But now his daughters had become victims, and Zara thought it best to seek advice from ISIF's Council of Ten. He spoke with his father Faaz that night. Father and son agreed. Best for Zara to fly to Baghdad in the morning, and more importantly for Zara to be prepared for action.

Night had fallen on Cairo, but the day's ending would not take with it the hollow feeling in Zara's heart. Zara went into his library, sat down at his desk, reached for his diary binder, opened the three rings holding the pages and inserted another page, entering the day's events. He wrote in his most favorite secret language; Egyptian hieroglyphics; the language of the Pharaohs. His passion for this art form had taken hold many years ago at school in Switzerland, and over the years, Zara had improved on encoding secrecy into his diary. He developed smart encryption that would add to further complicating the deciphering of his entries should anyone ever try. He was convinced no code breakers would ever know what he wrote into his book of secrets. The ancient Egyptian symbols would forever hold tight all that was ISIF; what it stood for, its philosophy, and the fine details of ISIF's plan to control the American government.

That night when Zara lay down beside Nawar, he said to his wife, "Nawar tomorrow I shall go to Baghdad. I will find answers there, ask me not how, but I will. You must take time away from the university and watch over the girls. I shall return in four days."

Zara kissed his wife good night but could not sleep. They both lay in silence holding hands, staring into the darkness, and then Nawar said, "I feel like I'm in a fully awake coma," and she began to cry again.

In the morning Eldon, Kimberley, and Billy made their way to the airport, as did Zara. Only he was flying to his boyhood home; Baghdad on commercial airlines, while Eldon and Kimberley were being flown back home to Florida by Billy on their private HJHC jet.

Nawar was also on the move, she was heading out to be with her two daughters at Cairo General Hospital, she would be with her girls until sundown, praying to Allah with all of heart and soul to comfort her girls in their time of great need.

The flight back home to Florida would require two fuel stops. Eldon's Lear 85 jet had a range of three thousand nautical miles or almost thirty-five hundred statute miles. Cairo to Ft. Lauderdale was six and a half thousand miles. Billy would refuel in the Canary Islands, then hop part way over the Atlantic to Bermuda, refuel again for their final segment. In Bermuda, they would take one day to get the cobwebs cleared from their minds. Eldon thought this would give them the opportunity in preparing for the next day's arrival back home and dive into it all. Their resort properties in Bermuda would be a welcome change from the events in Cairo. The three of them would take a break, maybe even enjoy the beach at Horseshoe Bay on the south shore. Kimberley loved strolling the pink sands of Bermuda's beaches. It might just be what they all needed after what they'd been through. Billy too needed a break. Eldon knew that Billy was fond of the Ram's Head Inn on Front Street and Henry the VIII's on the south shore. They all needed a break.

With the setting Bermuda sun shimmering over the darkening turquoise waters of the Atlantic, Eldon, and Kimberley looked out from their hotel balcony onto the horizon wondering what the next few days would bring.

Eldon looked across the balcony dining table at Kimberley holding her wine glass looking out across the ocean. The gentle Bermuda wind, blowing through her hair and a warm glow on her face from the afternoon sun brought out her inner beauty once again. He could plainly see that a calmness had returned to his gorgeous wife, and thankfully she was beginning to be herself. It was evident that the afternoon walk along the beach at Horseshoe Bay had a rejuvenating effect, and it was good to be in Bermuda; Eldon's favorite place to destress in the entire world.

"You know Kimberley, I'm going to ask Cathy again to come back to Cairo with us when we return in a few days. She already offered her help when I talked to her earlier," Eldon stopped talking for a minute and looked inwardly, being thoughtful. "

"I think I may be taking this too personally and wanting to make things right immediately. I know my daughter can't do miracles, I'm grabbing at straws," Eldon said to his wife.

"She will insist on helping out any way she can Eldon, you know that," Kimberley replied. "I'm willing to bet Eldon that Cathy will want to leave for Cairo right away after you explain the severity of the injuries Talia and Afraa sustained. She will want to consult with Doctor Nabel the minute after you tell her. You know what she's like Eldon when there are children involved, there is no one better than Cathy Davis, your daughter to provide the expertise these two children will need," Kimberley reassured her husband.

Eldon reached out across the table and took Kimberley's hand into his, saying, "I know sweetheart, I know she will. I hope she can shine a sliver of light into the Ahmed's world of darkness. Their two girls will need all the light they can get in the coming days and weeks," He paused and standing up from his chair leaned over the small table-for-two and kissed Kimberley. Sitting back down, he continued, "we will somehow figure things out, we always do Kimberley."

They both sat in silence for a moment.

Then Eldon started in again while gazing out over

the Atlantic. "You know, there was a time when my vision was blurred when it came to seeing things right in front of my eyes. My dad and I were walking the beach on the Jersey shore one windy summer afternoon when he suddenly stopped and asked me to look out onto the horizon and tell him what I saw. I did what I thought he asked me to do, but I missed the mark completely. I told him I saw the waves and seagulls soaring on the brisk winds. My dad figured I had gone blind."

Kimberley sat looking into her husband's eyes with intrigue.

"Yeah, he certainly opened my eyes that afternoon. I remember it like it was just yesterday. He told me I only saw what was immediately visible and I had to learn how to see over the horizon. He said when looking out on the horizon, he clearly saw his hotels in Spain and London. He could see guests checking in to his properties and envision his business flourishing.

Kimberley, I close my eyes, and I can still feel him placing his hands onto my shoulders, leaning in close to my ear - and there's that "whispering into my ear-thing" again, telling me that I needed to open my eyes. He said I had to learn how to see past what lay in front of me; to become a visionary. He encouraged me to check into the hotel business, teaching me how to look beyond today and into the future. I checked into one of his hotels and never ever checked out of the business. When he passed, I was ready to take control of the company he built. He honestly did open my eyes. Ever since then Kimberley, every time I look out onto the horizon over the ocean, I think of that day."

"And what is it you can see over the horizon now Eldon?" Kimberley asked.

"I can see trouble ahead sweetheart, our Jewel of the Pharaohs resort will have a tough time of things going forward after what happened," Eldon replied.

"Yes Eldon, yesterday morning, before we left the hotel, Fatima Alexander, our Director of Sales and Marketing caught me in the lobby and pulled me aside for a quick one on one. She told me that calls were coming in the world over from travel agents and tour consolidators Eldon. They were calling in to cancel room reservations, and the online booking services were tearing up the internet canceling bookings throughout Egypt. Our projected occupancy for the upcoming thirty days out has dropped by sixty percent, overnight; it's a mass exodus from the hotel industry in Cairo, and we're not immune," Kimberley said with an element of alarm in her voice.

Eldon replied, "yeah, blowing up buses full of tourists isn't good for the hotel business. The hotels in Cairo will suffer from this, especially the resort properties. We will have to find a way to soften that blow to our property, and I think I know how we might accomplish that Kimberley."

"Oh really, this ought to be interesting," Kimberley replied, her eyes wide open, "well fill me in."

Eldon replying said, "I was thinking on the plane about this before we landed in the Canary Islands and by the time we got here to Bermuda, I was convinced we might stand a chance in replenishing those gloomy room occupancy forecasts. You know this will affect all of Cairo, every hotel will suffer and I'm sure some will even end up having to close their doors until things settle down and tourism starts picking up again, that may take six months, maybe even a year. But that's assuming no more incidents like this happen," Eldon paused a moment, taking a sip from his wine glass.

"Well, we're not going to close Kimberley, and neither will we curtail the level of service excellence the Jewel is already famous for throughout the market. We will persevere no matter how challenging things get, we will not lay off our employees. I've got a plan in mind but will need your help, specifically your diplomatic State Department connections to get it off the ground," Eldon paused, for a moment waiting to see a reaction from Kimberley and it came.

"What have you got up your sleeve my dear husband?" She asked squinting her eyes at Eldon, with a smile forming on her face. "Knowing you Eldon as I do, I just know you have thought up something bizarre unique, even outlandish! What I love about you, my dear husband is that your plans always seem to need me in them. We pulled off a beauty of a plan in Moscow twenty years ago to rid the Russian Mafia from all our city hotels, and the way we put an end to the corrupt Caribbean hotel labor union was masterful. I'm sure you've come up with something equally as grand for Cairo. I want to hear all the crazy details," She replied.

"Okay baby, listen up." Eldon reached for the wine bottle, topping up her glass with her favorite Mouton Cadet. She leaned back into her chair and listened as Eldon laid out his plan to save The Jewel of the Pharaohs Resort and Spa, and maybe the entire Cairo tourism and travel industry following this disaster.

Zara, his father Faaz, and the Council of Ten gathered in the stone chamber of the ISIF cave, deep in the Iraqi desert. Upon their arrival, traditional greetings were exchanged between Faaz, Zara, and the ISIF group. Zara's position was still situated in front of the Council of Ten. The other ISIF members who were present at the first meeting Zara and Arish attended years ago, were not in attendance this night.

Faaz began, "son, we are deeply saddened to learn of your loving daughters' injuries. "Eye-sif" prays to Allah for quick recovery and healing to come in Allah's name to Talia and Afraa. Allah's will shall be done, come what may," Faaz stopped, waited a few moments, then on to business.

He started in again, and while speaking turned his head to the left and then to the right acknowledging the council members.

"The incident at the pyramids was not something we approve, it served no purpose other than to further aggravate the powers that be in Egypt.

This act will only intensify the authorities' search which will lead to their discovery and eventual elimination.

Our best information from the region leads us to believe this action was carried out by members of the ISS, (Islamic State in Sinai), a well-known affiliate of ISIS caliphate. They have for years been a constant thorn in the side of the current government trying to do everything they can to bring them down. Deliberately targeting and killing mainly children in mass is not the way of Islam, and we do not approve. Let that be known," Faaz stopped speaking. He paused for a few moments, then nodded, looking at one of the other members whom Zara recognized as his second uncle from his father's side; Turik Ahmed.

Turik spoke, "the Council of Ten; eye-sif, has decided the time to act is upon us. The time has come close for a revised new world order to come into effect. America shall no longer lead the way, ISIF shall change everything and restore the glory of Iraq. All is in place," Turik finished speaking, and he too then nodded, for another to speak.

As Turik lifted his head, another council member began at the far-left end of the group to speak, it was one of his uncles from his mother's side this time; Kabir. He addressed Zara directly.

"Zara, tomorrow will see the arrival of your brother Arish from the United States. He has been called back to sit with us. ISIF will be together as one, and we shall lay out the course of events to come. You have prepared well Zara over the years. Allah will bless us with great success."

Then Kabir paused, unfolded the flag sitting in his lap to show the swords of victory, bent down and kissed it.

He then passed it down the line until everyone else did the same. It finally came back to Faaz, who handed it to Zara, he kissed the swords on the flag, then gave it back to his father.

Faaz then said with a loud voice, "we are eye-sif, Islam, Saddam, Iraq, Forever," followed by everyone repeating in unison, "we are eye-sif. Islam, Saddam, Iraq, Forever"

The meeting for tonight was over. Faaz and Zara drove out of the desert and back home to Baghdad. Arish would be with them tomorrow. Knowing he'd be seeing his brother the next day, caused some momentary excitement for Zara, but just fleeting. His thoughts and heart were far away in Cairo with Nawar his loving wife and his two daughters lying unconscious in Cairo General Hospital.

ZARA-ELDN

***

CHAPTER
ELEVEN
ISIF

It was close to ten years since Arish Ahmed immigrated to the United States from Baghdad. Time enough to establish himself as a reputable businessman running a specialized type of company serving the needs of city planners throughout the country; building and structure demolition-implosion services.

Arish had initial hurdles to clear in obtaining special licensing to operate such a tightly regulated line of work. There were several security background checks for him to pass; Federal-DHS, FBI, as well as CIA since he was a foreign national and Iraqi. But Arish had no problem. He aced the various security checks. He was recognized and honored by the US Military for his contribution to the American effort in Iraq saving countless GIs from being blown up by IED's. Arish sailed through all the background check without a single blip on the screen. His license to operate a restricted business was granted and renewed annually.

Since having started his company; Confederated Building Demolition Industries, Arish contracted dozens of implosion jobs across the USA. His company had demolished football stadiums that had long past their time, entire government housing projects that had quickly deteriorated into eye-sores on the community and were to be replaced with new modern buildings.

Recently his Las Vegas-based company had won contracts to bring down hotels and casinos that had outlived their use and no longer fit into the Vegas strip evolution. Confederated Building Demolition Industries (CFBDI) was also engaged in bringing down highway overpasses, along with bridges spanning rivers and gorges. Arish was already involved in blowing things up all over the US.

Arish Ahmed, a demolitions expert, Iraqi Immigrant, now a US citizen had infiltrated ISIF's will into sections and sectors of American society just as ISIF had planned for the brothers to do when they first kissed the flag in 2002.

Zara successfully arranged to transfer over a thousand hand-picked ISIF recruits, Iraqi refugees through Egypt to the USA as new English-speaking Iraqi immigrants. Before leaving for Egypt, the Iraqi refugees received specialized training by the ISIF Council of Ten, in the setting of explosives; those explosives to be supplied by Arish. After the refugees arrived in Egypt, Zara held training classes for select chosen would-be immigrants in the secret language of his favorite pass-time, now incorporated into ISIF communications methodology; Egyptian Hieroglyphs. The training, in fact, was simple; each symbol represented a specific letter in the alphabet, everyone picked up Zara's teachings in a matter of minutes and was decoding hieroglyphs into English words within an hour. Without having successfully completed their training to Zara's satisfaction, immigration to the USA was not possible, but every ISIF recruit met Zara's requirements, the process was straightforward.

The key, however, in establishing the link between the individually chosen hieroglyphic symbols and the conversion of the symbols to the alphabet would lie in the source code key that only Zara controlled. Without the source key, the deciphering of the glyphs into letters of the alphabet was impossible. The Rosetta Stone from 1799 provided the clue to deciphering the Egyptian Hieroglyphs, and today, Zara would re-encode the secret all over again with his own personally developed variable source code key.

The explosives trained ISIF sleeper cells were now intricately woven into the fabric of North American society; The USA and certain sections of Canada. No, ISIF was not about to let Canada off the hook. Canada too shall pay for aiding the Americans in the destruction of Iraq, even if their role was a limited one.

Arish Ahmed's access to virtually unlimited amounts of industrial explosives paved the avenue to supplying the ISIF sleeper cells with all the bang they would ever need. His industry, however, was tightly regulated. The storage of explosives had to meet specific security parameters as well as special inventory maintenance accounting requirements. His company was required to keep accurate records of incoming product and outgoing product designated for demolition sites or used in training sessions. Arish always oversupplied the need for all jobs by at least fifteen to twenty percent. The extra unused explosives, Arish kept as his personal stash. He then little by little distributed the undetected inventory to the sleeper cells throughout the nation. Government audits of inventory whether scheduled or unannounced surprise audits visitations always proved to be in perfect order. His company's storage and inventory practices and procedures maintained an A level rating. Because all explosives used by Arish's company were commercial in nature, no identification taggants were required in the manufacturing of the C4 used by Confederated Building Demolition Industries. Even if the ATF (Alcohol Tobacco and Firearms) or the FBI (Federal Bureau of Investigation) forensics looked for taggants in exploded C4, none would be detected leading back to his company.

"Brother, my heart bleeds. When I learned of the news about my nieces from father, I tried calling immediately, but you must have been on the plane coming home brother. Peace be upon you, may Allah speed Talia and Afraa's health back into your arms." Arish pulled his brother Zara close, hugging him with all the affection they had for one another. "It is with sadness I must see you now, but my heart is filled with hope Zara," Arish finished greeting his brother.

"Thank you, Arish, and may peace be upon you. It is good to see you brother. We have much work to do," Zara said replying to Arish's greeting.

"Zara, we have done all our work, now we will

need to control and guide what lies ahead. Father and the Council of Ten will finally have the power in their hands for us to change the world. Zara, the time is fast approaching," Arish responded.

"That it is brother, that it is," Zara added.

Faaz and his two boys arrived back at the ISIF center in the desert. Once again, only the Council of Ten, Arish, and Zara were present. After greetings and prayers were concluded, the meeting was to get underway but not in the same immediate location. Neither of the boys had noticed before but just around a slight bend in the cave wall, a large stone wheel covered an entrance way to another chamber. Two men rolled the stone wheel to the side further along the stone wall, exposing an entrance to the inner room. Everyone went inside. The room was different than the main exterior area. This chamber was finished inside with paneling and electric lights powered by a bank of batteries connected to a voltage inverter. A large wooden boardroom table occupied the center of the room. The room was further equipped with laptop computers. On the wall at the far end of the room was another framed picture of Saddam Hussein with an ISIF flag underneath his portrait and underneath it; a huge wall mounted sixty-inch high definition television monitor connected to the laptops. The boardroom table was set so that the television faced the far end of the boardroom table affording a view to everyone.

Faaz took his seat at the head of the table and motioned for Zara and Arish to sit immediately in the first chairs closest to Faaz, facing across from one another. Two laptop computers were on the table placed in front of Zara and Arish. The Council of Ten was now prepared to set into motion the course of action that would change the world forever. The steps to making that happen would be discussed and approved this night.

Faaz began, "brothers, the rain we send in the coming days will have the flowers of death blooming across America. The steps we take today will see glory, prosperity, and power returning to Iraq. Yes, brothers, Iraq will be feared by its enemies as no nation has ever been in the history of the world. We will take the power that is America and make it our own. America shall suffer as we have suffered but times ten, and thus the balance of power will shift into our hands, Allah willing," Faaz paused, then suddenly stood and declared, "we are eye-sif, Islam, Saddam, Iraq, Forever."

After that, all members of the Council stood, as did Arish and Zara and repeated, "we are eye-sif, Islam, Saddam, Iraq, Forever," together as one voice.

"And now my brothers, my sons will speak. Arish, my first-born, will be the first to speak. Tell us of your work in the heart of the beast." Faaz said, sitting back in his chair, and listened with pride.

"Peace be upon you, father. It is my honor to sit at this table with the Council of Ten, all of mine and my dear brother Zara's uncles. We have come far, and now all is ready and in place. We have planned well, picked our members wisely. Eye-sif now patiently waits for the day to arrive when our presence on the world scene will be felt for the first time," Arish said, looking around the table at each one of his uncles.

After having made momentary eye contact with everyone, Arish continued addressing the Council of

Ten. He touched the laptop keyboard, and the large wall mounted television came to life. The screen displayed a coast to coast map of the continental United States, Canada, and in a corner section of the graphic, a separate map showing the Hawaiian Islands and Alaska.

"Brothers this is what we have," Arish talked as he worked the laptop. "Over the years we've waited, we've been planting. ISIF seeds have blossomed into our sleeper cells throughout the United States and a part of Canada. We are now finely woven into every aspect of American society. Brothers, we are, carpenters, bus drivers, truck drivers, we are accountants, sanitation workers, city council members. Yes, brothers, we are airport workers, grounds crews, luggage handlers, aircraft mechanics, train conductors, electricians, travel agents, engineers, restaurant managers, IT workers and hotel managers, in short, we are American society, but we are ISIF! Brothers, we have over one thousand sleeper cells waiting! My good brother Zara has assigned each cell its own unique identifying number. And brothers, as we planned and as you have instructed, all is ready to go, as of this day. All venues and targets are armed with detonators ready to be set off with radio frequency triggering devices," Arish said and then watched for the reaction of the council. They all reacted together, clapping and nodding their approval to Arish's update.

The Council of Ten listened intensely, focusing on the graphical map which now displayed highlighted names of cities with sleeper cells. To the right of the map, were three drop-down menu boxes. The first drop-down menu description was *Jobs.* When hovered over the job categories displayed, and further selecting a job category, example; *Airport Grounds Crew*, resulted in the map highlighting the corresponding cities: Buffalo, Boston, Memphis, San Francisco, Miami, Atlanta, Denver, Seattle, New Orleans, Los Angeles, Honolulu, Anchorage, Charlotte, Tampa, Cleveland, Cincinnati, Detroit, Minneapolis, Salt Lake City, as well as smaller cities and towns including one town in Canada; Gander Newfoundland.

The second drop-down menu box, was "*Targets*" which displayed a category of targets alphabetically, starting with "Airport, Arena, Bank, Bridge, Casino, Church, Country Clubs, Department Store, and down the list including such structures as; Overpass, Shopping Mall, Theme Park, and finishing with the last item; Zoo. Arish selected the first target category, "*Airport*," this resulted in thirty-four cities being highlighted across the US, such centers as Miami, Dallas, New York, Seattle, St. Louis, Atlanta, New Orleans, Tacoma, Indianapolis, Cleveland, Pittsburg, Nashville, Charlotte, Norfolk, Boston, Las Vegas, San Diego, to name a few. Also, each target highlighted was tagged with a unique sleeper cell numeric identifier linking to target, job description, and venue; 559- Airport-Airport Grounds Crew-Seattle.

The third drop-down menu box was "*Dates*." This opened another table with an interactive calendar. Hovering over a selected date, displayed the targeted categories (e.g., *Train station*) with the corresponding cities set to be activated on that day in the designated locations highlighted on the map. All calendar dates remained unpopulated at this time. That final step would change as of tonight.

Arish then continued addressing the group,

"brothers, the initial set of activation dates and target categories will be selected by you this night. After I enter that data into the calendar, Zara will take over and communicate the information to those waiting in America. I will now let my brother Zara speak," Arish concluded.

Zara then started to speak, "thank you and may peace be upon you brother. This has been many years in the making. In the year 2008, I moved to Egypt and Arish went to live in the heart of the beast. Now, brothers, we are here. The time has come, praise Allah.

Once the council selects the targets and the dates, I will communicate the will of the council to our people awaiting your instructions across the ocean. I wish to take this moment to once again thank the council for approving my communication protocols that will convey our wishes to those waiting. The information will originate from an internet domain website hosted on a server in the USA, but the location of the business is in Cairo; The Jewel of the Pharaohs Resort and Spa."

Zara then took over with his laptop, and although not connected to the internet, he brought up The Jewel of the Pharaohs website he earlier saved as "*HTML*" pages and showed the Council of Ten how the communication process will happen.

"The domain name and website is that of the resort. Although the property is located in Cairo, all online internet traffic runs on servers located at the resort's head offices in Fort Lauderdale Florida USA. Brothers, there are many good reasons why this venue is more than perfect for our needs. I might also remind you that we have a number of our ISIF brothers who immigrated to Egypt set up and working in the I.T. Department of The Jewel of the Pharaohs. Once again, a perfect set up. As you know, my communications language is embodied in the ancient hieroglyphics of the Pharaohs. I need not explain why this makes sense. My sleeper cells now in the USA await a call from the tomb of Tutenkamen. Praise be to Allah," and with that Zara looked to his father, Zara was finished.

Faaz then spoke, "thank you, my sons, for your words. The Council approves of your work and preparation. America will come to know the *Shock and Awe* Iraq felt, the thunder of American bombs and missiles that rained on Baghdad March 21st, 2003 at exactly 12:15 PM eastern standard time in the United States. In thirty days, *ISIF's Shock and Awe* will happen in America. It will be the anniversary date; time for the beast to pay." Faaz paused for a moment and again, the council exploded with applause, "in thirty days, the world will change.

"Brothers, as we have decided, the categories to be targeted on March 21st at exactly 12:15 PM eastern standard time in the US, are as follows," Faaz said as Arish started entering the data into his laptop.

"We will first give the beast a sampling, make it scramble, watch as it tries to run in all directions at once. We shall start with the four corners of the continental United States and one centrally located city. Also, we shall target a small airport in Canada. American planes on route will no longer run to Gander Newfoundland as they did in 9-11. It will also give the Canadian appeasers a wake-up call. Yes, brothers, Canada only played a small supporting role in shock and awe, but play they did, and now we play.

The airports to be activated are Boston, Miami, San Diego, Seattle, St. Louis, and the heart of the beast itself: Washington D.C. When the time is right, we shall reveal ourselves, and the beast will know ISIF," Faaz; ISIF's leader then paused, looking around the table and reminded everyone, "remember brothers, we have chosen not to communicate directly with any member of the US Government. Eye-sif will use one of America's own home-grown citizens to speak for us, Zara has chosen.

Praise be to Allah, Islam, Saddam, Iraq, Forever, we are eye-sif," Faaz concluded, and immediately the Council of Ten, Zara and Arish repeated, "Islam, Saddam, Iraq, Forever, we are "eye-sif."

It was now Zara's turn. He'd soon put the wheels in motion but first, he would spend much-needed brother-time with Arish.

ISIF

***

CHAPTER

TWELVE

ADRES

The American President wasn't exactly known as the great communicator as were a few of his predecessors. Trenten indeed did need the help of his speech writers. Without the speechwriters' well thought out compositions the President would come off sounding almost inept and incapable of conveying compassion. Even with the speechwriters' help, heartfelt conveyance of the human condition would be hard to see in his face or hear in his voice. When reading from the teleprompter, he was cardboard and monotone. But the time had come to address the nation.

The White House producer prompted Trenten by starting the countdown to going live. He pointed at the President, moving his arm back and forth, holding up five fingers, closing his fist, then opening his fist holding up four fingers, three, two, one, then pointed at the President signaling… go!

Trenten sitting behind his oval office desk started in, "my fellow Americans, this day marks one of the gravest and most horrific days in our nation's history. My heart and the heart of the nation bleeds with sorrow and rage with what happened to our children and citizens in Egypt this afternoon." Trenten paused and strangely started looking around the room, appearing very uncomfortable.

Pete Jericho, the president's chief of staff, turned to his assistant looking puzzled asking, "what's he doing?"

Then suddenly Trenten stood up and started into one of his rants, "Okay, America, I was going to read off the teleprompter the very properly prepared words written for me by my very proper speechwriters. Ladies and gentlemen, people of America, I'll be the first to admit that I'm not a Toastmasters International speech class graduate, but I have to say what is on my mind.

This bombing today, well, I've had it. You've had it. Here is what I have to say to those bastards, we're coming for you, and we're going to get you bastards!"

Jericho couldn't believe his ears, this was going right off the rails. On the other hand, he wasn't that surprised, it had been like this ever since he took over as chief of staff for this president.

The President's blood pressure was rising, and his face turning red with rage. He continued after a pause, seething!

"Whatever holes they are hiding in, we'll get them all just like we got Saddam Hussein. We pulled that son of a bitch out of his spider hole deep in the ground in 2003. America, when they blow up eighty kids and more, I'm no longer nice addressing the world,"

Trenten paused for a moment, then pounded his oval office desk with a clenched fist saying, "the world will know that America is coming for you bastards! God bless all Americans, and God bless The United States of America. Good night."

Jericho was stunned. He turned to his assistant once again and said, "holy shit!"

One would rarely find Greg Armstrong; the National Security Agency Director down at foggy bottom visiting with Drew McCoy the Secretary of State. But on this day, one would, as well as Web Moss the CIA Director and Mindy Beaton the FBI Director. On most occasions, the four would only be seen together when President Trenten called on all to attend a meeting at the White House.

The three men and one woman met in a sealed quiet room at the State Department.

"Well, that was quite the speech last night. He is really pissed, and I'm not too far off in agreeing with him this time," Mindy Beaton said.

"We'll have to produce something concrete here in the next day or two. We cannot let this go much longer without something from the four of us. I've got my section chief Al Munson in Cairo, working on this night and day," the CIA Director stated with a tone of confidence. The three federal agency directors sat looking at Web Moss almost breathing in at the same time as a choir, with a "*let's hope we get something look*" on their faces.

"Thing is, I wouldn't have been surprised if he had started firing each one of us on the spot after not having anything on the pyramids massacre. Sure, he would have been shooting himself in the foot, but yesterday Trenten was utterly unhinged. Fuck North Korea, nuke the fuckers… what did he call them – fish head motherfuckers? I've never heard him that pissed! Can you imagine the fallout if this had leaked to one of the networks or cable news reporters? Web finished saying.

"Well don't be so sure that that cannot happen. We've all been surprised before," Armstrong noted.

The FBI Director, Mindy Beaton then piped in, "I don't have much on my end. I honestly have nothing now. This type of terrorism on foreign soil involving American victims is pretty much in your three areas. Once we think it might have spilled over onto our shores, I'd have more of our people on it," Mindy said.

"But this time, I've assigned a legion of FBI agents looking to scour anything on our end that may link us to the Jihadists who carried out this horrific bus bombing. Mother of God…targeting children, just beyond the unthinkable," Mindy said with compassion and disbelief in her voice.

"Well my friends, as far as the State Department is concerned, our embassies in the middle east and greater region will be uploading their daily reports in the next hour. I've asked Munson to be especially vigilant on what's been going on there.

Earlier in the day when I spoke with him, he was leaning towards a group; a fringe group, a faction of the now-banned Muslim Brotherhood organization.

You'll recall they used to form the government over there in Egypt. Well now that they are banned after the coup, some of them are truly pissed. Those seeking revenge on the current powers that be in Egypt have lashed out ever since with ruthless acts of localized terrorism trying to unseat the president. There is this one group, that goes by the name of ISS, a fringe group perhaps of ISIS or ISIL.

Yes, it gives us something to go by but not a whole lot. So far, knowing the possible name has gotten us nowhere fast. But we'll get'em eventually. We're working on it and something ought to break soon." Drew finished briefing the group at the table.

"The NSA is listening to everything. We're virtually recording the whole world every minute, capturing everything from birthday party plans to movement of opium from Kabul Afghanistan to Chicago.

Our A.I. algorithms evolutionary progression is now incorporating cluster analysis. We think this will help in ferreting out some of the culprits currently hiding in plain view if that makes any sense to you. Trust me; it makes perfect sense to our information engineering gurus," Greg informed the group.

"We're all working hard as we can on this, here in the US and globally," Mindy added. "One last thing I need to say from my point of view." Now she had the men's attention.

"Let's not get bogged down on the territory as we have in the past. We're all on the same team. I can assure you, as soon as I know something, you will know it.

Playing it close to the vest no longer works or is in our best-combined interest, do we agree?"

The three men all nodded saying, "we agree."

Mindy Beaton then replied, "good, now let's get these bastards as Trenten said."

ADRES

***

CHAPTER

THIRTEEN

HLSINKI

"HJHC 01 ready at runway 12/30," Billy announced to Bermuda air traffic control.

"HJHC 01 cleared for takeoff, fly heading 050, climb and maintain 5000 HJHC 01," responded the controller.

Billy had the Lear 85 in clear skies with unlimited visibility. The two and a half hour flight home to Florida would be a smooth one this morning. They will have gained an hour, their ETA, 8:05 AM. Eldon and Kimberley had made this flight dozens of times over the years visiting their three resort properties, one in St. Georges and two on the south shore in the parishes of Paget and Southampton. Eldon loved Bermuda so much that they had talked about making the island their future home address whenever that day might come. Most of the island's residents had a need to get away after being on the rock for several years, but Eldon and Kimberley looked forward to rock-fever allowing them to get away from it all. That time had not yet arrived; a few more years left in the game.

Having reached cruising altitude, the Lear smoothened out.

"Hey babe, would you like a cup of freshly brewed coffee? I'm having one and taking a cup up to Billy," Kimberley asked Eldon.

"Sure I'll have one, thanks."

"Then I want to hear all about your idea on how to ease the fallout for The Jewel of the Pharaohs," handing Eldon his coffee and looking at him with anticipation as she walked by up to the cockpit.

"Thanks, Kimberley. It's looking like smooth sailing all the way home," Billy said, reaching for his coffee and taking a sip.

"Okay Billy, we'll be in the back if you need anything," they both started laughing.

Kimberley sat down facing Eldon. He looked her directly in the eye, sitting motionless for a few moments looking thoughtfully at his wife trying to gauge the level of her curiosity. Eldon sensed she was more than interested, he knew this sort of thing intrigued her – how they can avoid international disasters. It was one of her specialties. Having had a long career in the US State Department, Kimberley was a natural in the art of diplomacy and handling international incidents. He needed her buy-in, but only if she felt it worth the effort… she'd know.

"So let me run this by you, see if there's a snowball's chance in hell getting this to roll."

"I'm all ears, " taking a sip from her cup of coffee.

"The coming few days will test us both in facing the news media. I'm sure many will say, I told you so, about moving into Egypt. I know things will be difficult. I cannot imagine what all those parents are going through, but whatever you and I can do to meet our moral obligations, well it goes without saying Kimberley, we will do whatever we need to in their time of need. It was our bright idea in the first place to send them to Egypt," Eldon said.

"I know how you feel. I think the same, but I also know we cannot blame ourselves, and you know what… I don't think even one of the parents will lay blame at our feet. Remember how excited they all were being able to send their kids on such a learning adventure? I know this will not ease the feelings of guilt we both have, but from a State Department perspective; there was no travel advisory issued for Americans planning to visit Egypt, it was considered safe.

If there are to be daggers pointed at us, it will come from the news media. You know how they love to run things over and over again, especially the twenty-four-hour news channels. They've been looping the video our helicopter captured for days now. It's disgusting Eldon, and now they'll have an even bigger field day with you and me having returned home. They will be camped out in front of our place you can bet on it," Kimberley replied.

"You're right about the media. I wish Felix were flying back with us today so we could discuss our approach, but I asked him to stay in Cairo after arriving from Moscow. He is handling things there for the next couple of days battling with the press. We left in a hurry, and I'm sure all those reporters who met us at the Jewel are clamoring for more than just the statement I gave them. Felix will do a good job as he always does. It's what he's good at, but we sure could use him back home. Anyway, we'll face whatever we have to face, but here's what I was thinking," Eldon said, taking another sip from his coffee.

"Next month there's that huge international anti-terrorism conference in Helsinki Finland. There'll be over three thousand attendees from dozens of nations not to mention the news media, probably another two thousand of them."

"Okay, this is sounding interesting," Kimberley replied.

"What if we could get them to come to Cairo instead?" Eldon posed that question to Kimberley.

"Wow…now that would be the chess move of the century!"

"Yes it would be, here's what I have in mind," Eldon grew excited. He sensed Kimberley's keen interest right away. His idea immediately hit the diplomatic nervous system that ran through her every fiber. She could hardly wait for him to continue.

"I think we still have time to make it happen, but you would need to work the phones right away and probably twenty-four seven for the next two weeks. We only have three or maybe four weeks at the outside to make this happen, that conference is set to start on March 20th."

Kimberley listened and thought while Eldon spoke responding with dejection in her voice. "But, all the arrangements for all those thousands of delegates and attendees have already been made months ago, hotel bookings, travel arrangements, everything - deposits sent to secure the rooms, you know the drill babe. Helsinki is not going to want to give that up, and the logistics would be complicated to move the entire convention to Cairo. It's too late," Kimberley replied with a look of "*that's impossible*" on her face.

"No it's not, and that's where you come in, your diplomatic talents and your magic abilities in convincing the powers that be in doing the right thing."

Hearing Eldon challenge her negativity perked up her interest up again, setting her skepticism aside.

"Hear me out, here's what we have to do." Eldon dove in.

"The Helsinki convention is the first of its kind in addressing the chaos brought about by international terrorism. Terrorism affects virtually every nation on earth. It's no longer only bus bombings in Israel or nightclub bombings in France, or sarin gas in Tokyo subways or for that matter holding Russian theatergoers hostage in Moscow. It's all around the world now. Its fallout can be devasting to the economy of any particular country, whether it's in Bali or Egypt, and this time it was Cairo.

One of the hallmark philosophies in reacting to terrorism no matter where it may occur is for society to continue on with their lives as normally as possible so that the terrorists can't win. We bear the loss of loved ones and press on with our daily lives, that is the axiom. But in the meantime the local economy suffers, people lose jobs, governments may falter, especially tourism-based economies, as is the situation in Cairo. It's a significant portion of the economic pie for that city. If this convention in Helsinki indeed is what it's claiming to be, then let's put them to the test and see if they're willing to put their money where their mouth is," Eldon paused for a moment looking at his wife. He felt he was starting to get through to her. Kimberley was paying closer attention. So he continued, "The idea of these nations coming together like this for the very first time is two-fold. First to send a clear message to terrorists around the world, that all countries stand together in fighting and eradicating this blight around the planet, and second to support one another in coming to each other's aid in times of crisis. As did France with America after 9-11 and as America did with France after the 2015 Paris attacks.

Now would be the time for all nations attending this upcoming convention to stand with Egypt and show their support. I ask you babe, what better way for them to show their unified support for a recently attacked country than bringing their convention to Cairo instead."

Eldon continued, "Sure, it would be an economic blow for a little bit of time to Helsinki, but it's only one convention. They aren't facing a plunge in tourism over the coming year or years for that matter. Their city would lose one conference but on the other hand, gain the respect of Cairo and Egypt that might repay Helsinki in ways not imagined for years to come. Babe, this is the international community's opportunity to shine, like never before. This is in fact what terrorists hate and abhor; cooperation amongst nations. They want chaos and anarchy to ensue after an attack. Helsinki couldn't send a better message than this to terrorists around the world! And you're the one who could pull this off, Kimberley.

You already know most of the diplomats

scheduled to speak at this conference. Call them all and get them to change the venue. Appeal to their morals and vanity, how it will make them shine on the world stage, not to cower in the face of adversity. Terrorists will not win.

Our hotel in Helsinki, the Baltic Jewel would suffer some business loss. But with no terrorism threats in Finland, they can rebook those canceled rooms quickly. Considering March is traditionally a busy month for concerts and sporting events, the hotels will soon make up the fallout. Moving the convention to Cairo isn't going to kill our Helsinki hotel, but if no business comes to Cairo for the next year, it will destroy the Jewel of the Pharaohs along with twenty other large properties," Eldon said with conviction in his voice.

"Bringing the convention to Cairo could save the day and the month along with the year. As awful and shocking as the event at the pyramids were, it might only prove to be a blip on the economy if we could pull this off," Eldon said, waiting for Kimberley to respond.

Kimberley inhaled with a deep breath, raising her eyebrows, and then blowing out the air from her lungs saying, "wow… that is some plan!"

Before she could comment further, Eldon jumped right back in, "We can even sweeten the pot so that they might jump all over this," Eldon said, now becoming more excited seeing that Kimberley wasn't so negative any longer and apparently more open to his idea.

"Look, we will lose a lot of money if Cairo isn't able to bounce back. Not to mention the jobs lost.

What if we were able to soften the blow so that instead of having to close our doors, we manage to break even. I'm not so concerned about making a profit for the coming few months in Cairo. If we could just stay afloat and break even, that would more then solve our immediate problems.

Here's what I will do to sway their decision; offer the delegations and convention planners fifty percent off the room rates they agreed to pay in Helsinki. I mean for all their accommodation requirement including hospitality suites, breakout rooms, meeting rooms, banquet halls and on top of that, complimentary food and beverages for their entire five-day convention."

Kimberley now jumped in, "you're suggesting we giving away the hotel?"

"No, not quite, but almost, listen up. We present our offer of free food and beverages as a gesture we are making in harmony with their desire to cut their costs. Couple that with half of what they would pay for their rooms in Helsinki - we will have their attention. We emphasize how our newly formed partnership would meet our mutual interests, forfeiting revenues, a move in the spirit of fighting terrorism and saving the tourist industry in Egypt. From a business perspective, we sell the entire convention as an all-inclusive package planned piece of business.

As you know, we can maintain an eighty-three percent profit margin in the Rooms Department, while Food and Beverage Departments at best will only deliver maybe twenty percent if we're lucky. So we lose some now to gain some later. But even at a lowered room rate, we can still cover the housekeeping costs and have enough left over to cover food and beverage cost or at least get close. Even if we end up losing a little now, we'll all end up smelling like roses while having filled most of the hotels in Cairo. The news media will help as well showcasing Cairo's enhanced security measures and vigilance ensuring the safety of this international delegation. This would make the whole tourist industry much less jittery in the months to follow allowing us to make up for these initial losses," Eldon finished saying and now sat looking waiting for Kimberley's response.

"We'd have to contact the Finns about this first before we call any of the delegations. I think that would be the key to drive your plan."

Kimberley's response was like music to his ears. He was beginning to think he'd won her over.

"You're absolutely right, without the Finns' approval, this will not fly. But I think they'll go for it. As a matter of fact, if we approach this in the right manner, they may even champion this idea and offer assistance in expediting the complete transfer of the convention from Helsinki to Cairo, are you in?"

"Eldon, you did it again you're really something you know that?" She leaned forward over the table between them and kissed Eldon, again saying, "yeah, really something, and I love you for it, I'm in."

◇◇◇

West Palm Beach International Airport was only a seventeen-minute drive from home on Jupiter

Island. Billy brought them in on time just a couple of minutes after 8:00 AM. Eldon's car was parked next to the corporate jet hangar facility and having pre-cleared US Customs in Bermuda, they were on their way blending in with the traffic on I-95.

After refueling the Lear and booking it in for a mechanical checklist, Billy too was heading home to Sewel's Point in Stuart, just a few miles north of Jupiter Island.

Eldon and Kimberley figured they might have most of the day to themselves after they dealt with any news media that might be camped out Jupiter Island waiting for their return home.

"You know Kimberley, I have no problem facing the parents, but I'm not crazy about talking to the press today. I actually considered asking Billy to get the Stinger, pick us up in Juno Beach at Tradewinds Marina on the Intracoastal Waterway and coming home on the water, avoiding the road altogether. But then I figured it would have been too chicken-shit of a move, so I didn't. Maybe after turning onto our street, I will have regretted not asking Billy to do that," Eldon said, looking over at Kimberley, signaling his exit off I-95 to Jupiter and on to Jupiter Island.

"Well at least you thought about doing it, but it might have made things worse if the press figured out that we were home and avoiding them," Kimberley responded. "But it does show that you're still thinking," she let out a little laugh.

"Yea, not a good idea," Eldon replied with a smirk on his face.

Turning onto their street, and now just a couple

of hundred yards from their driveway, Eldon slowed the Jaguar anticipating a gathering, but nothing ahead as far as he could see. The road was empty of traffic, and no news vehicles were parked anywhere that they could see yet. Eldon reached the entrance to their driveway and not a car in sight, no trucks, no police, nobody around. They were alone.

Kimberley turned to her husband and said, "you see, all that worrying for nothing, still would have been a nice boat ride though," she said jokingly.

Eldon replied, "yeah, yeah, yeah,… laughing," as he touched the remote button on the instrument panel, and opening the driveway gate. He then leaned over to Kimberley, placed his right hand gently behind her head and brought her in closer, caressing the back of her neck, and kissing her on the lips for the first time in days, saying, "we're home babe," and drove the Jag up the driveway.

Neither Kimberley or Eldon ever traveled with luggage when visiting one of their hotels or resorts - a briefcase at the most and for Kimberley, her purse. They maintained private suites at all their properties already containing full wardrobes for both Kimberley and Eldon, they never needed to carry clothing with themselves unless of course, they happened to be visiting a city where no HJHC properties existed, and there were a few, but not many. Coming back from Bermuda this morning, their Lear Jet was luggage free, other than Billy's belongings.

"Feels good to be home," Kimberley said, walking in and stepping out of her shoes. Eldon, closing the front door, and turning towards Kimberley was suddenly caught off guard when she stepped up to him, pressing her body against his, tippy-toeing to wrap her arms up and over his shoulders passionately kissing Eldon on the lips, and then whispering, "I missed you, come with me." Kimberley was back!

HLSINKI

***

CHAPTER

FOURTEEN

BRUDRS

"Ahhh, to be back in Baghdad again after these many years brother," Arish said, gazing out over the Tigris River.

"Living in America for these past years has proven to be a hollow existence, much more than I ever realized. Sitting here now with you takes me back to when life was good for us. I remember when we were little, mother, and father, you and I would come to restaurants such as this one, perhaps twice a week. We could all enjoy a dish of our favorite *masgouf.* Now, it is rare to see a family enjoying a dinner of flame-roasted carp as we are tonight. Just looking down on Abu Nuwas Street, and the corniche, I remember how vibrant things were back then Zara, but now, today: only the well to do can afford a meal like this.

In America, we lack for nothing when it comes to material things. But I find myself with an emptiness in Nevada. I miss home Zara, I miss Iraq, I long for Iraq, its culture, history, to walk the streets every day with other Iraqis, and most of all to live in the land where my soul is anchored in the teachings of

Muhammed and Saddam. The spirit of the desert sands flows through my very veins brother. That is why I have decided to come back home to Baghdad for good, not right away, but when things settle down, perhaps in few months-six, maybe a year when Iraq is once again strong and respected as in the time of our great leader."

The look of longing was unmistakable on Arish's face. Zara saw it clear as day. There was no mistaking, Arish had only become American on paper, but not in heart and not in soul. There was no doubt about it, Arish would return to Iraq.

"My wife and I have prospered in Las Vegas Zara, as I say we lack for nothing, but my life remains empty, as empty as Las Vegas is of morals and soul, it thrives on broken dreams. I choose to no longer live in the belly of the beast, soon it will be time to come home," Arish stopped and looked at his brother across the table and said, "but first I shall fly to Egypt with you tomorrow, to see my nieces no matter how injured they are, I will come with you, Zara."

"But Arish, father, and mother will want to come as well," Zara replied.

"Yes, when I told father that I will go to Egypt with you to see Afraa and Talia he said they wanted to come as well. I suggested they wait until your girls have healed enough so that they can once again see the sparkle in their eyes, then the trip will be worthwhile. Talia is in a coma and Afraa is sedated, there would be no point. It would only bring more grief and sorrow to mother and father. Father then agreed, they will visit when the time is better.

But I will come with you, we have more to

discuss and a few days in Egypt will do me good, brother." Arish concluded.

"My heart sings with joy that will come with me to Cairo. Nawar will also be overjoyed to see you brother. I have many things to show you, and you shall understand when you see with your own eyes. I have chosen a spokesperson to speak for us Arish, tomorrow you shall know who this person is. We have much to talk about Arish, let us now eat."

Flight time from Baghdad to Cairo was two hours and forty minutes. They would gain one hour arriving in Cairo.

EgyptAir MS638 arrives in Cairo at 15:00 UTC or 3:00 PM in the afternoon. Zara was not about to bother Nawar about picking him and Arish up at the airport, it was more important for Nawar to be with the girls in case one regained consciousness and needed their mother. Nawar had virtually lived by the girls' bedside for the past three days, only returning home to clean up and try sleeping.

By 5:00 PM Zara had returned home, picked up his car and was driving in Cairo rush hour traffic to Cairo General with Arish to see his girls.

"You know Zara, I feel more at home even here in Cairo, where I don't live, than I do back in Las Vegas where I do live. There is no question, this is the region of the world I need to be in." Arish said as he watched the passing shops and people going about their business on the streets of Cairo. "You will be close to me again, with me living in Baghdad."

Zara, turned his head for a moment to look at Arish, then pounded his chest with a clenched fist saying," brother you are close to me every day of my life, you are right here brother, right here, day and night, right here in my heart."

"As you are in mine," replied Arish.

"Father was right about suspecting, ISS. The Islamic State of Sinai laid claim for the for the Giza bombings last night. What should we do about them Arish?" Zara asked looking over again at his brother.

"I know you and Nawar are broken now, as I am for your girls, brother. I don't know what we can do now. But time has a way of allowing for justice to come around, no matter how long it may take, you and I are proof of that my brother, and our justice will come in twenty-eight days on March 21st, the Council of Ten has decided. No Zara, we shall wait, for our avengement on ISS and when the time comes into our favor we will know, and we will act. Now is the time to be with your girls and over the years to come, make their lives worthwhile. Allah will see it happen, that is why he has chosen for them to live."

"Egypt is set Arish, change will not come here and needs not to. The country is now stable, and life has become better for all Egyptians. It is only the jealousy of the ISS leadership after being ousted from the country that they seek revenge on the ruling party. They cause much damage to the economy with these senseless bombings. The authorities know who the leadership is, and they will hunt them down, they have no chance in toppling this regime, they are only an irritant, a bad one they are but just an annoyance. But we Arish, we will get our pound of flesh when the time is right."

Zara drove into the hospital parking lot, picked a spot and shut the Mercedes' engine off.

INN FORMATION

"Come Arish, let us visit your nieces but be prepared, Talia will still be in the medically induced coma. Afraa, she might be awake. Nawar will be surprised to see you.

They walked into Cairo General Hospital and headed straight for the ICU.

"Peace be upon you, we are here to see my daughters, Talia, and Afraa Ahmed, this is my brother Arish," Zara informed the ICU desk attendant.

"Peace be upon you," Arish said to the lady attendant.

"Peace be upon you, Mrs. Ahmed, your wife is now with your daughter Afraa, but she has been moved to Ward B two floors above us, You will find her in room number ah, 15. Mr. Ahmed, Afraa is in stable condition, and you will be glad to know she is awake. When Talia improves, she will join Afraa in the same room, we will make sure your daughters remain together, but for now Talia must remain here in constant care, she is not yet ready and still sedated," The attendant finished saying.

"Would Doctor Nabel be available by chance, Allah willing?" Zara asked.

"I will check for you Mr. Ahmed, and if he is, I will ask him to see you in the ICU at Talia's bedside. He shouldn't be more than a few minutes if he is available."

"Thank you, peace be upon you," and they walked into ICU heading for Talia's bedside.

Approaching Talia's bed, Zara was relieved to see that Doctor Nabel was making his rounds and was tending to his daughter.

"Peace be upon you Doctor Nabel, this is my brother Arish."

"Ah I am glad to see you Mr. Ahmed, and peace be upon the both of you," Nabel replied. The three men shook hands.

"Can I touch my daughter now Doctor?"

"Yes, but only her hand and arm, her face and head are still very critical and will remain so for some time."

Zara, then reached over the bedside railing and took Talia's hand into his and prayed. Arish stepped beside his brother and put his arm over both his shoulders. With his other arm, he reached down over the railing and placed his hand onto Zara's as his brother held onto Talia.

"Allah will bring her back to us Zara, she will smile once again,"

After a few moments, Zara placed Talia's hand gently back down onto the blanket and turned to speak with Doctor Nabel.

"What can you tell me, Doctor?"

"My colleagues and I have been carefully watching and assessing both Talia and Afraa. The good news for Talia is that her vitals are strong. You know, both your girls had already lost more than half their blood when you brought them in almost four days ago now. They've both had time to recover in that area. Talia, we've had to keep sedated, we cannot have her moving her head for a while longer, it's best she stays sedated for a few more days. She is receiving nourishment intravenously so she will be fine in that respect. She will need many surgeries to restore functionality of the jaw and plastic surgery for her face. It will be tough for her, I hope she is of strong will. A lot of her ability to recover will depend on her. Pain, that too will be severe, but we can manage that with drugs to some extent," Dr. Nabel explained and stopped for a moment.

"As for her arm, we've cleaned where it was severed, and it should heal within a few months properly at which time we can look at having her fitted with a prosthetic. There have been some groundbreaking advances in prostheses even just in the past few months. I'm sure she will be able to take advantage of the remarkable science in that area of bionics. Remain steadfast and secure for your daughters, they will draw strength from you.

"Afraa is awake and has been talking. Your wife is with her now," Dr. Nabel said with a smile forming on his face.

Zara and Arish, listened, glued to every word Dr. Nabel was saying.

"Good news for Afraa, after we removed the shrapnel from her eye socket, it appears she will retain her sight. The eye muscles and nerves in the eye region have been damaged, and the prognosis is unclear regarding eye movement and coordination with her other eye. There are miraculous advances in that area as well Mr. Ahmed, microsurgery will come into play, we have great hope. As for her leg, same as Talia, it has been cleaned, and we expect normal healing in a few months when she will be ready to be fitted with a prosthetic. Crutches for the first few months, afterward she may even learn to run again."

Zara reached out with both his hands, shaking Dr.

Nabel's hand, bowing his head, saying, "Allah be with you Doctor Nabel, my wife and I have faith in our girls' recoveries, we are indebted to you and your dedication."

"You are not indebted to me for anything, we are both indebted to Allah for his mercy, now go and be with your wife and other daughter they will be happy to see you," Dr. Nabel replied.

Nawar was sitting at Afraa's bedside, gently holding her hand, resting on her Afraa's chest. Afraa had fallen back to sleep. Zara and Arish walked in.

Seeing her husband walk into the room brought a tremendous sense of relief for Nawar, she needed Zara's strength, she was exhausted and spent. Over the past four days, Nawar had not slept more than perhaps two or three hours each day.

Although Nawar was tired beyond her stamina, she stood and hugged Zara with much love, and not saying a word hugged Arish forming a circle of three. No words were needed. They stood holding onto each other. Then Nawar said, "Afraa will be fine, she is strong, and she is not afraid, Zara, she is not afraid!" Nawar looked at her husband and Arish, with amazement on her face, repeating it, "she is not afraid Zara."

Zara saw that Afraa was in a deep sleep. "She fell back asleep not long ago Zara." As Nawar was saying that, the attending nurse entered the room. Greetings were exchanged, and then the nurse said, "yes… she will now sleep for a while, we have sedated her again and will not wake till the morning. This might be a good time for you to think about going home and getting some rest, she will sleep through the night."

Nawar, Zara, and Arish kissed Afraa good-bye, and they left Cairo General Hospital walking out into the Cairo night air. There was hope in their hearts, and it had only been four days.

BRUDRS

***

CHAPTER

FIFTEEN

RGYL

"It's being compiled now, even as we speak Mr. Secretary," General Milton replied. We should have a definitive within the next few minutes.

The US Secretary of Defense; Roger Andrews, Central Intelligence Director; Web Moss, and National Security Agency Secretary; Greg Armstrong were gathered in the CIA's strategy center in Langley waiting for incoming intelligence from the Argyle System Special Operations Commander.

"General, give us the rundown on Argyle again, so we understand it's intel gathering integrity.

"Certainly, Secretary Andrews,' General Milton replied.

"Argyle is a Defense Advanced Research Project (DARPA), top-secret surveillance platform. We decided to deploy it six months ago, on a mission to gather intel on known terrorist ISIS organizations and suspected ISS cells throughout the Mideast.

Ever since then Mr. Secretary, Argyle has been actively storing live real-time video should we ever need to review activity. Sixteen days ago, Mr.

Secretary, the NSA picked up chatter that we believe to be ISIS or ISS communications over Egypt coming from Cairo. In response, the Argyle platform was repositioned over the greater Cairo area.

Argyle can maintain day or night continued 24/7 high definition surveillance, with the ability to track several moving targets miles apart from one platform located 17 thousand feet above the ground. We can maintain Argyle's stable positioning for weeks at a time. Argyle can capture objects as tiny as an eye-glass case from several miles away without refocusing on moving targets. It sees and catches everything in motion or not; birds, dogs, cats, mice, cars, or people, even bits of blowing debris in the streets, such as tossed away bits of tissue paper. All of this is made possible with its real-time (WASP) Wide Area Stare Persistent, 370 independent camera system composed into one single image of 1.8 gigapixels.

The one single Argyle image Mr. Secretary would be equal to one hundred predator drone images combined. Argyle's single image captures continuous video covering a seventeen square mile area of all ground and above ground activity.

Argyle's massive data storage system gives us the ability to zoom into any one section or block of a city and replay all activity down to six inches. Argyle's cameras capture real-time, second by second, minute by minute, 24/7 history of everything over a designated area. Washington is watching the world."

General Milton paused and let that sink in once again. Everyone around the strategy room table knew of DARPA, but just how amazing this newly advance top-secret information gathering capability had become was still somewhat mind-blowing to even these three men charged with protecting the United States of America.

"Mr. Secretary, we've been concentrating on suspected terrorist cell hideouts located in Egypt for the past two months. We, meaning the DOD (Department of Defense) and with the cooperation of the CIA, we believe with a high degree of confidence that our intel obtained from Argyle has led us to the operations center for ISIS or ISS. We are not certain at this point, which group, but we are sure to have a location, relating back to the bombings at the Great Pyramid of Giza." General Milton paused as a CIA special agent entered the room.

"We are ready General," said the CIA agent and exited as quickly as he entered, but holding the door open for Rudy Carr, the DOD's lead on Special Ops, and Argyle Commander.

"Ah, good, gentlemen, this is Commander Carr, he is mission leader on Argyle surveillance. Commander Carr will go over what we have…Commander," the General said, introducing the DOD's top man for Argyle ops.

"Allow me to explain how the Argyle surveillance and tracking system can at times be most useful, that gentleman is after an incident has taken place, not during or before, but after. Unless already have identified a target and are looking for a said target, that is one thing, but if the target happens to be unknown, or unidentified, that is when Argyle comes into its own as a very potent tool. Either way, the technology is revolutionary; fifth generation.

INN FORMATION

Gentlemen, we have the target location as of a few minutes ago. By target location, we know precisely where the bombers live, which we also concur, with the CIA is their operations center."

Carr paused for a moment, then continued by activating a hand-held laser device. The screen covering the wall in front of the group came to life, displaying Argyle's imaging system.

"What you see in front of you is the city of greater Cairo as captured by Argyle on the day of the bombings at the Great Pyramid of Giza. In fact, I will start the replay with the HJHC Sikorsky helicopter's landing on Cairo General Hospital's air ambulance helipad," Commander Carr said.

The complete image of Cairo was composed of several stitched rectangles fitted perfectly together. Each rectangular segment was a slightly different shade so one could select a specific area of the city contained within that square. Commander Carr pointed the laser device on the rectangular section containing Cairo General Hospital and began zooming in on the square until a clear image of Eldon's helicopter came into view on the helipad, and alongside the chopper, frozen images of the trauma teams tending to the care of the rescued children. In the top right-hand corner of the zoomed-in image was a digital clock showing both local Cairo and UTC time and date.

"Okay, now here we go, I will put Argyle into motion, and run the day and events captured in reverse," Carr said.

The trauma team could be seen backing away from the chopper and running backward to their holding position waiting for the HJHC helicopter to land. The video was in super high definition resulting from the 1.8 billion pixel compilation. Commander Carr pointed the laser at the helicopter, and the video continued running in reverse all the while holding the chopper in the center of the screen. Argyle was amazing. Secretary Andrews had seen it in action once before, but even he was totally blown away by Argyle's capability. The video followed the chopper and automatically switched into the adjacent rectangle containing the next sector of Cairo. As the helicopter flew into the new rectangle zone, Argyle auto-zoomed to the same scale. It now showed the helicopter touching the ground as it was really leaving the field with the children aboard.

Argyle had captured everything, in fact, it had obtained all that took place in Cairo for the past few weeks, literally everything.

"Now this is where things get interesting. As horrible as the bombings were, what we in special ops and Argyle command are looking for is what led to all of this. And gentlemen, we have it," Carr said with a massive dose of confidence in his voice.

Carr continued playing the video, but now reassigned Argyle's auto-tracker onto the lead bus. The four coaches were shown backing out of the parking area.

The video kept playing seeing the buses retrace their route along the Cairo highways and streets leading back to the staging area where all one hundred sixty students, the two American teacher-chaperones, and the two Egyptian children's minders embarked.

The video kept rolling showing the buses arriving

at the staging area, and all the way back to the bus company's fenced-in parking area and following that, the drivers accessing their buses.

"We good so far?" Commander Carr asked.

"Keep rolling Commander," General Milton said.

"Now from this point on, I will speed up the video playback, so we can rewind the rest of the day to 2:17 AM, but holding at the bus company parking lot location.

The video played back into the morning and then early into the morning, until 2:17 AM showed on the digital clock.

Carr paused the video and said, "now observe, I will slow things down. watch the sides of the buses, there are eleven buses in the parking lot."

Carr started the video, quarter speed. "Right there, see that person crawling out from underneath that bus, he is on his back, you can actually make out his eye sockets. He was clearly underneath it, now keep watching, and you will see another human figure captured by infrared as he too crawls out from the side of the next bus, there.. you see that?" Carr stopped Argyle's video.

"Those two men and I assume they are men, planted bombs underneath all eleven buses as you will see as I continue rolling. Reason for that: they couldn't be sure which buses would be dispatched for the school group, so they armed them all. There had to be someone close by when the buses arrived at the Giza parking area to remotely trigger the detonator for the buses to explode.

But that is not important in the big picture right now. Gentlemen; it gets better," Carr said and continued rolling the video.

As the video played, the two human images could be seen crawling out from underneath the buses holding packages, which they just placed underneath the coaches, but running backward, showing them with packages in hand.

"As you've seen, during darkness Argyle's advanced infrared composite focal plane array sensor, picks up the human images very clearly and in high definition, I said it gets better, and here it comes."

Everyone was on the edge of their seats, Web Moss and Greg Armstrong actually looked at one another both saying wow at the same time, as Carr continued on with the briefing.

As the video rolled backward the two infrared highlighted images could be seen walking backward towards the gate of the fenced in bus yard, closing the gate and getting out of their cars, arriving at the bus company.

At this point, Commander Carr auto-targeted the two men's vehicle. He then backtracked their drive from the bus company located on El-Sherbiny Road, on the Giza side of the Nile River running through Cairo, all the way across the river to the Islamic section of the city to a street across from the Al-Azhar Mosque, a little more than ten kilometers away.

"Now observe again gentlemen, I will slow down the video."

As their vehicle was leaving it started from a parking spot adjacent to the second house from the corner, and the two men got out of the vehicle, an

SUV, and walked backward into the house.

"That's it, that is where the terrorist cell is located gentlemen, and we have more, a verification of sorts," Carr said.

"This will be quick. The video we just saw is now ten days old, but let's go back just a few days, and two nights after those two men planted all the bombs on all those buses, well let me show you."

Carr then moved ahead in the timeline to two nights later in the video, once again, after 2:00 AM, same bus company parking lot, but this time, the two men are removing the explosives packages from the remaining seven buses. The vehicle that they arrived in, also originated from the same house and same parking spot; two houses from the corner opposite Al-Azhar Mosque Mosque.

CIA Director Web Moss then said, "yes, excellent work Commander Carr, excellent."

At this point, we still do not have a positive ID on the group, but we anticipate info on that incoming soon. We now need to bring the Egyptians on board and begin the I.D. process. They can determine who lives in the house, who visits, and precisely who they are.

We will need to run this by the President and get his approval to confer with the Egyptians. We will have a delicate matter in explaining how we obtained the information, which of course will have to remain classified. I don't think the Egyptians will have any other options than to play. They might want this more than anything they've ever wanted. Gentlemen, time for a White House visit," Director Web concluded.

"Commander Carr, thank you for your briefing, I

will be in touch," General Milton said, excusing the Commander.

The three men then got up from the table, with Greg Armstrong saying, "let's go see the president."

RGYL

***

CHAPTER

SIXTEEN

DUTEZ

"Oh my god, Kimberley, I've been seeing you and Eldon on television for the past three days now, they keep showing it repeatedly, here in Finland too. My heart goes out to all those parents, I just cannot imagine…Kimberley, how are you and Eldon holding up after this horrible thing in Cairo?" Ursula Latvala asked her friend.

"Ursula, Eldon and I, we are doing all right I suppose, and thank you for your concern. It has been an awful few days, worst days of our lives honestly but we are back in Florida now and trying to get on with things as regularly as we can.

Eldon is handling the fallout here regarding the grieving parents, whatever we can do, we are trying," Kimberley replied to her friend.

"This terrorism situation is putting the whole world on edge Kimberley. Things have changed so much over the years; the world is not what I remember it to be. We here in Finland must thank our lucky stars that we've been spared from such events, just horrible, just horrible.

These terrorists Kimberley, whoever they are, they just cannot be allowed to win, to keep disrupting our lives like this. And I can imagine how this will hurt the economy in Cairo, especially your industry, it will have devasting effects on those in hospitality. I wish the world could do something about them." Ursula added.

Kimberley listed to Ursula, and with her last statement thought that perhaps Ursula could be convinced, so Kimberley dove in.

"Ursula, my dear friend, you are so right, and that is precisely the reason I am calling you this morning."

"Really? How can I help Kimberley?" Ursula seemed genuinely intrigued.

"Well, Ursula, Eldon and I believe that you, being the Finnish Minister of Economic Affairs and Employment, hold the power in your hand to change world events and help bring about the end to international terrorism. At the minimum, forge the strength of nations to stand together as one, in the face of adversity" Kimberley said, with a sense of discovery in her voice.

"But you, Ursula, you and Prime Minister Peeka Karvonen would need to spearhead the effort, and it would need to happen now," Kimberley added.

She didn't wish to bowl her friend Ursula over with such maverick suggestions but wanted to make an impact, and not a light one. Kimberley pushing ahead then asked, "are you open to what I just said Ursula?"

"Well, that is something, I must say that is something I wasn't expecting to hear Kimberley. Yes, I'm open to..." Before Ursula could finish her sentence, Kimberley jumped in, not giving Ursula a chance to object.

"I'm so glad to hear that you are. You know we haven't had a chance to talk in person since Eldon and I were in Helsinki four years ago to open The Baltic Jewel Hotel and Convention Center. I'm flying to Helsinki immediately by company jet, and will see you tomorrow afternoon in your office, see you then Ursula," and Kimberley ended the call.

Ursula Latvala was entirely taken off guard by Kimberley. Perhaps a bit outplayed, in the way she invited herself to Ursula's office but Ursula was at the same time lost for words, trying to be polite in her initial response showing interest in Kimberley's suggestion that she could change world events.

Coming from Kimberley Ashton-Davis, those words were not to be taken lightly, and she was intrigued. Ursula thought about calling Kimberley back to postpone, but the intrigue of it all got the better of her. She'd meet with Kimberley. It must be something extraordinary for Kimberley to fly to Helsinki so quickly.

Then Ursula started thinking about Cairo again just as her office television once again looped to replay the video of the Giza bombings as captured by Eldon's helicopter. Ursula turned off the television's audio, and sat at her ministerial desk, watching in silence.

It was even more horrifying with the sound off. Ursula watched for a while longer, then picked up her telephone and called her direct boss, Peeka Karvonen; The Prime Minister of Finland, and depending on how that goes, the Finnish President; Oli Larsen may also be needed.

Kimberley would be Helsinki bound this afternoon to meet with the Minister of Economic Affairs and Employment late tomorrow afternoon. She'd be jet-lagged for sure, but she needed to expedite Eldon's plan.

She had given the whole idea some serious thought and believed if mountains could be moved, this one would be a good one to move. It would take all her diplomatic skills in bringing this about. Kimberley believed in Eldon's vision, and the fact alone that Eldon and Kimberley also had significant financial skin in this game, spoke volumes as to their sincerity and belief in what they were proposing.

The Finnish travel-tourism and hospitality industry came under the purvue of Ursula's ministerial powers and responsibilities for Finland

. Kimberley would need her buy-in before anything could move ahead in relocating the international conference on terrorism from Helsinki to Cairo. Kimberley's first step was underway, the next ones would not be easy.

She had to get in touch with Billy. She was hoping he wasn't halfway to The Bahamas deep sea fishing or having a few drinks down in the Keys at the Marathon Raw Bar. Kimberley dialed Billy's cell.

"Hey Kimberley, what's up?" Billy answered.

"She could make out the sound of music in the background as Billy answered his cell. It sounded like a reggae band. Kimberley's heart sank, *Billy must be in the Keys as she thought he might already be. God knows he deserved a little R&R, she couldn't blame him*, she said to herself.

"Billy, where are you?"

"I'm at home, why, should I be somewhere?"

"No no, I just heard some music in the background thought you might be out, glad I caught you at home," Kimberley replied.

"No, I've got some Bob Marley on, just trying to relax a little," Billy answered.

"Billy, I need to be in Helsinki tomorrow afternoon, can you get me there?" Kimberley asked, almost afraid to; knowing what they'd all been through.

"It would be my life's greatest pleasure in getting you there on time," Billy responded, saying it with a "*you gotta be kidding me*" tone, but all too happy to get Kimberley there and not a minute late, and Kimberley knew it.

Billy, Eldon, and Kimberley along with Felix were a unit; a team. Over the years, she had gotten to know Billy like one knows a brother. Billy would not hesitate one moment in having to take a bullet for Kimberley if need be or for that matter for Eldon or Felix, that was the strength and nature of their relationship.

"Kimberley, meet me at the airport jet hangar. I can be there in two hours, Helsinki is in the flight plan."

"I owe you one Billy," Kimberley replied.

"Okay, well then you can buy me a cold Heineken in Helsinki, and we'll call it even," Billy laughed and said goodbye.

Kimberley stood in her living room, looking out

onto the back patio and down the pathway leading to their dock on the Intracoastal Waterway. She felt so grounded once again being back home, she wished she could stay a few more days and enjoy it all, but that was not to be. But even so, a day or two at home had helped. She'd be on her own for a few days as would Eldon. Their duties were now twofold with both looking after what needed to get done.

Eldon was in a meeting with the State Governor even as Kimberley had just gotten off the phone with Billy and now she was about to fly away leaving Eldon again. It wouldn't be the first time their attention was needed in two places at once, sometimes three or four at once.

They always seemed to win the war in the end, even if a battle here and there might be lost. The events in Cairo resulted in a battle lost for now, but Kimberley and Eldon were soon to be fully engaged in war.

"Hi, hon, it's a go Eldon, Billy is flying me to Helsinki, we're leaving in two hours. I'm meeting with The Honorable Ursula Latvala, Minister of Economic Affairs and Employment, you'll remember her at the Baltic Jewel opening," Kimberley said.

"Yeah, I know her, we had a most enjoyable chat with her that evening, nice lady," Eldon replied.

"Eldon I set the table for her, I brought up Peeka's name and involvement as well, I think Ursula is a smart cookie and can read ahead a few chapters. I'm hoping she'll bring the Prime Minister in on this. I didn't want to spook her, so I kept our conversation short not telling her our whole idea, just enough to whet her appetite. Oh, and I sort of weaseled my way into her office - not giving her a chance to say no."

"That's my girl," Eldon replied. "I knew you could do it."

"How are things coming along on your end?" Kimberley asked.

"The Governor and I are arranging to charter a plane to fly all the parents to Cairo so they can bring their children's bodies home. They will all be staying with us at The Jewel of the Pharaohs, we'll take care of everything for them of course. I'll be meeting with the families in Boca Raton later this evening where we will go through the details with them.

The governor has also arranged for emergency passports to be issued to those parents who are not currently in possession of one. The plane for Cairo will leave in three days. Felix will greet the group at the Jewel. Kimberley, that's about where we stand at the moment.

Oh, and by the way, the press is leaving us alone. The Governor and I, we gave the media a statement, and that seemed to satisfy them for now, so they're not hounding the Governor or me. For once… they're doing the right thing. Anyway, sweetheart,

I have to get going here, they're waiting for me. We have to prep for this evening's meeting with the families.

Also, Cathy is here with me Kimberley. She's been helping big time, already had a video conference with Dr. Nabel at Cairo General today. They are welcoming her involvement as I knew they would. We can catch up when you get back, we both have so much to do and such little time. God's speed babe, Kimberley, I love you. You're in good hands with

Billy."

"I know I am, I love you too Eldon, see you in a couple of days, maybe three, bye hon."

DUTEZ

***

CHAPTER

SEVENTEEN

HYROZ

"His name is Imad Mahmoud. He was hired on long ago Arish, almost a year before the hotel was scheduled to open. Imad has been working in the hotel's I.T. department from the very beginning as part of the pre-opening team in getting this huge resort ready. He is one of our two in ISIF to have a job here. Yaseen Bashir is our second implant, he works as one of the managers in the hotel's Banquets and Catering area. They are both perfectly positioned for our needs," Zara said while he and Arish drove up to the Jewel of the Pharaohs parking lot. I sent them to apply for positions here as soon as the word was put out that the hotel was hiring for a pre-opening team. Both got appointed shortly after and have been here ever since. Yassen has been setting up the restaurant service areas and the dozens of choices on the restaurant and banquet menus.

"Come Arish, you will see why I picked this new hotel as my funnel for communicating our needs. I think you will notice almost immediately as we walk into the main lobby. But I have an even greater surprise for you Arish, something quite unbelievable, perhaps willed by Allah himself! That I will have to tell you, it is nothing I can show you. Zara could hardly contain his excitement, as the brothers walked up the sidewalk leading to the resort's main entrance.

The roadway and sidewalk leading to the hotel's main entrance and porte-cochere were lined on both sides with a row of twenty Egyptian Obelisks identical to those found at Karnak, erected by Thutmose I (1520-1492 BCE), with every second obelisk in the rows replicas of the Obelisks of Hatshepsut (1479 – 1458 BCE). The first two Thutmose obelisks on either side stood eighty feet high, as the original at Karnak, marking the entrance to the Jewel of the Pharaohs Resort and Spa.

"Well this is quite spectacular Zara," remarked Arish as they walked by the row of obelisks and through the front entrance into the lobby.

Walking inside, they found themselves in an extensive open-air concept reception area which Arish estimated to be fifteen thousand square feet. Directly ahead thirty yards was a replica of the mask of Tutankhamun, but it was huge, covering the entire back wall. The replica mask must have been thirty feet high, dominating the atrium. Set directly in front of and below the mask was a bank of eight hotel check-in kiosks. They were of sphinxes made to resemble the avenue of sphinxes in Thebes linking the temples of Karnak and Luxor. The immediate visual impact upon entering the lobby was breathtaking, even stunning.

Standing well inside the lobby area now, Zara extended his right arm directly ahead and gestured with his hand as he turned a full circle pointing at the thousands of hieroglyphs adorning the walls and pillars. He said to his brother, "behold, look, brother, look at what Allah has put into our laps, I could not have imagined something better than this, absolutely amazing!"

Arish was now starting to get clued in as to why Zara was so excited. He recalled Zara showing the Council of Ten, the web pages he downloaded onto the laptop from the Jewel of the Pharaohs website. Arish now figured things out; Zara's use of hieroglyphs to communicate ISIF's instructions could be hidden amongst the thousands of symbols located or originating from the Jewel of the Pharaohs.

"Yes, yes, I see it now Zara, I see it plain as day. I think this might be the ultimate definition of hiding in plain sight, yes indeed brother, this fits," Arish said as he too had now turned a full three hundred sixty degrees at least twice taking in the thousands of hieroglyphs adorning the walls.

"Oh, but brother we are just getting started," Zara said with even more excitement building in his voice.

"Come let me show you, we came here to have lunch, and that is precisely what we will do. There is a lovely casual restaurant here that serves wonderful local delicacies, and best of all the menu is a work of art," Zara raising his eyebrows as he said the words, works of art. "Come, brother, let us eat."

Arish couldn't help but love the way in which Zara built excitement and intrigue with his cleverly placed double meanings and innuendos. He marveled at his brother's ability to see things in ways few people could and then coaxing you along to guess what he knew. Their two brains worked in different ways but were connected in loyalty and devotion to one another for eternity, of that he had no doubts.

They approached the restaurant greeter's podium. "Peace be upon you Amir," Zara said to the host as he walked up.

"Peace be upon you Mr. Ahmed, two for lunch today?"

"Yes please, and perhaps we could have a table out of the way," Zara replied.

"I know just the spot, Mr. Ahmed. Mr. Bashir had alerted me earlier today saying you would be coming in for lunch and asked me to make sure you received this folder. I have been holding it for your arrival," Amir said as he handed Zara the folder, then said, "please follow me, gentlemen."

"Thank Mr. Bashir for me if you would," Zara replied.

The host showed them to a table close to the far wall of the restaurant, but with a side window overlooking the Gardens of the Pharaohs. Before the host departed he laid down two sets of menus with colorful covers of Pharaohs depicted on papyrus.

"They know you here?" Arish asked, sort of surprised.

"Yes they do brother, and that's how I wanted it to be, and now it is so," Zara replied.

Both Arish and Zara took their menus in hand. Arish glanced at the art on the cover when he started to open it to look inside at the items when Zara suddenly reached over putting his hand on Arish's menu saying, "wait Arish, look at the cover again. Look at the design they used to frame the cover, there must be fifty different hieroglyphs."

Zara continued, "That's the beauty of this place Arish; it's saturated with hieroglyphs. No matter where you look, what you pick up, like these menus, or where you are in the resort, you are bound to be looking at hieroglyphics. There is so much of it everywhere and on everything that after the first few hours of being here you become oblivious to it. It becomes like normal wallpaper almost. Sure, at first they're interesting but after a while, well their hieros, big deal!" And that my brother is how we hide our messages in plain sight! You cannot find that which is hidden when it is not hidden."

Arish listened and learned. Zara's plan was now taking shape in Arish's mind as well but still needing more of what Zara was about to reveal. Whatever it was; it was sure to be revolutionary. Arish knew that his brother was smart, but this was starting to look genius, and apparently, Zara was just getting started. Now Arish was growing excited and very much intrigued by everything Zara was showing and telling him.

"I have become a regular patron of the establishment ever since it opened. I have lunch here with my lawyer colleagues and sometimes embassy officials probably twice a week. I think I bring quite a volume of business. Strangely I have been repaid already more than I could have ever imagined, but I will put that aside for now. That will be talk for another time.

Let me tell you more about these menus brother." Zara paused, and then said, "we should decide on what to eat in the meantime, let's have a look inside."

Shortly after the waiter had brought their food

orders, Zara reached for the folder left for him by his implant; Yaseen Bashir, the hotel's banquets manager. Zara extracted the contents and handed them over to Arish.

Arish started looking through the stack of thirty pages, and then said, "these are banquet menus from the hotel's catering department. I see breakfast menus, lunch, brunch menus, all sorts of dinner menus. There must be several dozen options for dinner available and then all of the ala carte items. Pricey, they sure don't give anything away do they?"

"Look again Arish what else do you see on those menus?"

"Oh, you mean the hieroglyphs decorating the perimeter of each page right?" Arish asked.

"Yes, that is exactly what I wanted you to see," Zara said.

Arish, nobody cares about the hieroglyphs around the perimeter of the menus, those are just pretty little pictures, what everyone is focused on are the items contained on the menus and the corresponding prices, nobody gives a hoot about the hieros."

"And you are telling me this because…" Arish remarked.

"Because my dear brother, that is where I will embed my messages and instructions. On the frames of the banquet menus and the restaurant menus. But let me tell you how that will be done."

Arish was glued to every word Zara was saying. He would usually interrupt if he had a question, but not so far.

INN FORMATION

"First you have to realize that the hiero symbols placed around the page, to create the framing design of the menu are in random order. There is no order to the way they're placed so long as the spacing is pleasing to the eye and symmetrical. There are no hidden messages. Sure, each symbol has been given a corresponding letter of the alphabet that anyone can look up, but so what, they're just random, forming no words unless by fluke," Zara was doing his best to explain, so he went on.

"The messages that we need to send will be hieroglyphs not randomly placed any longer onto the menu frames, but specifically placed in a particular order that will spell out words Arish, but not in the way you might think. Yes, the symbols will represent letters of the English alphabet but not traditional associations. I will hold the source code for which letter each symbol represents, and without the source code association key, the hieros are once again just mumble jumble."

"Ingenious!" remarked Arish, "and in plain sight, even more ingenious, how will you change the symbols?"

"All the menus from all the restaurants as well as every banquet menu are on the hotel's website. Here, let me show you," Zara took out his cell phone and accessed the internet browser app. Now just so you know, I am not accessing their website. I am loading the web pages from the Jewel of the Pharaohs website from previously obtained HTML files given to me by Imad Mahmoud who works in I.T. I never access the hotel's website and view their online menus. I want to avoid any internet traffic trace bots from knowing that I ever visited the Pharaohs website. The clearer I stay away from their internet domain, the better for us all, got that?" Zara asked of Arish.

"Oh I got it all right, nice and clean, but still you haven't told me how you change the symbols on the menus," Arish replied.

"I don't, Imad does. Here's how it works. I create rectangular .jpg images on my computer at home, one identically sized pixel image file for each jpg menu-image on the Jewel of the Pharaohs restaurant and banquet pages. My menu images only have the hieroglyphs on them, nothing else, but the hieros I placed onto the frames of the menus are in a particular order. I can do as many new menus as I need, sometimes it may be just one menu change sometimes ten pages with new frames, are you with me?" Zara asked.

"Yes, I'm with you."

"Okay, I then save the new images onto a micro SD card. I come for lunch to the hotel as I have been twice weekly since the hotel opened, nothing new there, and hand off my micro SD card to Yaseen Bashir the food and beverage manager. Yassen then places the envelope with the sd card into Imad's hotel inter-office mailbox. Imad picks up his mail and transfers my hieroglyphics from the SD card precisely as I have placed onto the specified menus tagged to be updated. This way Arish, I never need the administrative access to the hotel's website. Imad does it all, and he works in the I.T. department. Furthermore, with Imad being the hotel's webmaster responsible for maintaining and updating their web pages…well, you couldn't ask for a better arrangement." Zara added.

"Perfect again!" Exclaimed Arish.

"So then our brothers in the US will access this hotel's website to retrieve their instructions?" Asked Arish.

"Yes but not directly, that may leave a digital trail leading back to our brothers from the Jewel of the Pharaohs website. I have created an off-ramp for that as well. Arish, as things have turned out over the past number of days, my off-ramp so to speak, has been now enhanced by recent events. When we initiate action in a few weeks, all suspicion will be directed at ISS. It is with high probability their organization will be blamed, giving us even greater freedom to operate as we please. This unexpected timing of events couldn't have turned out better. We shall take advantage of their blunder and use it to our advantage.

"You have thought this through very well Zara."

"There is one last item I will not discuss at this time, because I have not quite decided, and you know what that item is."

"Yes I do brother, I know you shall pick well," Arish replied.

HYROZ

***

CHAPTER

EIGHTEEN

RSULA

When Kimberley arrived at the jet hangar facility at West Palm Beach International airport, Billy had already pulled the jet onto the taxi tarmac. Lear 85 HJHC was ready to roll. It was noon when Billy had "wheels up."

"You best be thinking about getting some sleep on the way over Kimberley, you will be jet-lagged if you're thinking of working throughout this flight. It's just over eleven-hours flight time in the air. But add in the two refueling stops; St. John's Newfoundland, and Reykjavik Iceland, that will put us into Helsinki close to nine in the morning providing our refueling stops go smoothly."

"Billy I really appreciate this, I know you were looking forward to some quality downtime after everything we went through in Cairo."

"No, I'm happy to do this Kimberley, and if you and Eldon can get the powers to be over there in Finland to move the conference to Cairo, well…that would be amazing. So, who is it you will see in

Helsinki?" Billy asked.

"This was Eldon's idea as I told you, but after we discussed it we both agreed we'd need to have the Finns buy into it for this to grow legs," Kimberley replied.

"I'm meeting with a woman who is sort of a friend, more of an acquaintance. I suppose, but if this flies, she will become one of my best friends ever! Her name is Ursula Latvala, she is the minister of economic affairs and employment. We chatted some and then ended up having dinner together at the opening of The Baltic Jewel. Tourism and travel in Finland come under her ministry. She is expecting me sometime tomorrow morning, I'm shooting for ten or elevenish," said Kimberley.

"Well do try getting some sleep in about five hours because when we land in Finland, it will be 2:00 AM Florida time but 9:00 AM Helsinki time and you'll have the whole day and evening ahead of you, while I will be able to get all the sleep I need," Billy replied.

"I will Billy, I need to be sharp when I meet with Ursula."

"Billy, I'll catch up with you at the hotel sometime, thanks for the smooth flight over," Kimberley said as they completed being processed through Finnish Customs.

"Yeah, will do, I'll be looking after the plane for a bit anyway, catch you at the hotel later and good luck Kimberley," Billy replied.

Not knowing just exactly when they'd land in Finland, Kimberley came prepared. She had brought a fresh change of winter attire on this flight. A winter overcoat, appropriate footwear, hat, and gloves. Kimberley changed on the Lear before deplaning, she was planning to go straight to Ursula's government offices directly from the airport.

Billy brought the Lear 85 into Helsinki International Airport at three minutes after nine in the morning. Kimberley was glad she had the whole day in front of her, and thankfully she managed to get six hours of sleep altogether, broken into segments but still a good six. She'd be fine until at least ten or eleven tonight.

It was late February, the Finnish sky was overcast and grey with a light snow falling. Kimberley took her cell phone in hand and dialed Ursula's number.

"One moment please Mrs. Ashton-Davis, the minister is expecting your call, I will put you through straight away," the telephone operator said.

"Kimberley, you're here already!" Ursula said with surprise in her voice.

"Yes, I'm at the airport and about to leave for your office," Kimberley replied.

"Kimberley, I have been thinking about what you said to me over the phone and how cleverly you cut me off before I had a chance to react."

Kimberley cut in, 'you're angry with me Ursula?"

"No-no-no, I'm not angry with you at all. In fact, I admire your courage and your strategic smarts. I think it was a calculated move on your part. Knowing you as I do, and thinking of what you and your husband Eldon have been through, I believe you have something vitally important to tell me otherwise you would not be flying halfway around the world at the drop of a hat. Am I correct Kimberley?"

"More important than you can imagine Ursula," Kimberley replied.

"I thought so. You know us Finns, we are a perceptive bunch, and that is why you will not be coming from the airport to my office," Ursula said with a tone of redirection in her voice.

Ursula caught Kimberley off guard with that comment, and she couldn't help herself asking Ursula, "No? So where am I going then?"

"Kimberley, I've had a Government car and driver at the airport awaiting your arrival. We weren't sure when you would arrive, but we checked with Helsinki International, and air traffic control told us your ETA was about twenty minutes ago, they were right. I was hoping you would call me when you did. You are still at the airport is that right?" Ursula asked.

"Yes, was just about to hop into a taxi," she replied.

"No, don't do that, my driver will be there momentarily, he is being notified now even as we speak. You should see our car come into view any second, it will have a police escort vehicle. Are you close to the taxi stand at arrivals?

"Yes, that is where I am, Kimberley replied.

"Walk a few yards farther down the sidewalk. Our driver will meet you there Kimberley," Ursula said. "He will bring you to Snellmaninkatu Street; to Government Palace," Ursula said.

"But that's the Prime Minister's and Ministry of Finance offices," Kimberley replied.

"That it is Kimberley, and I shall meet you there in approximately forty-five minutes, welcome back to Finland my dear friend," and Ursula ended the call.

The Finnish government car pulled up to the curb where Kimberley was standing and stopped. Kimberley wasn't quite sure how the driver knew, but he seemed to. The chauffeur got out of the vehicle, came around, greeted Kimberley, and opened the rear door of the Mercedes for her.

"Welcome to Helsinki Mrs. Ashton-Davis, please enjoy the ride through the city. With a police escort, it shouldn't take longer than fifteen minutes to Government Palace," the driver said with much courtesy.

"Kimberley Ashton-Davis, to see Mrs. Ursula Latvala," Kimberley said to the receptionist at Government Palace.

"Yes, Ms. Ashton-Davis, please make yourself comfortable in our sitting lounge, the Minister will be with you shortly. She may be a few minutes, can I get you a coffee or a tea while you wait?" the receptionist asked.

Kimberley thought for a second, *maybe coffee would be good. She'd been in such a rush ever since Billy woke her an hour before landing in Finland; the quick shower on the plane and getting ready she hadn't even had a coffee or even a croissant for breakfast. She was in such a rush not to waste even a minute, and now the sound of a warm cup of coffee sounded good.*

"Yes, that would be nice, thank you very much," Kimberley replied.

Two minutes later the receptionist brought Kimberley a beautifully arranged lounge tray with Finnish government china coffee service array and a side plate of morning pastry selections.

Just what the doctor ordered, Kimberley thought.

"Thank you so much, that is very kind of you," as she placed the tray onto the table beside Kimberley's chair, Kimberley indulged, the pastries hit the spot.

"I must thank you for clearing your schedule this morning to accommodate this urgent unexpected meeting. I know you have not met Mrs. Ashton-Davis, Mr. Prime Minister, but I think you will be very impressed. She and her husband Eldon Davis were the driving forces in bringing change to the Moscow hospitality industry and much of the hotel business throughout the Russian Federation.

No one is sure about the intricate details; how Eldon and Kimberley managed to drive the Russian Mafia and former KGB operatives out from the Moscow hotel business, but they did. Not just from their three properties in Moscow but from every western hotel in the Russian capital. You know Mr. Prime Minister, they actually got the Russian President: Viktor Orlov at the time, to demolish all the Mafia houses of ill repute with Russian battle tanks bringing all their standalone buildings down to rubble. Orlov then arrested the mafia bosses, as well as his KGB/FSB Director. That is who Eldon and Kimberley Davis are Mr. Prime Minister, and that is why I accepted Mrs. Davis's urgent request to meet with me today.

They have built their company into being one of the most respected in the world. Their company motto is *Service with Integrity*, and I for one believe that is what they deliver globally no matter wherever they might operate. The Baltic Jewel and Conference Center here in Helsinki is one of the finest hotels in Finland and arguably in all of Scandinavia. Eldon and Kimberley are industry leaders Mr. Prime Minister, and when they talk, I listen. I need to Mr. Prime Minister, tourism comes under my watch for our country, and Mrs. Ashton Davis is about to speak. Let us hear what she has to say. If you are ready, I will go and get her, I understand she's been in our lounge enjoying some of our pastries," Ursula said, smiling at Prime Minister Karvonen as she got up out of her seat to fetch Kimberley.

"Kimberley, so good to see you in person," Ursula said, walking up to greet her with a warm cheek to cheek embrace.

"Hello Ursula, thank you for seeing me, and thank you for that unexpected airport pickup, I certainly wasn't expecting anything like that Ursula."

"Kimberley what you have been through over the past week, well…that is the least we could do for you. Come, let us go and talk, I have someone I'd like you to meet," replied the Finnish Minister of Economic Affairs and Employment.

INN FORMATION

Kimberley followed Ursula down the corridor. A few meters down the marble hallway, they came to a door marked with the emblem of the Flag of Finland. Ursula did not knock, she opened the door and motioned for Kimberley to step inside, Ursula followed closing the door behind her.

"Prime Minister Karvonen, Mrs. Kimberley Ashton-Davis," Ursula said gesturing to the Prime Minister as he stood from his chair, walking towards Kimberley, extending his arm and the two shook hands.

"My pleasure to meet you Mrs. Ashton-Davis," Peeka Karvonen said to Kimberley, looking her directly in her eye. Kimberley noticed a strong but soft handshake, and he had a pleasantly disarming smile, Kimberley felt welcomed.

"Mr. Prime Minister, what an unexpected pleasure to meet you," Kimberley said, pausing and turning towards Ursula, "I had no idea the Prime Minister would be joining us, Minister Latvala," Kimberley added.

"Please won't you sit down, may I call you Kimberley?" Peeka asked.

"Oh please do Mr. Prime Minister, that would make me much more comfortable."

"Me too Kimberley, please call me Peeka, now what is it that Ursula and I can help you with?"

Kimberley was not about to mince words. The Finnish Prime Minister had just asked her what they could help her with. She hadn't flown across the Atlantic to have just coffee and pastries, she would come at the Prime Minister and Ursula with guns blazing, Kimberley responded.

"Peeka, Ursula, the question is not what you can help me with, the question is; how can you help the world. Not in ten years or five, but now, today, as of this moment. You hold power in your hands to change the manner in which the civilized world responds to acts of international terrorism. The window of opportunity is only open for a few days, perhaps for just the next two weeks but in this period the world must act, or this once in our lifetime opportunity will have been lost forever. Finland has the chance to make world history if you act now," Kimberley had given it her best shot, went for broke, stopped talking and looked at both of them sitting in front of her.

Silence filled the room for a moment. Ursula and Peeka looked at each other. It was not too often such definitive and dramatic statements were directed at the Prime Minister, and one of his cabinet members with such force and conviction as Kimberley just delivered.

Peeka Karvonen remembered that Ursula had told him that he would be impressed with Kimberley Ashton-Davis and after hearing that delivery, he had to admit to himself that he was. *Now to see how she would back up her dramatic preamble.*

"Well Kimberley, you have our attention," Peeka said.

"Peeka and Ursula, this will not be easy at first, but if approached in the right manner, it can happen almost on its own, but you will need to spearhead things and get the ball rolling. So this is what I have for you to consider and you must decide one way or the other by tomorrow morning," Kimberley paused.

All right Kimberley, what is it you have for us?"

Peeka asked.

"The terrorism that hit Cairo Egypt last week; now they are killing children, you know it could have very well been Finnish children, or Greek children or Chinese or whatever country you can name on this earth, they were our children, humanity's children of tomorrow and we must stop this madness plaguing our civilization.

You, here in Helsinki have the very first conference of its kind, on international terrorism with over two hundred countries of the world slated to come to Helsinki. Mr. Prime Minister, move the convention to Cairo Egypt! Let the terrorists know that the world will not be intimidated by their murderous acts, we shall meet them where they are today, and each and every day wherever they go we will follow and eradicate them from the face of the earth. Moving the conference to Cairo will send a message like never before!"

Kimberley was spent, she had given it her best, now she needed it to sink in. She stopped and waited.

"And how do you propose or suggest we go about moving such a huge international event booked months in advance, with such negative economic impact to our economy, picking it all up and moving it to thousands of miles from here to Cairo? Is that even possible?" Ursula asked, looking somewhat shaken.

Kimberley sensed that both Ursula and Peeka were so blown away by her suggestion of moving an international conference about to take place in three weeks to Cairo, neither one really knew what to say. But they hadn't yet said no! So she jumped in again.

"This is what's needed to make this happen," Kimberley said and proceeded to tell both Peeka and Ursula all about Eldon's plan. How to make it work, what economic impact it would have on Helsinki, the resulting effect on Cairo if this did not happen, how both cities could cooperate in jointly sharing some of the burdens for the overall good. Kimberley pointed out that making this historic move would surely bring new international respect and cooperation to both countries with unexpected future payoffs and benefits. The world community would be ever stronger by sticking together in the face of adversity. Kimberley went through it all, everything she could think of over the next two hours with Peeka and Ursula. But most importantly the key to all of this would be Peeka's and Ursula's efforts in managing the transfer of the convention from Finland to Cairo. Once they kicked off the idea and the delegations began seeing the light, things would move fast, with countries trying to outdo one another in their willingness to be amongst the first to make a move. Part of it was psychological, and part of it was bravado. Peeka and Ursula would need to lead the way.

Kimberley also emphasized that Cairo was already prepared to host the convention since all their hotels would now be almost empty after this latest act of terrorism. Booking the rooms for all attendees would not be an issue, and it would save Cairo and only impact the hotel business in Helsinki for a few weeks at the most.

Kimberley had delivered her best diplomacy dance. Ann opening dance of international unity ending with a saber dance into the heart of the terrorists. Now she would wait. Prime Minister

Karvonen had promised to give Kimberley an answer by noon tomorrow.

Kimberley left Government Palace and headed to her hotel; The Baltic Jewel. It was now early afternoon. She would call Eldon as soon as she got to her hotel suite. She could hardly wait to hear his voice, even if he were five thousand miles away.

"Hi Kimberley, were you able to meet with Ursula?" Eldon asked.

"Hi hon, yes, I met with her all right, but not in her office. Eldon, I was picked up at Helsinki International by police-escorted limo and driven to Government Palace," Kimberley replied.

"Wow, you were taken directly to the Prime Minister's office, they just cleared their schedules and placed you as a priority?"

"Seems like they did just that hon, and Peeka Karvonen listened, both he and Ursula listened to every word I said. I think they were well aware of our past accomplishments, especially in Moscow and decided to take my request for this sudden meeting as seriously as I did," Kimberley replied.

"So, how'd it go, are they on board?"

"Oh, Eldon I just don't know, I came on pretty strong. After I left the Prime Minister's office, I had mixed feelings. To be honest, I either won them over appealing to their humanity and better wisdom to act, or I came across as a paranoid lunatic; no middle ground on this one babe." Kimberley replied, with a deep sigh in her voice. "I told them I needed an answer as soon as possible and Peeka said he would have an answer for me by tomorrow noon."

"So, what is your next move, Kimberley?" Eldon asked.

"My next move Eldon is to wait for their response, and in the meantime, I will meet with Lars Kaarlson our managing director here at the Baltic Jewel and give him a head's up just in case things are a go. We will need to be ready to rebook all the delegates from our hotel in Helsinki to the Jewel of the Pharaohs. In fact, seeing that Cairo is emptying out, I'd have him transfer everything over tentatively and then hope the delegates all agree. I'm sure if the US and British delegations agree, then all delegations will follow suit, that's my hope anyway," Kimberley replied.

"After that, I'm having Billy fly me back home so we can get on with things there. I can always video conference in with Ursula if need be, but I think they will handle things on their end just fine. Now for the big wait hon, what's going on in Florida, any new news?"

"The local stations in Florida are still focused on the Giza bombings, as they should be," Eldon replied.

"They've begun interviewing grieving parents, the ones who are willing to be interviewed and the sadness is all-encompassing as you can imagine. Kimberley it seems like all of South Florida is suddenly a huge mega family. Reminds me of the 9-11 aftermath when we all came together as Americans, showing kindness and compassion to one another. That's what it's been like here for the past couple of days, but the sentiment has apparently really taken hold now gripping West Palm and Ft. Lauderdale. People of South Florida can be seen walking about their business with tears in their eyes, even a week later."

"It's going to take a while for normal life to resume, but it will never be the same again Eldon," Kimberley replied.

"But I'll see you tomorrow hon, I've got dinner this evening here at the Baltic with Lars and our sales and marketing director; Elsa Talus. Even if our push to move the conference doesn't pan out, it will be good to catch up with their plans for the coming year," Kimberley replied.

"Kimberley, remember I said that Cathy's been talking with Doctor Nabel at Cairo General…well, Cathy insists on coming with us when we return to Cairo next week. She says that after consulting with Nabel, she may be able to help in the microsurgery needs for Afraa's eye muscles and after reviewing x-rays of Talia's facial injuries; most definitely will be able to restore movement to Talia's jaw, but she needs to examine the girls herself. Cathy is very positive about their prognosis. Zara and Nawar will be overjoyed to hear this news directly from Cathy, that's my news, Kimberley. I think we need to be back there in three days max, so when you arrive in Florida, we fly back out to Cairo." Eldon replied.

"Oh, that's amazing news hon, yes, Zara and Nawar will be thrilled."

"There is one thing though, both girls will have to be flown here to Florida, Cathy needs to have her medical team with her, and she can only perform this type of microsurgery with the computer-aided link to the procedure only available here and a few other facilities in the US."

"Well then, that's what we do, we'll bring the girls to Florida, I'm sure our good Governor can arrange special clearance for these two girls' admittance to our medical center. The whole world will be watching their progress," Kimberley added.

"Eldon, I love you, see you tomorrow! I sure hope this flies."

"Love you too Kimberley, see you when you get back."

Kimberley stirred in her bed hearing her cell phone's ringtone, it was Eldon. Reaching for it on her bedside night table she quickly glanced at the time, 3:19 AM.

She swiped the answer icon, and before she had a chance to say anything, Eldon was on saying, "Kimberley, baby, you did it." repeating it again, "you did it, Kimberley!" The excitement in Eldon's voice had Kimberley sitting up in her bed, could hardly get a word out.

Eldon went on, "it just came over on WINN as breaking news, just this last minute!

"It did?" Kimberley asked. She was somewhat bewildered. She wasn't expecting this, not at all, and she still wasn't quite sure what Eldon was referring to, but it sure sounded like the news she was waiting for, just not at 3:19 AM, and least of all for it to come from Eldon in Florida.

"It's on WINN as breaking news?" Kimberley asked Eldon again.

"Yes Kimberley, you know it's almost eight thirty here. It just hit the airwaves. WINN is reporting that the Finnish Government is asking the international community to move their conference on terrorism from Helsinki to Cairo Egypt to show their undivided support for Cairo in their time of need!" Eldon said with excitement in his voice. "There's more to it, but that's the gist of it. You did it Kimberley, whatever you said to Peeka and Ursula, they didn't think you were a paranoid lunatic, they felt what you felt Kimberley, you got through! Not only did you get through, they too thought it through. They issued an immediate press release just in time for it to hit prime time in the US here on the east coast," Eldon said, now calming down with a sense of great satisfaction and accomplishment coming through. Kimberley could feel it.

"Oh my god, that is wonderful news Eldon, just wonderful. There is no way any of the delegations will oppose this request from the Finnish government. For any single delegation to object would bring ridicule and shame on them, no this will now grow legs, Eldon, we are almost there. Oh, I am so thrilled, there's no way I can get back to sleep now, what time is it?" Kimberley looked at her bedside clock again.

"Ok, it's three thirty here. Oh god, Billy's going to kill me. I'm going to call his room and wake him, I want to get on the plane and get back home right now. I can call Ursula from the plane later to thank her, there's no turning back now, they've made the commitment and announced their decision, I'm sure it's all over Reuters and the A/P by now. Well, if WINN has it, everyone's got it. Eldon, I'll call you from the plane just before we take off from Helsinki. I'm coming home, I love you."

"I love you too Kimberley, just get back here, and as for Billy, don't worry about him, he's our man and we will make it up to him, see you back home, bye sweetheart."

Oh my god, it worked, Kimberley said to herself, as she hopped into the shower.

RSULA

***

CHAPTER
NINETEEN
BLOMUP

Pete Jericho walked into the oval office, closed the door behind him, saw that President Trenten was sitting on the sofa leafing through a magazine of some sort. He walked up to the sofa and looked down at Trenten. Pete stood for a few moments until The President finally looked at him and asked, "what is it, Pete?"

"Mr. President we have significant progress on the Giza bombings. We need to push your schedule back two hours for this afternoon sir, you are needed in the situation room."

"What, like right now?" Trenten asked looking at his chief of staff, with a *you-gotta-be-kidding-me look* on his face.

"Yes Mr. President right now, this cannot wait," responding to Trenten's question like he was addressing a recalcitrant teenager. *Jericho wanted to slap his boss on the side of his head and tell him to get his ass in gear before he knocks his block off.* But of course, Jericho just thought that, *well… maybe one day.*

"This better be fucking good Pete." Trenton stood, reached for his suit jacket draped over the back of the sofa, and was out the door with his chief of staff heading to the White House situation room.

Walking down the White House hallway, Trenten turned to Pete saying, "do we have a bead on those fuckers?"

"I don't know Mr. President, I just know your presence is required, I'm sure this will be something we've been waiting for," Pete responded.

Trenten and Pete walked into the situation room. Much to Trenten's surprise there were only a few people there waiting for him.

"So, what's the urgency, you have something for me this time around or am I going to be leaving in another minute?" Trenten ranting already, not even having had a seat.

While everyone else was retaking their seats after standing for the President as he entered the room, they remained quiet except for Web Moss, the CIA director. There were just three other people around the table. Web Moss's boss; Greg Armstrong, Secretary of the National Security Agency, the US Secretary of Defense Roger Andrews and Mike Lance, the Secretary of DHS (Department of Homeland Security)

"Mr. President we have a positive location on the terrorists who committed the Giza bombings in Egypt," Web Moss said looking directly at the President, expecting some sort of outlandish response, and he got one.

"Well blow up the motherfuckers, blow 'em to kingdom come! What the fuck are we all waiting for?"

Roger Andrews, the Secretary of Defense, then piped in, "we can't just blow the motherfuckers up with all due respect Mr. President." Before Andrews had a chance to get another word out, Trenten cut him off.

"Sure as fuck we can, we can do anything we want. Do I need to remind everyone just who we are? We are the United States of America or did everyone around this table all of a fucking sudden come down with amnesia? We can do anything fucking thing we want to in this fucked up world. Let me ask you, Mr. Secretary, who the fuck is going to stop us? That's an order Roger, blow the fuckers up now if we know where they are."

Roger Andrews responded saying, "Mr. President we'll blow them up all right, but we need to bring the Egyptians into this. We cannot just go around blowing up buildings in sovereign nations, especially allies of the United States. We have to pursue this with their involvement, that is how we operate sir. The United States does go into Canada or Britain or one of our other Nato allies or for that matter, friendly nations and start blowing shit up, do you understand Mr. President? Together with the Egyptians we will launch an operation and eradicate those fuckers like you say," Andrews lectured Trenten.

Surprisingly, Trenten backed off some.

"Well those bastards sure didn't ask the Egyptians if they could come in and blow up their buses, they just did it, and our kids!" Trenten retaliated.

Web Moss then countered with a logical approach, "So Mr. President, our next step needs your approval for us to proceed. Yes, the CIA and DOD will work together on this effort. We need your approval for our proposed plan of action, and then call the President of Egypt and tell him what we intend on doing. He will agree Mr. President," Web said emphatically.

"And why do you think he will just willy-nilly agree?" Trenten asked, obviously still wanting to go it alone without the Egyptians' involvement and just blow up the fuckers.

"Mr. President, the Egyptians will agree because they want them as much as we do, but only we know where the terrorists are, they will have no choice. We can also insist that we take the lead on this once the action begins, but we will need the Egyptians to do some serious recon work on this group to make sure we get them all. That is something we cannot do Mr. President. On-ground recon needs to be Egyptians, they know the lay of the land in Cairo better than we do," Web Moss replied.

Finally, it appeared Trenton was beginning to see the light, he asked, "all right then, what is your proposed plan of action in getting these motherfuckers?"

Roger Andrews then responded to Trenten. "We need to place eyes on them 24/7 and not lose them. That we are doing already from the sky, but I mean eyes on the ground as well. Once we have them, they all need to be identified. That is the primary reason we need the Egyptians. Establishing who they are, the nature of their network and leadership structure is essential. We were correct in our initial assessment that the bombings were carried out by the ISS Jihadist group, but we need to identify which individuals make up this group especially their command and control. Knowing the organization's name alone does not give us much, we need to identify them all to the point of recognition.

The ENP (Egyptian National Police) will come into play on the ground. Their counter-terrorism unit would be conducting the 24/7 ground surveillance on ISS now that we know where they are. Mr. President, we have eyes in the sky that give us the capability to follow each one of the members.

We can follow and track, but only if they stay in the open, once they enter a building, we cannot be sure it's the same person coming out. This mandates ground-level surveillance.

Our combined aerial and ground surveillance will allow us to find where the terrorists live throughout Cairo. We will know where each one lives, their families, and their friends, but we need some time to gather this information."

"All right, and when do we blow them up?" Trenten asked defiantly.

CIA director Moss then spoke up. "We might never blow them up, Mr. President. We aren't really in the blowing up business. If we bomb their control center that is one thing, but they move on to a different location. We need to find them and capture them Mister President. Also, don't forget that the Egyptians want them as much as we do. They lost their children as well. The counter-terrorism game is an international effort Mister President. The Jihadist can act on their own, but countries of the world need to combine their resources in hunting these fanatics. Without international cooperation, the terrorists can run loose."

Mike Lance, the Secretary of Homeland Security who had been sitting silently by then chimed in. "Talking about international cooperation in the global effort to combat terrorism; we're all aware of Finland's move to relocate the international conference from Helsinki to Cairo?" Everyone nodded. Trenten sat at the head of the table, not really reacting.

Lance pressed on. "I for one, being the head of DHS was very impressed by this idea of moving the conference to Cairo. What this does, is not only send the obvious message to would-be terrorists that the world stands together as one, but it actually emboldens the international delegations and their individual members to an actionable commitment by their nations coming together wherever terrorism raises its ugly head. I instructed our delegation coordinators to immediately accept the proposed relocation to Cairo from Helsinki, and I am sure every other nation will follow our motion to relocate."

"Yeah, pretty ballsy move by the Finns to come up with this idea. I think we missed the train on this one, too bad it wasn't our idea and it had to come from the Finns who've never had to endure an attack on their soil," replied Armstrong the NSA director.

"Well, in fact, it was us, Greg, no, not anyone in DOD or DHS or from this administration, but it turns out that it was us. By us, I mean two Americans Mr. President," Lance said, now looking at Trenten.

"Yes Mr. President, in the backstory to the Finn's

requesting the conference be relocated to Cairo Egypt, it turns out it was two Americans who convinced the Finns to initiate the move."

"You boys sure missed the boat on this one," remarked Trenten.

"That we did Mr. President. I have to admit, we were all still asleep while Eldon and Kimberley Davis were waking up to the light. They are the two Americans with hotel properties around the world, they are HJHC, Holiday Jewel Hotels, and Casinos

. They just recently opened their new eighteen hundred room mega-resort and casino complex in Cairo on the doorstep of the pyramids; The Jewel of the Pharaohs Resort and Spa. Mister President, Eldon and Kimberley Davis have much more skin in this than you might know," Lance said.

"Oh, how's that?"

"Well sir, they are the ones who sponsored the cultural exchange trip to Egypt and the Pyramids for the American children, they feel personally responsible for this tragedy."

"And they are making it their mission to fight terrorism? What the fuck!" Trenten responded.

"We can't allow civilians to run counterterrorism operations or strategy, that needs to come from you people and me!" Trenton was now starting to unwind.

Lance responded, trying to hold things together. "No Mr. President, they aren't running our operations, they were just the driving force in getting the Finns to see the light in moving the conference.

I'm thinking they are both extremely savvy business people as well, in fact, that goes without saying. After all, they do have hotels in virtually every major city on the planet. They are a force to contend with when it comes to the hotel and resort industry. When they talk Mr. President the business and tourism industry listens. I wouldn't be a bit surprised if their thought process had something to do with saving some of their own skin in Cairo after the bombings put a damper on traveling to Cairo."

Lance kept pressing on, everyone was listening, "Sure, their idea is something we can champion, moving the international terrorism conference to Cairo, but it gives me great concern now for us at DHS."

"Yeah, I see where you are going with this Mike," Web Moss the CIA director commented.

President Trenten sat looking at the three men not really following where Lance was going with this and obviously felt upstaged by Web Moss's comment, but he didn't say anything, so Lance went on without addressing The President directly, he just continued on from where he left off.

"I'm afraid now with the word being out, that Kimberley and Eldon Davis, Americans were the ones behind spearheading to move the conference into the city where the Jihadis live in this latest attack, that it may cause them to react. In my mind, this raises our threat level here in the homeland.

Kimberley and Eldon may have gotten the international community to spit into the eye of the terrorists but may have inadvertently brought about a greater threat to the US.

We can never assume we know how they might react to such bravado and may lash out here in the homeland with bombings. As the secretary of Homeland Security Mr. President, I have to assume the worst at all times, I cannot afford to let even one drop of nitro fall between the cracks."

"Are we done?" Trenten asked.

"Yes Mister President, we are done, the only thing left is for you to call the Egyptian President and tell him that the United States of America requests his cooperation in joining us in the apprehension of the Giza bombing Jihadists."

"Okay I can do that," Trenten responded. He then stood, and motioned to his chief of staff to come with him saying, "come on Pete, let's give the Egyptians a call, what's the name of the President over there again?"

"His name is Ramses Nero, President Nero, sir," Pete replied as the two of them walked back to the oval office.

Andrews, Moss, and Armstrong, and Lance sat back down around the situation room table after Trenten and Jericho had left.

Roger Andrews then turned to his colleagues, the CIA director, Secretary of DHS, and the NSA director, asking them, "how'd this guy ever become President? My God, he'd have us in a war with our allies in a heartbeat if he was left to go out on his own."

"Well Roger, that's why we're here, to prevent that from happening.

Right now America needs us more than America needs our president, let's make sure we don't let our country down," replied Moss.

And the four men left the situation room

wondering what the next day would bring in the life of the President and America.

BLOMUP

***

CHAPTER

TWENTY

MOM

"We're ready to roll," Billy announced over the Lear 85's fuselage PA speaker system.

Eldon, Kimberley, and Cathy were on their way to Cairo in their private jet as it lifted into the warm Florida sky over West Palm Beach International Airport and east over the Atlantic.

Just north of Grand Bahama Island, Billy turned northeast heading once again for Bermuda; their first refueling stop.

Eldon thought of taking another breather in Bermuda where the three of them could discuss their plan of action in comfort at their Shelly Beach resort, but Cathy wanted to press on as soon as possible, so Bermuda would only be a fuel stop.

From there, it would be the Canary Islands again and then Cairo Egypt five and a half hours later. They'd have more than enough time to discuss their strategies and approaches to getting things done.

"Billy, what's our ETA into Cairo?" Eldon asked using the onboard communications to the cockpit.

"If the weather holds and we need not do any go-arounds, with our two fuel stops, the flight computer indicates 10:20 AM Eldon. You might have to come and relieve me for a few hours up front, I may need a catnap or two."

"Oh sure Billy, just let me know when. I'd like a few more flying hours under my belt. Actually, why don't you let me take over flying out of Bermuda, I'll take the next leg to the Canary Islands. I'll probably engage the autopilot anyway, but still, I would welcome a few hours flight time." Eldon replied.

"You got it, Eldon," Billy replied.

"So, tell me about Talia and Afraa's parents, what are their names again; Zara and Nawar?" Cathy asked. "I'm not that familiar with Muslim names, I take it they are Muslim, is that right?"

"Yes, they are Muslims, Sunni I would think, ninety percent of Egypt are Sunni Muslims. Both Zara and his wife Nawar are very humble people Cathy, I think you will like them. Eldon and I haven't really had a chance to get to know either of them other than the hospital visitation and introductions by Dr. Nabel, but they did come across as being good people, they certainly love their daughters, and as you can imagine Cathy, they are totally broken in spirit," Kimberley replied.

"Yes, sweetheart, your initial findings and evaluations based on the x-rays you examined will bring great relief in knowing there is hope for both their girls. How soon are you thinking of bringing them over to Florida?" Eldon asked his daughter.

"Just as soon as I can. I think that will depend on how soon our government can expedite the paperwork for these kids to come over, but like you were saying, dad, I think that paperwork might already be in the approval stages. I know Governor Warner is looking after that for us. If I can arrange for the girls to fly out say in three or four days that would be ideal. That would give me time to review all of the medical procedures to date, arrange the transportation details and give time for Nawar to make arrangements to accompany her daughters to Florida," Cathy said, but then continued.

"Their mother will have to be put up at our hotel in West Palm Beach, that shouldn't be a problem, I think you've already taken care of that dad."

"I haven't yet, but that won't be an issue, well have her stay at The Boutique Jewel."

"You know this is not going to be a short stay, I'm thinking three months at the minimum. Things will be difficult for Talia. I expect three surgeries in three months, there may be more needed, but the follow-up surgical procedures can be done back in Cairo. Both girls will be ready in three months to be fitted with a prosthesis. The trickiest part will be the microsurgery I need to perform on Afraa's eye muscles and nerves. That most definitely I can only do in Florida. I need my surgical computer linkup for that procedure," Cathy finished.

"All right sweetheart, three months it is, that's what we will shoot for. I'm hoping their mother can arrange for all that time away from her position at the University. Seeing the unique circumstances and their daughters' healing process being covered by the whole world's media, I'm sure the University will grant her a leave of absence in this matter," Eldon replied.

Kimberley reached over to take Cathy's hand into hers and said, "Afraa and Talia are so fortunate to have you in their corner Cathy, I know you will do everything in your power to restore dignity back into their young lives. We'll all do everything we can, won't we hon?" Kimberley said looking at Eldon.

"Absolutely and more, Eldon replied.

"Mom, dad tells me that your trip to Helsinki has turned into a dam burst with flood waters flowing into the Egyptian desert. Looks like all the international delegations have made the switch and then some!" Cathy said with excitement in her voice.

Kimberley welcomed Cathy calling her mom. Cathy started calling Kimberley mom when she realized her birth mom; Linda was never coming back from heaven. That was about sixteen months after Eldon and Kimberley rescued Cathy from her kidnappers in the Bahamas when she was just six. Later the following year, when Cathy started grade two, and Kimberley took her to her school bus the very first day of the new school year, that was when Cathy hugged Kimberley around her neck as Kimberley knelt down, and kissed her goodbye. But before boarding the school bus, Cathy said "I love you, Kimberley, you can be my mom," then she turned and boarded her school bus, heading off to grade two.

That moment brought tears to Kimberley's eyes and great joy knowing that Eldon's darling little girl had accepted Kimberley into her life. Kimberley thought of Cathy as her own and guided her young life with Eldon, parenting her along the way in shaping her into the woman she was today. Kimberley couldn't have been more blessed than to have Cathy come into her life when she did.

"Yes, once the DHS (Department of Homeland Security) delegation from the US jumped on board to make the transfer, every other country fell into line and within a week all had made the switch. We owe Peeka Karvonen and Ursula Latvala our endless appreciation for their cooperation. But no doubt about it, they too saw it our way. I think once they realized it was the prudent thing to do, they really stepped out and championed the move.

I talked with Felix earlier on, and he says the hotels in Cairo have never been busier. There's an atmosphere of unity throughout the hotel industry with all the major properties starting to fill up. It turns out that this switch from Helsinki to Cairo has kickstarted an influx of law enforcement agencies and organizations of all sorts now wanting to join the conference coming to Cairo, not just the expected conference delegations. Felix says the hotels are having to scramble finding enough rooms to accommodate the onslaught to Cairo.

He's been keeping a list of the range of related businesses booking at just our property. Some of them are private security companies, law firms, transportation companies who have security concerns such as airlines, rail companies, the cruise industry, container shipping companies. Even Amtrak is sending a contingent. Insurance and reinsurance companies are booking rooms like no tomorrow as well. Apparently pirating off the African coast is still a considerable terrorism concern, resulting in risk management workshops having become a growing addition to this conference. The world is coming to Cairo, and the city is running out of rooms. The

B&B's are filling up, and private home rentals are showing sold-out for most of the city. It's a complete turnaround!" Kimberley said.

"Unbelievable, just unbelievable," Cathy responded with surprise all over her face.

"We thought moving the conference to Cairo would have a positive effect on things but honestly neither of us expected this, this is unprecedented. We have the Finns to thank for this and to be honest, we also have the media to thank. They did an outstanding job in promoting this event," Eldon added.

"I had a brief follow up conversation with Lars Kaarlson our Managing Director at the Baltic Jewel. Well, it turns out that the conference organizers had no problem about the hotels in Helsinki holding on to the fifty percent deposits on the rooms booked since most of the properties in Cairo were willing to take our lead reducing room rates by fifty percent throughout Cairo for all conference attendees. So it turns out that the hotels in Finland did well, not having to take a loss on the canceled rooms. The hoteliers in Helsinki are happy, and the hoteliers in Cairo are ecstatic about business coming back. Eldon, it was all your idea," Kimberley said looking at her husband with a huge smile.

"Yes it was, but you made it fly Kimberley, you gave it wings. Without you babe, I wouldn't have stood a chance. Now to see how this conference goes off, I hope great things will come of it leading to some answers in ending this craziness. The world has been in a tailspin, and we need to right it," Eldon said as he looked out the window.

"Ah, we're coming into Bermuda. God, it's such

a beautiful island, just look at the colors of the surrounding waters. It's never ceased to amaze me how this little island in the middle of the Atlantic is able to exist like an oasis exempt from all the worry in the world, I just love this place. One day, one day, we will live here and call it home," Eldon said with almost a dreamy look in his eyes. "But first we need to go to Cairo and get on with things, Bermuda will have to wait."

Billy brought the Learjet 85 into L.F. Wade International Airport. Their refueling stop would take forty-five minutes and then be on their way to the Canary Islands. Billy and Eldon exchanged places. Billy was ready for a little catnap. Eldon was eager to get some more flying hours under his belt.

"So which one of you ladies wants to be my co-pilot?" Eldon asked with a smirk on his face.

"We'll both come," Kimberley said.

"Come on Cathy, you can sit beside your dad in the co-pilot's seat, and I'll take the jump seat behind you. We can both watch your dad take us up."

MOM

***

CHAPTER

TWENTY-ONE

KHTY

The two brothers hugged one another standing just outside the stanchions leading to the airport security checkpoint and on to the departure gates.

"May Allah be with you brother," Zara said to Arish.

"Allah is always with me, brother as he is with you," Arish replied kissing his brother on the cheek and then heading for the security checkpoint.

The time in Cairo was 10:00 AM. Egyptair flight MS985 scheduled for a 10:19 AM departure non-stop to New York City.

Arish boarded the Boeing 777-300 taking his seat in first class. Settling in and before taking off, Arish thought, *he'd be back in the States by 3:30 in the afternoon. His connecting flight to Las Vegas would put him home before midnight and then…seven days from now, all hell will be unleashed on America. Allah willing, he'd have a front row seat to watch it all, right in the heart of the beast. America will soon know ISIF, what it's like to lose a country, bring chaos in the streets and send parts of American civilization back to the stone age. The time for ISIF has come.*

Zara, making his way back to the airport parking garage checked his wristwatch; 10:07 AM. *Good,* He thought, *time enough to make it to Cairo General by 11:30 for the meeting this morning with Kimberley and Eldon Davis, Dr. Nabel and a surgeon from the USA. Apparently, someone who has been consulting with Dr. Nabel on his girls' treatment."*

By now, of course, both Nawar and Zara well knew that Eldon and Kimberley who saved their daughters happen to be the owners of the Jewel of the Pharaohs. Zara was the most amazed by this unexpected stroke of luck or perhaps the will of Allah. He and his wife were now naturally developing an unintended relationship with these two Americans who made it their personal mission to see that his girls receive the most excellent medical treatment available in Egypt. In Zara's heart, he hated not Americans, but the warmongering government of the beast. And yet, Zara found this to be the most opportune of circumstances that he could not refuse. He would use Kimberley and Eldon as he believed their historical relationship to be a gift from Allah. *It was unfortunate, but some Americans would need to be sacrificed for the will of Allah, Kimberley, and Eldon Davis fit into this sacrificial requirement perfectl,* Zara though

But this new American doctor must be someone brought in by Eldon or Kimberley. Well, so long as his daughters stood to benefit, why not.

It had been almost three weeks since his girls first arrived at Cairo General and both were now in the same hospital room. Afraa had been awake, lucid and talking regularly since her horrible injuries. She was strong, not afraid and comforting her mother as much as Nawar comforted her.

Talia had only been brought out of her coma a week ago and was still being observed each hour as the days passed. Thankfully she was gaining strength and communicating via computer with a keyboard. Talia's right arm and hand were not injured so she was able to work the computer keyboard just fine when sitting up. Talia's computer was also equipped with an eye-activated on-screen keyboard. By looking at a particular letter of the on-screen keyboard and then blinking quickly; twice, the selected characters would then transfer to the document. This technology allowed Talia to type words, make sentences or even write a letter, thus communicate even while lying on her back. The past three weeks had been an ordeal for Nawar especially, who had been with her girls every day almost 24/7, but nothing like the daily ordeal her daughters endured. She gave thanks to Allah that gradual progress in her daughters' journey was being made and seen, albeit very slowly.

Zara arrived at the hospital and headed directed to the patient/physician consultation room. Checking his notes, it was room number C2. He found the room, opened the door to see his wife, Dr. Nabel, Kimberley, Eldon, and a lady he had not yet met.

"Ah, Mr. Ahmed, we had just gathered a few minutes ago," Dr. Nabel said as Zara entered.

"Peace be upon you all, thank you for waiting for me," Zara replied.

Everyone stood as Zara entered the room, walking up to Nawar, Zara kissed his wife on her forehead and shook hands with Kimberley, and Eldon. Zara's deceit ran deep.

"Mr. Ahmed, I would like to introduce you to Dr. Cathline Davis. Dr. Davis is a specialist in microsurgery and reconstructive plastic surgery," Dr. Nabel said.

"Dr. Davis, peace be upon you,"

"And peace be upon you Mr. Ahmed," Cathy replied.

Zara then, looking somewhat unsure, but making the connection, glanced at both Kimberley and Eldon with the unmistakable look and question on his face, which Eldon addressed.

"Yes Mr. Ahmed, Dr. Davis is our daughter. When we told her of Talia and Afraa's injuries and the specialized procedures they would be in need of, well Dr. Davis insisted on consulting with Dr. Nabel to see if she could be of any assistance," Eldon said while glancing between Zara, Cathy, and Nabel.

"May Allah be with you kind doctor," replied Zara reaching for Nawar's hand and sitting down beside his wife as they both settled in to listen. Now Zara's deceit was running even deeper.

Dr. Nabel started the meeting off laying out the current situation of the two girls.

"Right, it's been three weeks since the girls sustained their injuries. Both are starting to recover but at different rates. Afraa and Talia are in need of specialized surgical procedures to give them a fighting chance in recovering so they can lead relatively normal lives. As I have already pointed out, the fact that they are young and very importantly, still growing, we believe this will help in their prognosis," Dr. Nabel paused, taking a deep breath and continued.

"However the specialized procedures they require are not currently available here in Egypt but as things have turned out, thank Allah, Dr. Davis has offered her assistance as well as her medical facilities," Nabel said.

"Dr. Davis, the floor is yours."

"Thank you, Dr. Nabel. Mr. and Mrs. Ahmed, both Talia and Afraa as Dr. Nabel has pointed out will require surgery, microsurgery that involves specialized surgical computer interfaces. We are dealing with surgical procedures down to the micron level, surgery using microscopes in plain language. Talia will also need bone grafting procedures to restore her jaw and eventual functionality enabling her to eat, talk and even swallow without pain. The pain, for now, we can manage with drugs, but we don't want to have Talia on pain medication her whole life. Are you with me so far," Cathy asked affectionately.

Nawar, looked at her husband, squeezing Zara's hand, tears forming in her eyes answering, "Yes doctor we are listening," Nawar replied.

"They will both be ready to receive prosthesis for their missing limbs in about three months. Let me assure you that will be huge confidence builders for both girls. And by the way, advances in prosthetics have changed people's lives like never before. Truly amazing things are happening in bionics," Cathy added.

"The important thing is to not waste time, we need to start the surgical processes as quickly as possible. We had to make sure that no infections set in before we began, that has been addressed and both girls are ready for surgical procedures to start, but that can only happen at my medical building and facilities in West Palm Beach Florida," Cathy finished saying, held her breath and waited.

"Florida?" Zara exclaimed. "You want to take our girls to the United States?"

Everyone looked at one another sitting around the table, surprised at Zara's reaction.

"Yes, Mr. Ahmed," Cathy replied. "Otherwise Talia will never regain the use or movement of her jaw, will never be able to eat like you and I do. She will have a disfigured face for the rest of her life and Afraa will never see again out of her eye. Yes, Mr. Ahmed, I want to care for your daughters in our hospital back in Florida giving them a fighting chance," Cathy responded.

"Nawar, it would be best for you to come as well for an initial three month period. You would be close to your girls every day, helping them in their recovery," Kimberley added.

"Neither of you would need to worry about expenses, Eldon and I are happy to look after everything for you and your two daughters. Your temporary home while in Florida would be one of the suites in our hotel just two blocks from where the girls would be at Dr. Davis's facilities. You could even walk to see them every day. But you and Zara need to decide today, tonight because Dr. Davis will be returning to Florida in two days. The paperwork to allow your daughters entry to the USA have been arranged on a medical emergency special visa for an extended stay, and you can accompany your daughters as parent/guardian special status. You need to let us know by tomorrow so Dr. Davis can make arrangements to receive Talia and Afraa at the hospital in West Palm Beach," Kimberley said appealing to both Nawar and Zara, "Nawar, you need to be on our plane with your daughters back to Florida when Dr. Davis leaves in two days."

"Mr. and Mrs. Ahmed, you need to do this for your daughters," Eldon said looking at Zara and Nawar, with a *why wouldn't you?* look in his eyes.

Zara knew he would need to let his daughters go. Deep down he knew he'd have to let them fly into the belly of the beast, but perhaps not the belly, but instead into the loving care of this Dr. Cathline Davis. Zara calmed, he would go along with this. But he knew tonight he would not sleep.

"Thank you to you Dr. Davis for coming to see our girls and for your graciousness. Mr. Davis, Mrs. Davis, we are indebted to you for your generosity and humanity. My wife and I will give you our answer in the morning. We will now visit our daughters, peace be upon you," Zara said with warmth in his voice (*a sheep in wolf's clothing*). They got up and left the room, heading to see Talia and Afraa.

Nawar and Zara waited for the elevator to arrive. They got in, pressed the button for their girls' floor, the doors closed, and they found themselves alone inside.

"It's okay Nawar, you will go to Florida, our girls will go to Florida with Dr. Davis."

"Oh Zara, Allah be with you, our girls need this Zara, you see how wonderful this Dr. Davis is, and her parents Zara, they are wonderful people," Nawar said to her husband.

Nawar was oblivious to ISIF, Zara's involvement with ISIF and had no idea what really was going on. Zara had managed to keep his secret, secret.

"Yes they are Nawar, Talia, and Afraa will receive loving care, we shall see them now and tell them of the news," Zara replied, all the while with thoughts swirling through his head. Thoughts he could not control. *His mind was here with Nawar, and his mind was back in the ISIF cave with his father, in Iraq. Another part of his mind was with his brother Arish who was back in the belly of the beast, and now Zara was about to send his daughters and his wife to America.*

Zara's head was about to explode; in four days he would unleash hell upon America.

KHTY

***

CHAPTER

TWENTY-TWO

LYVYZ

"Go live-eyes with Argyle," Commander Carr ordered the Argyle, pilot navigator.

"Roger that commander, Argyle is now live-eyes video feed to DND Argyle control center," answered the Argyle, pilot navigator.

With that order given, Argyle was transmitting live video feed and simultaneous video data capture of all activity within a seventeen square mile area of Cairo Egypt.

Argyle captured and recorded everything. Argyle beamed the live video to its DOD satellites, and the NSA picked it up in Washington as if was coming in from down the block.

Argyle could see a shopkeeper making change for a loaf bread someone just bought from his sidewalk bread stand.

Argyle could also see the seven ISS terrorists gathering in the second house from the corner across from the mosque.

With President Trenten having obtained the

cooperation of the Egyptians after his talk with President Ramses Nero, the US special counter-terrorism forces were now in constant contact with the ENP and together they had closed in on the membership.

ENP having been provided the coordinates of the terrorists' location by US lead Argyle surveillance was successful in further identification of three individuals previously suspected of bus bombings in Egypt. This was now confirmed. The leadership seemed to consist of two individuals previously identified as suspicious by the Egyptian counter-terrorism intelligence.

"General Milton, we have confirmation of fifteen individuals gathered at the target house. This is the largest gathering of the group to date since we've been monitoring the house and activities.

We may not get another opportunity like this with such a large concentration of these terrorists. Argyle shows everyone gathered for what seems like a 1:00 AM meeting," Commander Carr informed General Milton.

"Standby Commander," the general replied.

General Milton knew he had to act, this was now the President's call. But he already knew what Trenten would say.

He called the Secretary of Defense, Roger Andrews.

"Mr. Secretary, we have confirmation, Argyle live-eyes and confirmed by Egyptian CTU, fifteen individuals gathered at the target location, do I have authority to execute Mr. Secretary?"

Secretary Rogers listened carefully to his Army General in command of US special forces. Fifteen terrorists, meeting at 1:00 AM at the target location surely isn't for a stag party, this is another meeting for some terrorist action, perhaps on the conference gathering in Cairo. He couldn't take a chance of having a terrorist attack on the anti-terrorism conference. That would be a disaster! Rogers could give the command, but he'd call Trenten, it would only take a minute.

Rogers thought for a minute. He was currently in San Diego, 3:16 PM on the west coast, it was 1:16 AM in Cairo, that makes it 6:16 PM in Washington. The President would be having his dinner or perhaps hosting an event. Perfect, at least he wouldn't be playing golf. Rogers knew he hated being interrupted on the golf course, such was the man.

"Mr. President, we have a situation in Cairo. Fifteen of the Jihadis are gathered for a middle of the night meeting at the target location.

Do I have your" … before Andrews could finish his sentence Trenten cut him off saying, "blow up the bastards Roger, and that's a direct order this time. I want to see it on the news in the next few hours, do it, do it now."

"Yes Mr. President, consider it done."

"Commander, release your birds, the target is hot, fire at will," General Milton gave the order to Commander Carr.

Two laser-guided bombs were delivered by Argyle on target and target eliminated. Argyle captured the bombing event. No movement of any sort or kind was detected after that from the target area.

ISS was dead.

LYVYZ

***

CHAPTER

TWENTY-THREE

KOD

Lear 85 HJHC touched down at West Palm Beach International airport. Time was 2:20 PM on Thursday afternoon March 20th. Nawar Ahmed had arrived in America with her two daughters to begin medical procedures that would restore their young lives to normalcy, giving them back the opportunities of the future they otherwise might have lost forever.

Cathy arranged for her medical team to meet their plane upon arrival. The girls were transferred to West Palm Hospital via ambulance. A short ride from the airport but one of the most essential trips they will ever take. Talia and Afraa were on the way to the rest of their lives. The first round of surgeries would begin tomorrow morning, March 21st, with Talia's ramus jawbone being prepped for bone graft procedure. Later in the afternoon, Afraa would receive her first procedure as well with an exploratory examination of her eye muscles. Their first day was planned and procedures scheduled, even before their arrival to the US.

The Jewel of the Pharaohs Resort and Spa had been enjoying full occupancy for the past week with new bookings arriving days ahead of the International Conference on Terrorism. The announcement by DHS that their delegation was making the switch to Cairo had created a sudden demand for rooms at Eldon's hotel.

The conference had officially kicked off yesterday and was to last another three days; Friday and the weekend with most delegates checking out Monday morning and flying back home.

Cairo news was abuzz with terrorism news and related articles. Early this morning, news had broken that the suspected the ISS Jihadist organization responsible for the Giza bombings had been attacked by joint Egyptian and American forces resulting in their control center being taken out by the US military, wholly destroyed with no survivors. It is believed that the head of the Jihadist group was also killed.

There was an air of justification and avengement running through the entire hotel. Every delegation seemed to be talking about the taking out of ISS by US laser-guided bombs early that morning.

"Well, Eldon, it might come as some comforting news to these families here picking up the remains of their children that the US has killed the Jihadists," Felix said.

Felix, Eldon, and Kimberley were up on the hotel's mezzanine floor overlooking the main open-air lobby through the large panoramic windows of a meeting room.

They were having a catching-up luncheon meeting. Felix had some news from Moscow he needed to update Eldon and Kimberley on, and there was the families issue to discuss. Their plane was leaving, going back to Florida later this afternoon. It was a somber flight back home. The parents who were able to make the trip were crushed with despair and anguish, taking their children's body parts home to Florida. It was just too much to even consider as being real and yet, that is what was happening.

Eldon and Kimberley had met with all the parents during their stay at The Jewel of the Pharaohs, there was no animosity. The entire situation was a historical human tragedy, but not one of the parents blamed Eldon or Kimberley for arranging the trip. No one could have known such a horrific thing could ever happen. The parents prayed together with Eldon and Kimberley before heading to the airport and back to the USA. They'd be back home, landing at Fort Lauderdale International Airport before noon tomorrow.

"I wonder how the hotel's bookings look for the coming month? Do we have any occupancy after the conference checks out on Monday?" Eldon said, more of a comment than a question.

Kimberley responded, "let's find out, I'll call Rida my assistant, she'll have the ten-day business forecast as well as the reforecast for the next thirty days. I'll ask her to print out hard copies for us to look over while we have lunch."

"Rida, Kimberley, would you please bring three copies of the business forecasts up to me, I'm in meeting room two on the mezzanine," Kimberly said.

"Yes Mrs. Davis I will bring it to you, also while you are on the phone, I was just about to call you. An envelope has arrived by local courier. It is addressed to you, marked urgent and confidential, would you like me to bring that to you as well?" Rida asked.

"Yes Rida, I'll have a look at that too."

A few minutes later, Rida knocked on their meeting room door and brought in the forecasts, and the envelope marked urgent.

Kimberley laid the computer printout business forecasts on the table and reached for the envelope. She opened the sealed manila envelope and extracted two letter-sized pages, one containing text the other page with Egyptian hieroglyphs around the edges of the sheet, with an additional row of symbols on the bottom paired with corresponding alpha characters under each one. It was some sort of legend.

"What the heck is this?" She remarked holding the pages in her hand, looking at both simultaneously but not reading any of the text.

"What have you got there hon?" Eldon asked.

"Well, I don't know," Kimberley placed the document with the hieroglyphic symbols to the side and started reading the text to herself, it read…

We are ISIF (ISLAM SADDAM IRAQ FOREVER)

We seek justice for the unprovoked aggression and military action against the sovereign State of Iraq that lead to the fall of our government, our country, and our beloved President Saddam Hussein. ISIF will now have justice. For close to twenty years we have planned and waited. The time has now come.

You Kimberley Ashton-Davis and Eldon Davis have been chosen to be the voice of ISIF.

ISIF will not talk directly with the head of the beast. We will make our demands known to you, Kimberley Ashton-Davis. Eldon Davis will speak to the head of the beast; the American President.

ISIF does not and will not negotiate. The demands of ISIF will be met. It is the will of Allah.

Your instructions are given in the language of the Pharaohs. Read from left to right, begin from the top left corner and follow the path of the perimeter. The code is provided on the bottom. Do it now.

ISIF has spoken.

Kimberley finished reading the note.

"What?" Kimberley reacted.

She looked over at Eldon and passed him the letter. Then she took the page with the hieroglyphs in hand looking at the blank page with the symbols around it.

Eldon read the letter and couldn't believe what he'd just read. He read it over again.

"What is it, Eldon?" Felix asked while eating his lunch.

"Not sure Lix, I'm not sure, let me hold onto this one for now," Eldon said to his close friend.

Felix knew when not to press, so he didn't ask again, instead went on with eating his lunch while looking over the business forecast, but knew something strangely unexpected had just happened. Eldon and Kimberley never acted like this. They hadn't said much, but on the other hand, had told a lot.

Eldon wasn't about to dismiss this as some sort

of joke. Too much had happened in the past few days for this to come across as a joke. No, Eldon took it very seriously. Apparently so did Kimberley. She was already pairing up the symbols around the edges with the alpha characters as indicated by the legend on the bottom.

She then wrote down the letters starting from the top left hand corner of the page, going across the top, down the side, around and along the bottom now proceeding right to left and straight up the left side of the page to the last hieroglyphic symbol at the top just underneath the symbol she started with.

The letters she wrote down were:

-

tumorouwilresevyrinstrkshnslukondakngtutrstmnuon yrwebsyt-

She saw it right away. It was a phonetic representation of English words. She then parsed the letters out into the English words.

-

tumoro/u/wil/resev/yr/instrkshns/luk/on/da/kng/tut/rs t/mnu/on/yr/web/syt-

That then translated clearly to; *tomorrow you will receive your instructions look on the King Tut restaurant menu on your website.*

Kimberley now shuddered. This wasn't shaping up to be a joke.

She passed her deciphering over to Eldon who read it and then looked back at Kimberley with alarm in his eyes.

Eldon then looked at his watch. Today's date was March 20th. Something was about to happen on March

21st.

Eldon then said to Kimberley, "I-S-I-F …Islam, Saddam, Iraq, Forever. March 21st. Does that mean anything to you, March 21st Iraq, Saddam?

"No, not really, wait, wait…yes," Kimberley said, "yes it does! Hon, you will remember this too,"

Eldon was looking at his wife, his eyes wide. Kimberley's diplomatic career had never left her and all global events of significance registered in her brain even though she no longer served in the State Department.

"Yes, you and I, Cathy too, she was still on March break from Harvard. We were home in Florida Eldon, I think it was a Friday actually, we were planning on going down to the Florida Keys. It was the second to last weekend in March remember hon? The lobster season always ends March 31st in the Florida Keys, but on the last weekend we had plans to fly Cathy back up to Boston, so we decided to go lobster fishing on the second to last weekend that year, but then we didn't. We decided to stay at home instead and watch the war in Iraq. We were getting things ready on Friday. That would have been March 21st. I clearly remember WINN interrupting their regular programming with breaking news. The full air campaign "shock and awe" was underway lighting up the night sky over Baghdad, the Tomahawk missiles were raining down on the city, hundreds of them," Kimberley said with a frightful look overtaking her face.

"This is not good Kimberley," Eldon said.

"What should we do Eldon?"

"Right now, nothing. We can't. If we did

anything, I think we might make things worse than they already might be. Reading that letter, apparently whoever this ISIF group is, they picked you and me for something or other. I'm thinking they might know what they are doing. The note is very to the point. We do now what scuba divers do when their regulators malfunction," Eldon said.

"And what's that," asked Kimberley.

"Don't panic," Eldon replied. "And I mean it. If this is serious and not a joke, we need to work it. We have no choice but to wait until tomorrow," Eldon finished saying.

"But Eldon, the message says something about our website, we should…"

"I don't think so Kimberley, we need to let this one play out. If we go messing around with our hotel's website, that may make these people angry with us, and angry is nowhere near the word I'm looking for, we may bring about another Giza. Let's let it play out. I think they might need us, otherwise, why pick us."

"I'm nervous Eldon."

"Me too Kimberley," Eldon replied.

"My God!" Kimberley remarked.

Felix sat listening to them both. "Is there anything I can do?" Felix asked.

"Yes there is Lix, I know you don't know what we're really talking about, but you probably picked something up on your radar, so what I'd like you to do is to say nothing at all, this stays here at this table," Eldon replied.

"Understood Eldon."

"Well I know what I'm going to do this afternoon," Kimberley said. "I'm going to study Egyptian hieroglyphs, that's what I'm going to do. God knows there's enough of it all over this building, all of a sudden they're not that pretty anymore."

"Lix, we'll catch you later, stick around, may need you," Eldon said as he and Kimberley were starting to leave.

"Okay Eldon, I'll be here at the hotel all day, not planning on going out anywhere."

Eldon and Kimberley walked out of the meeting room. Kimberley held onto Eldon's arm, and as they walked together, Kimberley whispered to her husband, "Eldon I'm scared, who are they? What's this got to do with you and me? Why pick us…pick us…for what, the head of the beast… speak to the beast? I'm really scared, Eldon."

KOD

***

CHAPTER

TWENTY-FOUR

FRSTWAV

March 21st Miami International Airport, 12:10 PM

Airforce One; The President's Boeing 747 was ready to receive President Trenten and his White House entourage. The press corp was gathered hoping to catch the President for some comments on the news coming out of Cairo from the night before.

Trenten was feeling good about having taken out the terrorist control center in Cairo. He was more than ready to tout his administration's success in taking revenge on ISS. He stopped to answer some of the questions the press corps was shouting at him over the noise of the 747's engines.

"President Trenten, do you have a message for would-be terrorist looking to harm Americans?" Shouted one reporter.

Trenten moved in closer to the group of reporters, all holding microphones close up to capture Trenten's comments. Trenten's remarks were live on local and national television networks and radio.

"When I said that America was coming for them,

I meant it. We will hunt them down and kill them where ever they are. Our bombing of their control center is a loud and clear message that terrorists cannot hide from the United States of America. That is why we are over there so that we kill them before they can come over here. We will not have another 9-11 under my watch!" Trenten said while pointing his finger into the camera.

Almost at the exact moment as Trenten finished saying "*under my watch*," simultaneous explosions could be heard coming from the terminal area. Jetways at gates F17, F19, F21, and F8, blew up collapsing parts of the jetways onto the tarmac below. Sections of Gates G10, G8, and G2 also fell to the ground with explosions happening all along the wing of the terminal. Seven jetways were exploded.

The secret service grabbed President Trenten and rushed him to his waiting 747. Airforce One taxied immediately into position for takeoff even before the President had sat down into a seat. All incoming flights were being diverted to alternate airports. Miami International was under emergency shutdown.

President Trenten looked out the window. Ambulances and Firetrucks were converging on Miami International, ISIF had struck.

At that exact time, identical bombings were under way at Logan International in Boston. Gates C30, C29, C27, C31 and closer towards the main terminal building Gates C25, C11, and C12. Boston's Logan airport also underwent emergency shut down procedures. No outgoing or incoming flights, other than those planes already on the flight path for landing. All aircraft in line for takeoff were grounded. Chaos set in throughout Logan International.

INN FORMATION

At precisely the same time, chaos had ensued in Seattle at 9:15 AM Pacific time, at Sea-Tac airport. Seven jetways were destroyed at each of the ISIF targeted airports, sending passengers scrambling, forcing emergency airport shutdown orders in Seattle, San Diego, St. Louis, and Washington's Reagan International.

The US Department of Homeland Security issued the order to the national air traffic control network; US airspace to be closed as of 12:31 PM eastern standard time. All aircraft in the air over the continental USA were to land at the nearest airport. All incoming international flights were to land at the nearest airport, avoid entering US airspace unless inbound from the Atlantic or Pacific.

At precisely 1:45 PM Newfoundland time, Gander International Airport in Newfoundland Canada was also hit with one explosion; a fuel truck, causing a huge fireball but the airport itself sustained no damage. The signal couldn't have been clearer. The news spread around the world in minutes of the US airport bombings and closure of US airspace at 12:31PM. Four minutes after the explosion in Gander, Gander's air traffic controllers were already well aware of the international incident. A half an hour later at 1:01 PM eastern standard time, The (RCMP) Royal Canadian Mounted Police, and TCCA (Transport Canada Civil Aviation) authority issued emergency orders closing Canadian airspace. North America was suddenly shut down to all air traffic. Only the military flew.

It was 9-11 all over again.

"Mr. President we are on our way to Cheyenne Mountain, NORAD command center," Pete Jericho informed Trenten.

"We need to get you to the safest location in the country. Cheyenne Mountain is impenetrable sir. You will be safe there until we figure out what is going on."

Trenten looked back at his chief of staff, with a complete look of terror and helplessness on Trenten's face.

"It's secret service protocol in times like this Mr. President, we have to get you to safety, and there is no safer place then NORAD command center."

Trenten just kept staring back at Jericho like a scared rabbit.

Jericho said to himself, *big talking loudmouth, chicken-shit of a man, that's who I have to deal with, his true colors were now vivid; yellow mainly.*

President Trenten looked out his window to see three F-18 super hornets escorting his plane, he kept looking for a minute or so.

"Yes Mr. President, we will have air force escort all the way to Cheyenne Mountain Colorado. We have six fighter jets to escort Airforce One Mr. President, you need not to worry, we'll get you there safely."

Pete found himself all of a sudden talking to his boss as if trying to comfort a six-year-old. Jericho wanted to throw up. The man was really terrified. The real reason for his Vietnam deferments was now clear as day; President Trenten indeed was a chicken-shit of a man, right through to the bone!

The President was accompanied by a number of his cabinet on this trip to Miami, and they too were on Airforce One heading to Cheyenne. Pete was glad about that. He needed some people around him with balls and ice water running through their veins.

He excused himself from the President's quarters. "Mr. President, I'll be with Secretary McCoy and Director Moss in the staff room if you should need me," and Pete left Trenten to brood on his own.

"So, how's The President doing Pete?" Web Moss the CIA director asked.

"The man is terrified Web, I'm not kidding, he looks like he's seen a ghost, no shit!" Pete replied, looking at Web and Drew McCoy the Secretary of State.

"To be honest Pete, I'm not surprised, that's very characteristic of loudmouthed braggarts. They like talking tough, but when faced with a real threat to themselves they recede back into their shells. If he's like you say he is, I suppose we have to deal with that as well. Don't forget, that is why we're here, to look after the nation, and not the President; that's the job of the secret service, not ours," McCoy pointed out.

"You're right Drew, thank God for straight thinkers like you," Pete replied.

"Airspace is closed across the US, you guys heard yet?" Pete asked.

"Holy shit, not again!" remarked Drew.

"Yeah, Mike Lance just called me a minute ago,

he issued the order. Department of Homeland Security just shut down the entire country. San Diego, Seattle, Boston, St. Louis, and Washington Reagan International were all hit. Oh yeah, and I heard that airport up in Newfoundland, Gander, took a hit as well. You'll recall during 9-11 there were over twenty US flagged carriers stuck there for days. Their little city had almost fifty aircraft converge there.

"So, we're shut down, nothing is moving throughout the country. That'll surely fuck things up really good," Web said.

"It'll fuck things up way more than really good. This incident is going to throw the whole country and a lot of the world into a tailspin, you watch. Trenten won't know what to do. We have to call everyone in on this. Trenten's going want to start bombing everywhere. It's apparent to me at least that *everywhere* happens to be right here in the USA this time.

"Stock market just tanked, it's down three thousand points in the last half hour," Web said looking at his cell phone.

"You knew that was going to happen," Pete replied, "and if this isn't yet over, it'll plunge, even more. It may even shut down or halt all trading, which they will probably do today if they haven't already. Three thousand in half an hour.. .yeah, trading will stop," Pete said.

"Okay, so what do we do?" Asked Drew.

"We get everyone together, all cabinet members, we bring them all to Cheyenne, it's either that or we all go back to Washington and forget Cheyenne altogether. I know the secret service is following protocol right now not knowing what's coming next, but for the President to be perceived as hiding, well that won't look good for him or us. I say we tell Trenten to give the order to go back to Washington tomorrow if nothing else happens."

"I think if anything more happens it will be something along the same lines, disruptive tactics. This isn't 9-11, but overall it could have much worse results than 9-11 ever did. Let's see what happens tomorrow if anything, then we can decide. From what I've seen with Trenten so far, he'll be quite happy to stay in Cheyenne," Jericho said.

Moss and McCoy agreed.

The first round of ISIF's attack on America was now completed. No air traffic and millions of Americans were now stranded throughout the US. Chaos was simmering soon coming to a boil.

FRSTWAV

***

CHAPTER

TWENTY-FIVE

SLPRSLS

In Cairo Egypt, the time was a little after 8:00 PM on March 21st. Cairo was seven hours ahead of the US east coast.

Usually around this time of night, if Eldon and Kimberley were in the hotel, they could be seen enjoying dinner, perhaps entertaining friends or a group of travel agents in one of the Jewel of the Pharaohs' six gourmet restaurants. Not so this night. Kimberley still hadn't gotten over the letter. The letter with the hieroglyphics. In fact, Kimberley spent the entire day reading and studying the Egyptian pictographs and hieroglyphic symbols.

After delving into the topic, she realized that once the code provided by the Rosetta Stone, had been broken back in 1822 by Jean Francois Champollion, the rest was easy. After assigning alpha characters to particular symbols, expressing words and creating sentences in English could be straightforward.

There were a group of hieroglyphs that stood out from over the thousand different pictures and drawings. This particular group was the phonetic sounding hieroglyphics. They were universally accepted to represent specific phonetic sounds, and these hieroglyphs were assigned corresponding letters from the alphabet. So it became effortless and straightforward to compose a word consisting of pictographs because each symbol or hieroglyph represented a letter, and the symbols for those letters never changed. It could still be a little tricky because it was phonetic. So a word such as Washington for example with ten letters would only require seven hieroglyphs corresponding to the letters w-s-h-n-g-t-n, forming the sound for the word, Washington. Kimberley picked that up in a few minutes, nothing complicated about that.

By the middle of the afternoon, Kimberley could write an entire letter using nothing but Egyptian hieroglyphs.

"So, this is how it works hon, simple enough," she said to Eldon.

Kimberley had kept herself busy all day long. Eldon, on the other hand, was waiting for something to happen, and his wait was not to be extended. They were both sitting together in their hotel suite when WINN broke in once again with breaking news.

On-scene reporters from six different major international airports were reporting in about bombings in all six cities as well as one airport in Canada. American airspace was closed as of 12:31 PM eastern standard time all across the US, as well as Alaska, and Hawaii.

Kimberley and Eldon stopped what they were doing. Kimberley squeezed in beside Eldon on the couch burying herself under Eldon's arm whispering, "my God, my God." Eldon held her tight as they both listened. All air traffic across the US and Canada was grounded to the nearest airports. Inbound flights from the Atlantic and Pacific were allowed to continue to the US so long as they'd already passed their halfway point, all others had to turn around.

"Oh my God, Kimberley said again, the parents on the charter flight, are they coming back here?"

"I don't think so, they are well past their halfway point, probably already landed before the bombings happened," Eldon assured Kimberley.

"Kimberley, I think this is our cue. I think this is when we are to have a look at our King Tut restaurant web page," Eldon said.

"I'm almost scared to Eldon."

Kimberley grabbed her laptop and placed it onto the coffee table, she accessed the Jewel of the Pharaohs website. The homepage displayed. Kimberley clicked on The Pharaohs' Restaurants and clicked again on King Tut.

The page displayed but there wasn't anything immediately unusual. She then took the sheet in hand with the letters she had parsed out yesterday and clicked on King Tut's Menu, and there it was, the first page of the six-page menu showing the selections from the restaurant. Both Kimberley and Eldon saw exactly what they were looking for. Each menu page displayed was framed with Egyptian hieroglyphs, looking very pretty and eye appealing.

This time, however, there was no legend on the bottom of the menu, the legend had already been provided on the sheet in the manila envelope,

Kimberley referred to that.

She took her pen in hand and a blank sheet of paper and started writing the letters represented by the hieroglyphs placed around the first menu page. She quickly flipped through all the pages to see if they all contained hieroglyphs. They all did, it was the artwork on all their hotel menus, not just the restaurants' but all catering and banqueting menus, food as well as beverage menus. Hieroglyphs adorned almost everything, even the carpeting had hieroglyphic embroidery designs.

She looked up at Eldon and said, "okay, here we go," and she started writing down the letters. When she got to page five of the menu, she felt it wasn't going right, things weren't making sense, and she was right. Starting with page five, the hieroglyphs no longer contained a message, they were just randomly placed, but the first four pages resulted in an unambiguous message to Eldon and Kimberley, it read:

werisifumstfoloowrinstrkshnsdontcntctenijwluvfaros orhjhcmplezevrabowtdisifudouwldiyrdotrwldialsodiy usawatwedidindaustudaduonliwaturtoldmorwilkumt omoroifdiswbpgiztmprdwthyuwilditomortranwilexpl disifhzspokn.

Kimberley parsed it out;

we are ISIF you must follow our instructions do not contact any US authorities or jewel of the pharaohs HJHC employees about ISIF. Death will come to you Cathy will suffer torture to her death. You now know what ISIF can do. Do only what you are told tomorrow train will explode ISIF has spoken

Kimberley read it out loud to Eldon, then put the

paper down and looked at Eldon with disbelief on her face.

"Eldon, is this really happening to our family?"

"I'm afraid it is, and they're dead serious, not only that, they will demonstrate to you and me Kimberley that this is real. Tomorrow they're going to blow up a train. You know if that does happen we're in for a horrible ordeal going forward," Eldon said looking at Kimberley as he placed his hand gently behind her neck and pulled her in close, kissing the side of her forehead, trying to comfort his wife.

"Kimberley let's have another look at the letter from yesterday. Look at what they say."

We are ISIF (ISLAM SADDAM IRAQ FOREVER)

We seek justice for the unprovoked aggression and military action against the sovereign State of Iraq that led to the fall of our government, our country, and our beloved President Saddam Hussein. ISIF will now have justice. For close to twenty years we have planned and waited. The time has now come.

"It's the last two lines that are the most telling Kimberley. These people are not fooling around, things will not end with just the airports being bombed today, look at what they say," Eldon said while pointing to the lines as he reread it, "for close to twenty years we have planned and waited. The time has now come," Eldon finished reading and took a long deep breath.

"What do you think they want Eldon?"

"Reading between the lines Kimberley, my guess is they want to bring down the USA, they've been planning and waiting for twenty years, I wouldn't doubt they have sleeper cells all throughout the US and then some, maybe even throughout Europe, in the countries that participated in the Iraq war, I'd go that far."

"God, do you really think so?"

"Yes I do," replied Eldon.

The gears were turning in Kimberley's mind. Eldon could tell that Kimberley was trying to process all this, as was Eldon.

Kimberley then said, "but why us, what have we got to do with this?"

This is only a guess, but I think it's because we are the ones, you and me, who came up with the idea, well ok… me, about moving the International Conference on Terrorism to Cairo, which was tantamount to me spitting into the eye of the Jihadis. They apparently weren't too impressed with you and me when Peeka Karvonen mentioned to the media that you and I of HJHC were the ones who convinced the Finnish Government to move the terrorist conference to Cairo. Now they're picking on us to put us in the middle of everything all over again. Look at their letter Kimberley, they're going to want me to talk directly to the President for them, they say it right in their letter. I wonder how they want me to do that.

Kimberley listened to everything Eldon said.

"Well Eldon, as crazy as it all sounds, I think you are right, I really think that's what they're going to have us do. Just like you say, put us both in the middle of everything acting as filters for the terrorists and threatening to harm our daughter and kill us if we don't. This is just awful Eldon, just awful."

"We have a lot more to worry about than just that. I think their demands will be the easiest part for us. I think that will be pretty much straightforward. They'll tell us what to say, I say it and be done with it. It's not like we're going to have back and forth conversations. Apparently, it will all come from these damn pictographs, hieroglyphs or whatever.

What I'm concerned about right now here is what's going to happen in the next few days. Nobody from Egypt will be able to fly back to the US with the airspace over the continental US closed, Canada too. We might have some guests who will have no choice but to stay put for a few more days."

"Surely the US will allow planes to come to get them," Kimberley replied.

"Well I don't know, the government might want some of their DHS key employees back home but everyone else, well they're just citizens like the regular tourists who won't be able to fly to the US from anywhere else on the globe. This will mess things up in a big way. Not to mention what may be coming down the pike, " said Eldon.

"Oh, my God," Kimberley said, letting the words roll slowly off her lips, like the end of the world was about to happen.

"I can't wait any longer, I'm calling Cathy," Kimberley said.

"Yes, do that, but not a word about this to her. I want to hear her too, put her on speaker."

Cathy answered almost immediately on the second ring of her cell phone, her ringtone signaled it was Kimberley.

"Oh mom, I'm so glad you called. I wanted to call you today, but I've been in surgery all day with Talia and Afraa. Oh my God mom, what's going on? Nobody is going out anywhere here in Florida, everyone's remaining in their homes. All the airports in the country are closed, mom, there are millions of people stranded all over the country!"

"I know honey, your dad and I have you on speaker, are you okay otherwise sweetheart," Kimberley asked.

"Hi, dad."

"Hey Cathy, things are pretty crazy over here too. Nobody thinks they can get back to the States. A lot of people are freaking out, even the planned conference meetings are falling apart. Turns out only about half the meetings scheduled are still a go. We may be looking at housing a whole lot of people for a while. Let's hope the airspace over the US doesn't remain closed for too long."

"Surely the government will allow people to come home who are stranded over there," Cathy replied.

"Yes, sweetheart, but don't forget, it's not just the people here, there are Americans stuck all over the world and somehow I don't think the airlines will fly just with Americans on board, that would leave most planes virtually empty, I really don't know how they will work all that out," Eldon responded.

"Dad everything is so messed up," Cathy replied with a voice of despair.

"Cathy we love you, stay strong, no matter what happens okay sweetheart?" Eldon added.

"I will dad. Nawar is freaking out, she thinks she will never be able to get back to Egypt with her two daughters. I think she's just overwhelmed with everything that's been going on. I'm not surprised some people are losing it. I'll stay strong, I love you and mom, let's talk every day ok?" Cathy said.

"We will sweetheart, we will call you tomorrow Cathy, we're sending our love to you," Kimberley said, as both her and Eldon said goodbye.

"I'm beside myself Eldon, not really sure what to do or say or how to even act. I might not be able to handle all this, it's just too much, and it apparently hasn't even started yet, this is just a taste of what's to come, Christ, I just don't know, I don't know," Kimberley was getting very nervous Eldon could tell. He hadn't ever seen her behave quite like this.

Eldon's phone rang. He answered.

"Mr. Davis, peace be upon you, this is Zara Ahmed, my apologies for contacting you this late but I am anxious about things over in the United States, I was wondering if I could speak with you for a moment in person," Zara said.

"Peace be upon you Mr. Ahmed, would you please hold for a moment, I'll be right with you," Eldon replied, looking at Kimberley.

"It's Zara, he wants to talk, what do you want to do?"

"Let's see him down in the lobby, he's probably scared out of his mind. God knows he's not the only one," Kimberley replied.

"Mr. Ahmed, not a bother at all, my wife and I will be down momentarily, we can chat in a quiet area of the lobby," Eldon replied.

"Thank you, Mr. Davis, I will wait for you by the reception area," Zara replied.

"After we talk with Zara, I want to have a walk around the hotel to get a feel for what's happening, there's bound to be tensions in the air. I don't really know what I can do, or how I can help but maybe I can calm some of our guests who might need someone just to talk to," Eldon said as they made their way to the lobby.

"Ah, Mr. and Mrs. Davis, thank you for seeing me for a few minutes, I felt it best to speak with you in person. I spoke to my wife Nawar earlier in the day, but she was frantic. I found it impossible to talk to her. She went on and on about not being able to come home with our girls. Have you heard anything at all? Peace be upon you," Zara said with a good dose of humbleness.

The crimson red ISIF blood flowing through Zara's veins ran deep with deceit. The closer Zara got himself to Kimberley and Eldon, the farther away the face of ISIF would be.

Kimberley and Eldon showed Zara to a seat in the lobby, and the three sat down to talk. Zara appeared to be very anxious for some news… if Eldon and Kimberley only knew.

"We did speak with Dr. Davis earlier. Mr. Ahmed, she has been in surgery most of the day with procedures on Talia and Afraa. We will have more news in the coming days. You must remain strong for your girls and your wife. At the moment things are very calm in the area where your daughters are. As you know, all the airports in the United States are down with the airspace closed across the continental US. There is no need to panic Mr. Ahmed. Nawar is in good hands, and not alone. She is with Talia and Afraa, and they are with her. In a few days, we will know better," Kimberley said to Zara.

"Thank you for your comforting words, Mrs. Davis. I will speak with my wife and try getting her to calm down. You are right, she must remain strong for our girls. I hope all will be well. Thank you again, for seeing me. I will be on my way, may Allah be with you," Zara said while shaking hands with Kimberley and Eldon.

"Have a good night Mr. Ahmed," Eldon said as Zara was turning to leave.

The deceit ran deep. Zara had accomplished what he intended to this first day.

SLPRSLS

***

CHAPTER
TWENTY-SIX
MNUZ

Darkness had fallen over Cairo. Zara drove home and went directly to his library. He sat down at his writing desk, against the far wall. He reached up to the bookshelf directly in front and took down his diary.

Zara began to enter the events of this day into his diary, but first, he would mark the day's entry with today's unique source code at the bottom of the page. Zara entered in numeric code #25-3-55. Then Zara began his events of the day update using the hieroglyphs. Even Zara would have difficulty deciphering his own written entry without knowing the unique source code he wrote at the bottom unlocking the secrets of the hieros. He could do it, but it may take some time, this was much easier. From time to time Zara would insert a page or two of random hieroglyphs with a fake code at the bottom of the page, just to throw things off kilter.

Zara aimed to maintain a living record of all events chronicling ISIF's step by step rise to power, the resurgence of Iraq, the expulsion of American troops from the Mideast and the subsequent effect of ISIF on American civilization. His diary would be a record for the ages.

He turned on his computer and accessed the original images he copied onto the micro SD card he passed on to Imad Mahmoud in the I.T. Department of the Jewel of the Pharaohs. He then copied those images containing the dates, sleeper cell identification numbers, and associated targets for the coming three months, each sleeper cell dedicated with its own unique source code.

The turning of the wheels having been set into motion would turn until the ISIF flag of Saddam's hands holding the *Swords of Qādisīyah,* pierced deep into the heart of the beast.

"I'm going to have a walk around the property Kimberley, talk to some guests as well as some of the staff. I know everyone must be under stress," Eldon said to Kimberley.

"All right hon, we'll catch up later. I want to check on something myself."

Kimberley couldn't leave it alone, she had been thinking about it all the while they were talking with Zara. She had to know, and now she was heading back up to recheck her computer.

She accessed the Jewel of the Pharaohs web site again. This time she clicked on the heading description Banquets, then on Banquet Menus.

There were many. Breakfast menus, lunch, dinner, and then tailored to a variety of different banquets and themes. Everything from traditional breakfasts and dinners to extravagant dinner parties with a Pharaohs theme, Nile River theme, Luxor theme, and the list went on, perhaps a hundred different menu pages. But all the menu pages had one thing in common; they were all framed with hieroglyphs. Kimberley took pen in hand and started writing down letters as per the legend.

She completed the first menu page, then went on to the next. Kimberley had completed ten pages and decided to stop to see if she could parse the letters out into words. She tried the first set from the first menu page. It just wasn't working. The letters seemed totally random, words were not forming. She tried the second page, the same thing, it was all just gobble-de-gook. But Kimberley was not one to give up, she worked another three hours until she had completed all the menus' hieros. She tried each page. Nothing.

She was determined, sat looking at the banquet menus all over again.

Eldon walked back in from his touring the hotel.

"Yeah, Kimberley, there are a lot of worried people out there. Nobody's been able to book any flights back to the States. Billy and Felix met up with me. They've been talking to friends back home. Everyone is down in the dumps in South Florida, people fear the worse wondering what's about to come tomorrow and next week."

"Come here hon, look at this. I couldn't sit still, I had to give it a try. All the banquet menus, I also went through all the other restaurant's menus, not just King Tut. There are 114 pages of food and beverage menus including the pool bars and lounges, did you know that?"

"Well no I didn't," Eldon replied.

"So, what did you find?"

"I found nothing, no other hieroglyphs on any of the menus form words or parse into words, just the one from King Tut. Have a look, can you see anything I'm missing?"

Eldon moved in beside Kimberley and started looking at the menus on the laptop display.

"Yeah, I see something, look, at the bottom of each menu in the right-hand corner, there is a document number, see that, this one here, look, Doc No.27 #04-4-08. Did you consider that?" Eldon asked.

"Well, yes I did, but I think that is to identify the menu for cataloging it. The Doc No.27 contains menu number 5, 4th page of 08. I don't think it's relevant to the hieroglyphs," Kimberley replied.

"Maybe not, maybe yes. It looks logical, but it could be designed like that to throw you off, it might be some sort of a code or something," Eldon replied.

"Ok, look at the next one, Doc No.28 #05-05-08. Yes, that makes sense too, it's Document Number 28 containing menu number 5, 5th page of 08. Now let's see the 8th page. Yes, same thing… Doc No 31 #05-08-08. Well, that's what it is hon, just a number system to keep things straight," Kimberley said, convincing herself. She wasn't the skeptical one; that was Eldon.

"Well okay, you're probably right, but still it's something I'd keep in the back of my mind."

"We could ask our I.T. Department," Kimberley said.

Eldon then looked at her, with a look that said, no. She realized suddenly what she had just said.

"No of course not, we can't contact anyone working for us about this. The letter said if we did, they'd hurt Cathy and us. Oh, Eldon, what are we going to do? I feel helpless."

"All right, I'll go talk to Trenten about going back to Washington, let's see how the scared rabbit reacts," Pete said.

"We'll come with you Pete, Web and I need to support you on this, so he sees we're unified. He can't be seen running from these airport bombings. I personally think the Secret Service overreacted this time. This was no 9-11," Drew McCoy said, standing up to come along.

"Okay, let's go see him."

Pete walked into the President's cabin without knocking, the Secretary of State and the CIA director followed. Pete thought it best to appeal to his ego, which was huge, but an ever-bigger tail between his legs.

"Mr. President, Secretary McCoy and Director Moss, agree that the best course of action would be for you to show your dedication for the values and way of life we hold so dear with all Americans Mr. President. America will never back down or run from any challenge it may face. Mr. President you must order Airforce One to turn around and head for Washington. You need to be seen running the country and issuing orders to combat these acts of terrorism from The White House. You cannot be seen flying off to a fortress inside a mountain, while Americans at home lock themselves away, afraid to go out. You must take the lead, Mr. President."

"Well yes, I suppose you are right," Trenten said after Pete had just buttered him up.

Trenten sat in his chair looking at the three men in front of him. He waited and waited.

Almost an entire minute had gone by and no response from Trenten.

"Mr. President?" Pete said.

Trenten then suddenly grew a backbone, something must have clicked in his brain.

"God-damnit, turn this fucking plane around now! Get me my Secret Service Agent!" Trenten ordered.

"Yes, Mr. President."

Pete immediately went to get Secret Service Agent Fisher from the cockpit. He was listening for any incoming updates on possible more bombings.

"Fisher, President Trenten wants to see you," Pete said.

Agent Fisher entered Trenten's cabin, and right away Trenten started in on him.

"This was no god-damn Presidential emergency to have me whisked away to a fucking mountain hideout! Now go and order the pilot to turn this plane around and head back to Washington right now! You got that, agent Fisher?"

"But Mr. President the threat level…"

Trenten cut him off… "now! Trenten yelled at Fisher.

"Yes, Mr. President," Fisher left and within a minute Airforce One was banking a right turn heading east.

McCoy, Jericho, and Moss then left the President's cabin. As Jericho closed the door behind him and the three men walked back towards their area, Jericho said under his breath, "all right, the ass is back," both McCoy and Moss heard it.

Moss then replied, "better an ass, than having a scaredy cat running the country."

"We run the country Web, and don't you forget it, without us there's little hope in hell."

MNUZ

***

CHAPTER
TWENTY-SEVEN
TRANZ

Zara answered his phone. It was 1:55 AM March 22nd in Cairo Egypt.

"Peace be upon you my son," were the first words spoken by Zara's father; Faaz.

"Peace be upon you, dear father," it is good to hear your voice. How is mother, father?" Zara asked.

"It is good of you to ask about your mother, joy will come to her heart knowing that you are asking of her. She misses you Zara, no matter how many days or months since she last laid her eyes upon her youngest boy," Faaz said to his son. "She is fine, we both grow old Zara, but our spirits remain ever young knowing you are doing Allah's work, my son," Faaz said.

"I am father, as is Arish."

"Yes, I heard how well you and your brother have been coming along. I am sure your work will not go unnoticed. I look forward to hearing more of your great work Zara. Peace be with you my son, we will talk again soon," Faaz said goodbye.

Zara's heart soared, his father had just called to say he was happy.

Zara made no mistake about it, he fully understood why his father was so pleased; he approved of Zara's work.

Morning had broken with the sun rising over Cairo at 5:55 AM on March 22nd. Zara was out at first light and on his way to a public internet café. When he arrived ten minutes later, the restaurant was already buzzing with the daily jolt of java seekers. Zara got his coffee and found himself a comfortable seat. He opened his throwaway laptop, accessed the free wifi and logged in to a public blogger website with his fictitious sign in. Using his forum nickname, he then entered eleven sets of sleeper cell identification numbers. To ward off possible snoopers such as the NSA or CIA, only every second digit in each set was counted. The other digits were there to confuse and hide. So one set, for example, 412671 activated sleeper cell number 161 and another set, 92166, enabled sleeper cell number 26.

As of March 21st, all ISIF sleeper cells across the USA accessed the same open blogger website from a publicly hosted wifi connection. There was never a need for them to log in, they could read the postings but could not post themselves. They never had a need to post, only to look. They'd look for their unique identifier numbers under Zara's nickname. If their number were part of Zara's entry for that day, the sleeper cell would proceed to a variety of third-party websites such as travel agencies, hotel review websites, hotel booking sites, and the like. Only from there, would they then select the Jewel of the Pharaohs website, eventually ending up on the banquet menus webpage, finding their identifier number on their designated menu, with the source code key unlocking the hieroglyphs' associated letters to read ISIF's instructions.

For today's targets, Zara selected the sleeper cells that had prepared Amtrack train station platforms. The eleven he decided upon were: Albany, Philadelphia, Baltimore, Sacremento, San Francisco, Memphis, Minneapolis, Columbus, Topeka, New Orleans, and Jacksonville. There were many more, but eleven would suffice for today. The specified time for all eleven platforms to explode simultaneously across America was embedded in the hieroglyphs to be decoded.

Zara looked at this watch as he finished entering the sleeper cell numbers on his blog. All was set, the current time in the United States was just past midnight, 12:09 AM. In Cairo, 7:09 AM, seven hours later, March 22nd.

In precisely eleven hours and fifty-one minutes, the beast would receive another shock from coast to coast. Zara aimed for a 70 percent success rate. He factored in allowances for some of the ISIF members not to be available, one might be hospitalized for whatever reason, another might be traveling, the reasons could be many. They all maintained inconspicuous lives within their communities but sworn to carry out ISIF's cause to their death if need be. Sleeper cells not being able to meet the call, would remain dormant for a future opportunity. Out of the eleven he enabled today, he hoped for at least seven, but he wouldn't get seven, he got'em all!

INN FORMATION

Eldon and Kimberley had to do something that seemed normal, like maybe even having dinner together. The events of the past few days had consumed them both so much they couldn't think straight any longer. Everything about their lives, their actions, no matter what it was they did or said centered around terrorism and how it had taken over their lives. Perhaps doing something normal like having dinner in a restaurant might reset their psyche into thinking straight again, allowing them both to think things through.

"Eldon, it's almost seven o'clock, do you want to have dinner?" Kimberley asked.

Eldon wasn't sure how to respond. He wasn't hungry, or maybe he was. His mind still running wild with recent events, but he also realized that Kimberley was suggesting something normal for a change.

"Sure that would be a good idea, here or down at one of the restaurants?" Eldon replied.

"One of the restaurants would be nice. Maybe it will put some of the staff at ease to see us out and about. But you know it is almost seven, this will be a busy time with the first seatings about to get underway," Kimberley reminded Eldon.

"Try it anyway, see if they can fit us in, any one it doesn't matter which one, although Italian would be nice. Try the Venetian," Eldon replied.

"I'll just call the concierge, ask him to fit us in somewhere."

Kimberley called down to the concierge and held the line for a moment.

"Okay, the Venetian it is. They can take us now." Kimberley replied.

"Great, let's go."

Kimberley and Eldon finally got to spend a little quality time enjoying a gourmet Italian dish, from a first-class Italian restaurant. The Venetian was becoming a favorite restaurant with patrons from the city. The Jewel of the Pharaohs was proud to offer a selection of international cuisine as well as classic Egyptian main courses and desserts.

Eldon picked up the bottle of Chateauneuf-du-Pape and poured some of the red Grenache wine into Kimberley's glass. Usually, Kimberley preferred white wine, but with this Italian course, the famous red French wine from the southern Rhone valley fit the bill very nicely.

"You know we're going to take a huge hit with everything going on Stateside," Eldon said after taking a sip from his glass. "Our airport hotels while they may be full right now, with no aircraft moving. In the next day or two, people will find alternate transportation, those hotels will be empty. If airspace remains closed, our airport hotels will close. That'll be a blow to the company but more importantly, a mega punch to the employees. But honestly Kimberley I don't care about all of that. If I could find a way to end this, they can have all our hotels, everything I've ever earned and built just to stop this madness and have Cathy safe.

Kimberley reached across the table, taking Eldon's hand, "I know honey, my heart aches as does yours. No question about that, it's not going to be good Eldon. Look, I know we're stuck here for a bit, but I'd really love to get back home," Kimberley said. "I'm concerned for everything, and yet the strange thing is I can't do a damn thing about any of it."

Eldon was looking out into the main lobby of the hotel, through the slats forming part of the Venetian's wall. He saw people all of a sudden running and congregating in the vicinity of the sixty-inch flatscreen television tuned to WINN. Eldon could see some people walking away from the area in tears.

"Oh my God Kimberley, something else has happened," Eldon said, starting to stand up from the table.

Kimberley turned in her chair to look out through the slats, into the lobby. As Kimberley stood up, she was startled as patrons from the Venetian started rushing their way out the doorway, into the hotel's lobby, heading towards the lobby television.

Then someone could be heard, yelling out "they've bombed the train stations, all over the country! They've bombed the trains!"

"Kimberley, come on, we'll go the back way, through the kitchen and take the room service elevator up to our suite," Eldon said, taking Kimberley's hand. The two of them left the Venetian.

The television was already on in their suite when they walked in.

Kimberley stood in the middle of the living room and just watched the horror unfold in front of her and the world.

"Eldon, they're at it again," she turned to see

Eldon already accessing the laptop. Kimberley quickly went to sit down beside him, and they started looking at the menus again. They flipped through all of them, but they couldn't see anything different. All the menus were the same as before. Eldon then went back to the web page with the King Tut menu.

No changes there either, it still had the same message as before..no there was a change, subtle but a difference. It was the final four hieroglyphs on the top left side of the menu. Kimberley quickly wrote down the corresponding alpha characters, and it spelled out in plain English; WAIT.

"Wait. That's it? Wait? Kimberley remarked, almost expressing disappointment.

"Damn, well we now know these guys are for real. Yesterday the message was that a train would be bombed. Kimberley we're in for it, this is about as real as real gets."

"Eldon, shouldn't we call the American Embassy to tell them the terrorists are communicating with you and me?"

"No Kimberley, ISIF will kill Cathy," Eldon said.

"What do we do, just wait like they say?"

"Yes, for now, we are safe, and so is Cathy. Kimberley…sweetheart listen, right now, they are in control. The main thing is that we are safe, they obviously need you and me for something, maybe there will be a way out of this we haven't even thought of. Like I said Kimberley…scuba divers, no oxygen, don't panic. That's what you and I need to do, breathe and don't panic."

"God, Eldon, I wish I had your nerves of steel.

How can you remain so calm?"

"Believe me, Kimberley, deep down I'm terrified too, but if I let that surface, we won't be able to think. So like I say, deep breaths, and we will get through today. Let's call Cathy, she'll be wanting to hear from us.

"Yes, yes.. call Cathy, call her now!"

Eldon saw that Kimberley was really shaken up. He was hoping, hearing Cathy's voice and that she was safe would calm Kimberley down.

"As soon as the US airspace opens we will fly back home Cathy," Kimberley said.

"Mom, dad, they bombed the Jacksonville train station and a bunch of other cities! I'd really love for you guys to come home!" Cathy pleaded, all the while knowing they couldn't. Cathy's voice was showing some real stress over the past two days' developments.

Even just listening to his daughter on the speakerphone, Eldon could tell that the country, in general, was taking on a mood of doom and gloom. The coast-to-coast fear factor was starting to take hold with the added train station bombings. It was more than evident in his daughter's voice. She voiced the feelings of the nation.

"Dad, mom, with these latest bombings happening on a Saturday, the injuries and deaths would be limited. But inevitably come Monday morning, nobody in the nation will want to board a train anywhere in America," Cathy said with surrender in her voice.

Eldon thought to himself as Kimberley and Cathy

talked, *the millions of people using the commuter rail system throughout the US will not be going to work come Monday morning. How long will this last? Well, anyone's guess.*

But Eldon had a feeling that ISIF will have a good deal to say about how long the chaos will last. Whether ISIF is caught or never caught, they will already have done more damage to America in the past two days than perhaps ever, and it's all about to burst at the seams come Monday.

The stock market alone will lose half its value, causing it to close indefinitely until normality returns to the country if ever. Yup, Eldon was a doomer and gloomer, thinking the worst but always looking for that ray of light to burn through at the last moment.

After Eldon and Kimberley said goodbye to Cathy a certain uneasiness filled the air.

Eldon then spoke up, as he made his way over to the bar, "I'm going to ask Billy and Felix over. I've been thinking about bringing them in on this," Eldon said as he poured himself some Jack on the rocks.

"Would you like a drink Kimberley?" Eldon asked.

"Sure, rye and ginger hon, I think I need something stronger than my usual Mouton Cadet.

Eldon brought Kimberley's drink over to her, they clinked glasses with Eldon saying, "Here's to our future, we'll figure out how to maneuver ourselves out of this, we always do Kimberley although I think this will be like no other.

Don't fret Kimberley. Remember what we did in The Bahamas and Grenada, we eventually got those corrupt officials. It was you and I who figured things out, as we will this time. These ISIF people Kimberley…they put us into the middle of this and we're going to get ourselves out of it, one way or another." Eldon paused for a moment. He saw that his words were starting to bring Kimberley around again, building up her courage.

He couldn't blame his wife for being down in the dumps about everything. After all, hundreds if not thousands of people had perished in the US over the past two days. No matter how far away your loved ones might be from the actual devastation, you always thought they were too close and worried for their safety. That is how Kimberley felt about Cathy. Eldon and Kimberley, both well knew Cathy was safe, but just being in the same State where bombs were exploding had put Cathy in harm's way in Kimberley's mind.

"You want to bring Felix and Billy in on this?" Kimberley asked, repeating what Eldon had just said.

"Yes, I do. You know Billy or Felix would be put out if either one discovered we were keeping this from them. Kimberley, they were in it neck deep in saving Cathy's life and in it neck deep again with the Russian mafia and KGB in Moscow.

We need to bring them into this. I'm convinced they can help us when the time comes. More importantly, they'd want to be involved. They may not be our flesh and blood brothers Kimberley, but they've become like brothers over the years," I'm calling them.

"Eldon, I trust Felix and Billy with my life, you know that. Call them both, I want them in on this too!"

"Hey, Lix, round up Billy and come on up, Kimberley and I need to see you guys about something," Eldon said.

"Sure thing Eldon, be there in a few," Felix responded.

Billy and Felix arrived a few minutes later.

"Can I get you, boys, anything?" Eldon asked.

Both Billy and Felix saw that Kimberley and Eldon were having drinks, so they accepted.

"Sure, I'll take a Heineken Eldon," Billy replied.

"Make that two," Felix piped in.

Eldon invited the two men to join him and Kimberley around the dining room table. Eldon had this thing when it came to discussing serious matters. He preferred the talk and conversation to be around a table.

Even as a child he envisioned himself in one of the chairs around King Arthur's roundtable. To Eldon, it was an intimate setting allowing greater focus by all on the topic at hand. This way everyone looked at each other all the time.

With the four now seated, Eldon looked at Kimberley, then at Billy and Felix for probably longer than expected, looked back at Kimberley when Kimberley reassuringly said, "go ahead hon," and Eldon began.

TRANZ

**

CHAPTER
TWENTY-EIGHT
HU

Late Saturday afternoon on March 22nd the White House situation room was full with every seat occupied. President Trenten for a change was much quieter than anyone had ever seen him to be in this room.

"All right people, what have we got?" President Trenten asked the group.

"We have a holy mess on our hands Mr. President that's what we have," replied Mike Lance, the Secretary of Homeland Security

"How's that Mike?" Trenten responded.

"The thing is Mr. President, we don't know squat. We do know that these are coordinated attacks, but as to whom is coordinating things, well that is still to be determined Mr. President," replied Mike.

"Is this some sort of retaliation by those terrorist bastards we took out, who were they, ISS or something like that?" Trenten asked.

Web Moss then replied, "it might be an offshoot of their former self, but we don't think so sir. These attacks, to be so well coordinated and to come so quickly after we took out the ISS control center in Cairo, well, these latest train platform bombings and airport bombings would have to have been in place long ago just waiting for a trigger command sir, that's how we see it."

"I agree with Director Moss, Mr. President," Mike Lance of DHS added.

"So, ladies and gentlemen, tell me what we are going to do about this. We're not just going to sit on our asses and wait for the next set of bombs to go off are we?"

"We have all of our agents and every police organization throughout America looking for explosive devices at every airport and train station and all vulnerable areas we can think of. We have all of America's law enforcement entities looking in every nook and cranny for explosives Mr. President, we're all mobilized," Mindy Beaton the FBI director noted.

"If I have to, I'll call out the army and the national guard to start looking for more explosives. We can't have our facilities being blown to fucking bits," Trenten responded.

"No sir, we can't. Already these two nationwide bombings have brought a good portion of our economic engine to a grinding slowdown. No planes are flying and as of today Mr. President most of the rail service in the country has come to a screeching halt. Come Monday morning sir, millions of commuters will not be commuting," the DHS Secretary said as he looked around the table.

Most everyone around the table had a look on

their faces that said, *we're really fucked this time*. This obviously wasn't like 9-11. America seemed to have a viable enemy to retaliate against. The Taliban who were hiding Bin Laden, and somehow Iraq eventually became a target, but this time, these attacks came entirely from unknown origins.

Web Moss then started addressing the group. "Mr. President, we in the CIA have been gaming this exact scenario for years now, and I am afraid to tell you, Mr. President, that we are faced with the worst possible situation you can imagine.

A situation that has the potential to bring this nation to its knees. I am not trying to scare anyone in this room, but this scenario is amongst the greatest threat that any free nation can face, and we are now facing it.

Do we all understand what I am talking about?" Web Moss stopped and looked around the room.

"Go on Web," Trenten said.

"Mr. President, Secretary Lance can best address this going forward… Secretary Lance, " Web replied handing things off to Mike Lance of DHS.

"We are no longer dealing with terrorists over there, we are now dealing with terrorism from within. I'm not talking about one Oklahoma bomber, a Timothy McVeigh or one shoe-bomber, I'm talking about hundreds, perhaps thousands, ready to be called into action.

And I'm afraid to say, it's the worst possible kind of action imaginable.

It emanates from a cancerous tumor that's been growing for years possibly decades. It has spread into our towns, our cities, our places of work, metastasizing throughout America, and now threatens to kill us. I am afraid to say, Mr. President, that within days, within weeks, our nation will come to a complete standstill choking off our economy and threatening our way of life. The scenario gets much worse sir, much worse, but I think we all get the picture. I will leave it at that for now," Mike Lance finished saying with much heaviness in his voice.

"So who's doing this to us?" Trenten asked.

Lance went on, "We in DHS, NSA, and the CIA, Mr. President have come to the conclusion that America has three maybe four potential enemies that could possibly do this. It, in fact, is a viable alternative to Nuclear war. This sort of well planned out action can have the same effect, maybe even worse because it allows for a nation to watch its own decline into a state of anarchy and eventual hell. Without even aiming one ICBM at our shores, the former Soviet Union or the Russia of today could have planned this years ago to defeat America and become the leading power on earth.

The second possibility is, of course, Islamic Jihadists, they too would have good reason from their point of view to bring chaos and anarchy to our shores from within. The third possibility would again be a potential enemy, China. But the Chinese are tied into our economy much too tightly to do that, they wouldn't have any customers left to buy their products. North Korea, well they know any move to undermine the USA would bring annihilation to their country, so it only leaves Russia or Islamic Jihadists.

My pick would not be the Russians, we're too closely tied in blood and money. I'd say this is the work of some long hidden, underground Jihadist group out for revenge." Mr. President.

"So what's your recommended plan of action, Mr. Lance?"

"We have to find the bombs, Mr. President. If more bombings continue in the coming days, the nation's business will quickly come to a halt. People will revert back to survival of the fittest, and that will bring chaos and anarchy in the streets.

You, Mr. President, will have to declare Martial Law throughout the nation otherwise we will disintegrate into a failed State," Lance finished.

The situation room fell silent. You could almost hear the collective heartbeats of everyone around the table.

Secretary Armstrong of NSA then added, "Soon enough Mr. President, when whoever is responsible for this, feels that we've initially have had enough, I expect we will hear from them.

Until then sir, unless something totally unexpected happens, we can only search for more explosives set to detonate and try finding clues from the ones that already have. When we do hear from them, then sir we may have something to go by, but for now, we should be ready for more of the same."

"All right, I hear ya loud and clear, but I'm not about to just sit and wait. Secretary Andrews, I want you to put all forces in the Mideast and NATO on high alert immediately. If we have another attack in the next few days,

I will declare Martial Law in the United States and will have further instructions for you all at that time." Trenten said as he stood up to leave the room.

Everyone then stood and watched the President leave. Everyone else remained for a few minutes longer looking at one another seeking answers, but none came.

HU

***

CHAPTER

TWENTY-NINE

MRSHLLA

Sunday came and went, there were no incidents on Sunday. The United States could breathe for one day and lick its ISIF wounds. The airspace over the US and Canada however still remained closed. Trains were moving on Sunday once again, but the ridership was minuscule, perhaps twenty percent of normal Sunday volume which was small anyway. But now it was Monday morning, 7:00 AM and commuter volume and ridership would typically be high. Amtrack executives decided to operate to keep the nation moving. People were staying home from work. The nation's news media reported barely fifty percent of regular train passengers in the New York-Philadelphia-Boston corridor. The bombings were having a significant economic effect already, and it had only been three days.

The White House staff and the President's Cabinet were all on pins and needles, was there to be another attack today? The answer to their questions would come again at 1:00 PM New York time.

Zara had issued another round of explosions to take place. Once again Zara targeted airports, while he still had the opportunity to do so. With all planes having been grounded, and people realizing there was no chance of flying out. Passengers would find alternate transportation, cars or buses and the airports would empty out. He wanted to keep the airspace closed to further cripple the economy, and while his ISIF cells had access to their workplaces. Zara targeted fifteen more airports across the USA. This time it would not be jetways, all those would already have been checked over thoroughly. This time the target was inside, terminal escalators, moving walkways, and airport automated cable-drawn people mover trams. The cities were, Atlanta, Charlotte, Tampa, Columbia, Chicago, Newark, Dallas, Las Vegas, Newport, Buffalo, Cleveland, Nashville, Orlando, Salt Lake City, and Detroit.

Zara also prepared a message to appear on the King Tut menu today for Eldon and Kimberley.

The time on the east coast of the USA was ten seconds to 1:00 PM. In ten seconds, some of the people still stuck at airports throughout the nation would suffer injuries and death. The bombings across the nation today would close every airport in the nation. People still stranded at the airport locations would have no choice but to walk away, out onto the streets and roads. And that is exactly what was happening. The nation's airports that served as temporary shelters for the stranded passengers who found themselves still stuck, now emptied into the streets and onto the highways.

The national guard and FEMA (Federal Emergency Management Agency) were called into action to provide buses in moving people out of airports and to temporary shelters now being set up nationwide. An unraveling of the country was beginning with chaos spreading across America. Zara's actions had the desired effect.

President Trenten declared Martial Law at 1:45 PM Monday afternoon throughout the United States of America.

Canada, meanwhile also having suffered one small explosion at the Gander International Airport in Newfoundland had not declared Martial Law, and found itself with a massive influx of Americans rushing the Canadian border. Traffic at all major border crossings coming into Canada was backed up for miles and miles so much so that vehicles were running out of gas while waiting in line to cross into Canada. Although Canada had not yet declared Martial Law, the Canadian Prime Minister, and his Cabinet were discussing the possibility of closing the border between the two countries. It was decided that once all visitor capacity was met, meaning those without relatives in Canada, or friends with who they could stay, and all hotels, campsites, and accommodations were full, the border would be closed. Only those who had family living in Canada would be allowed to enter after that.

The Canadian government considered reopening Canadian airspace once again since no bombings of any sort were taking place in Canada. The explosion in Gander was apparently to prevent US flagged carriers from landing in Canada as they did during 9-11. For the time being, it was looking like Canada had dodged this bullet meant for the USA.

By 8:07 PM Cairo time, the news of the additional airport bombings across the US was on the Cairo television and radio stations as it was already around the globe. Zara was successful in activating twelve of the fifteen cells, that was an 80% success rate. Zara was happy.

The Jewel of the Pharaohs still had most of its American guests attending the terrorism conference. The non-Americans were able to check out and fly back to their countries of origin, Americans could not. Most of the Americans stuck at the Jewel of the Pharaohs were with the Department of Homeland Security. Strangely enough, there was an element of major embarrassment running through the group. Here they were, experts on terrorism and being prevented by terrorists to go home. It was irony with a capital I.

Eldon heard earlier in the day that the US government was sending a plane to bring them back to the USA. By tomorrow morning the Jewel of the Pharaohs would almost have emptied out, but strangely enough, there were some expected arrivals. Seems like the world was realizing that this was a fight between America and whoever, but not affecting the rest of the world. These indeed were strange times, Eldon thought.

With the news hitting the airwaves in Cairo about the bombings in the US today, Eldon and Kimberley quickly accessed their computer to see if there was a message on the King Tut page. There was, and it was long. All the hieroglyphs on four pages of the six-page menu had changed. Once again, Kimberley and Eldon sitting down beside one another on the living room couch started deciphering the hieroglyphs containing the message.

This time the letters Kimberley wrote down filled half the page. After she had parsed the letters into words, she ended up filling the entire page. It was extensive.

Having parsed the letters, Kimberley understood what most of the message was, but now having written down the actual words, what she then read out loud to Eldon, well even she couldn't believe it, but there it was. This was actually going to happen. After she read it to Eldon, he asked her to reread it to make sure he heard her right.

She read,

Kimberley Ashton Davis, you are a former diplomat. You will go to the US Embassy in Cairo at 9:00 AM 03/25 Inform the US Ambassador that ISIF will make a statement to the US President   Eldon Davis arrange for live media coverage. You will read ISIF statement to the US President at 8:00 AM New York Time, 3:00 PM Cairo Time.

Eldon Davis is to read this statement and say no more.

Start of Statement. To the American President: Head of the Beast.

We are ISIF Tomorrow March 26 at 9:00 AM NY Time a major explosion will take place in an unnamed American City. ISIF   does not negotiate. ISIF has spoken.

My name is Eldon Davis ISIF forces me to speak their messages to America. Any attempts by you or your assignees to contact my family or me will lead to more devastation in America. You do not contact me, ISIF contacts you. ISIF will speak again through the media. End of Statement.

Kimberley and Eldon Do not ignore this

message, do not reveal how ISIF makes contact. If you do all of America will burn and your hotels will burn, Cathy will be tortured to her death, you shall die. Disable all video surveillance at the Jewel of Pharaohs now. ISIF has spoken.

The two of them just looked at one another not knowing what to say.

"Oh my God, they're still watching Cathy too Eldon, they're probably following her all the time, oh my God!" Kimberley was stunned.

Kimberley looked at her husband with terror filling her eyes, helpless to do anything or even say a word. She bowed her head into her hands whispering, "oh dear. God, what is happening."

Eldon too was alarmed; his baby doll five thousand miles away in Florida was being brought into this. Eldon tried thinking things through. His logic filtered through his emotions, and turned towards Kimberley, reached over gently placing his hand underneath her chin and turning her head to look into her tearful eyes.

Softly caressing the side of her face saying, "Kimberley, Cathy knows nothing about this. We must keep it that way. She can go about her everyday life, she doesn't need to find out. If she did, she'd live in even greater fear than she already is. What we need to do is keep her safe, we follow these fanatics' instructions to ensure her safety," Eldon said trying to calm Kimberley down.

"This Kimberley is what I call real terrorism. They're really putting it to our country and to you and me. But you and I are just small potatoes in all this, we're the message bearers, they stopped shooting the messengers a long time ago. But you, me and Cathy I think are safe. These people, whoever they are, have a hair up their butts about not wanting to talk to the Americans, they just want to force the President to do things, and they might get away with it. They've already caused a hell of a mess we know that. But you and me, and Cathy, we're safe for now. We just need to do what they want us to. And I promise you, Kimberley, they will slip up, they will, and when they do, they will run. Remember hon, when it's time to panic… don't," Eldon said trying to steady Kimberley.

"So, we just go ahead and do whatever the hell, they tell us to," she said looking at her husband.

"Yes, to the letter. Kimberley, tomorrow morning you will go to the Embassy and inform the Ambassador that the President needs to be available to watch the news at 8:00 AM NY Time. I will contact A/P and Reuters and WINN and let them know to have their cameras ready to go live satellite at 3:00 PM with a prepared statement from ISIF to The American President Clyde Trenten. We are not allowed to say anything else on live TV. The whole thing will take less than sixty seconds. Then we wait Kimberley," Eldon replied.

"Oh Eldon, how do we get ourselves in these situations. Honestly, when I decided to leave the US State Department, I thought that being in the hotel business was going to be a piece of cake compared to dealing with governments and organizations always wanting something from me. My God Eldon, this is more than I can maybe deal with," Kimberley replied with nervousness coming from every breath she took and word she spoke.

◇◇◇

Billy and Felix were in the Jewel of the Pharaohs having dinner together when things started going off the rails again.

"Come, Felix, let's finish up and go see Eldon and Kimberley, they're going to need our support," Billy said.

The knock came at Kimberley and Eldon's suite, Eldon got the door hoping it would be Billy and Felix, it was, he was glad to see them.

"Jesus, all mighty they're ramping things up big time," Felix said as he and Billy walked in.

"I'm glad you both came over, we could use some additional brain power. Billy, your military background might lend some insight into how our DND, CIA, and DHS might react to what's about to happen," Eldon said with a *you-wont-believe-this*, look on his face.

Billy and Felix, having entered the room stopped in their tracks, while listening to Eldon but looking at Kimberley. They had never seen Kimberley like she was. She sat on the couch with her head bent down, buried into her hands, she didn't even look up as the two of them came into the suite.

"God, Eldon, what's going on? Billy asked.

Felix went to sit beside Kimberley putting his arm around her shoulders trying to comfort her, he didn't need to know what was going on. He saw that she was at the end of her rope with whatever new developments Eldon was about to them him and Billy.

Eldon gave Billy the page with ISIF's message that Kimberley had deciphered. He read it and then walked over to Felix handing it to him. Felix read it while holding onto Kimberley, then placed the page onto the coffee table, bowing his head and squeezing his forehead with his thumb and fingertips, he couldn't believe it either. Both he and Billy now totally understood why Kimberley felt as she did.

"Look, I don't believe there is much we can do, but maybe we can brainstorm this, come up with something, anything at all," said Eldon.

"Come on Billy… think, tell me what you think the CIA and DHS might want to do after I go on air with ISIF's statement."

"Jeez Eldon, this might be a little under my pay-grade, I think Kimberley might have a better bead on this than me but let me think about this. When I was in special ops, our focus was on execution and tactics, not so much planning and strategy. I have to think about this." Billy started to slowly pace around the suite, looking around the room but not really looking at anything, he was thinking it through. Billy reflected on his special ops days, his training encompassed enemy infiltration, surveillance, and counter-espionage.

"I can tell you this Eldon, the CIA, they'll want to know everything about you and Kimberley. I mean everything, from how many cornflakes there were in your bowl for breakfast this morning to precisely what second your mother gave birth to you. But right away they'll want to know why you are still in Egypt, well that's an easy one, all the US airports and airspace are closed. They'll look for gaps in your usual routine or business practices, they'll examine everything.

They'll want to know why you… why you and Kimberley? That's an easy one as well. You two were the ones that spit into the eye of the terrorists, and now you must pay by being their gophers.

Now that Martial Law has been declared, your civil liberties will not exist, not for you or any American," Billy paused and let that sink into both Eldon and Kimberley.

"But you and Kimberley and Cathy will remain untouchable, no matter what they think they might have found, they will not be able to touch you. You and Kimberley and Cathy now, are the link for both sides. ISIF will not allow the US to access you in any way because you now know way too much, Kimberley knows the messages are hidden inside the hieroglyphs. ISIF will threaten the US with devasting carnage if they try interrogating you or even contacting you or Kimberley or even Cathy for that matter. As far as ISIF is concerned, Cathy knows as much as you do now, whether she does or doesn't, she is nevertheless by default part of the mix. ISIF will protect all three of you. The other side, us, the good guys, Americans, they will protect you as well, because they don't want to lose you, you're the only link to the bad guys. You are like honey and kryptonite rolled into one; something you must have but cannot get close to."

"Jesus Billy, I don't know if I'm feeling any better after what you just said, puts us all between a rock and that hard place and that hard place right now is everywhere I look, Jesus!" Eldon exclaimed with frustration and a no-way-out feeling. "Fuck!" Eldon said. He never swore.

"One of the first things the CIA will want is all the recorded video from the hotel, all of it from day one."

"Yeah, ISIF is keen to that already, you saw the deciphered message, they had me disable all the surveillance cameras throughout the hotel," Eldon replied.

Billy continued with his theory. "As to whether they get access to that is questionable. ISIF can lay down the law saying that if any attempts to do virtually anything at all, be that gathering video equipment or trying to access your website servers, snooping around inside your computers with stealthy sniffer programs, they will blow up more Americans. I'm not sure the US will want to be party to blowing up more of their own citizens.

To further safeguard ISIF's safety, they'll tell the US government if anything should happen to ISIF in this case, the individual sending these messages to you Kimberley, and he is prevented from sending out his "all is safe" code daily, then all hell will be leashed on the US, with even more targeted sites taken out. So, to some extent, the US government, that is the military, and the CIA will be hogtied to do much of anything, unless like I say they factor in the future loss of American citizens as acceptable collateral damage to saving the country. I would think with all the advanced technology in the arsenal of the CIA and NSA, they'll probably have a bead on whoever this is within a month or two but won't be able to do a damn thing about it," Billy said, trying to explain things as he saw it.

He continued, "The thing is Eldon, ISIF will no doubt forecast the consequences if the US government refuses to carry out ISIF's demands, whatever those might be since we don't know yet. Failure for the US to comply and then have more Americans killed the following day because the US didn't do what ISIF demanded will topple the Trenten Administration bringing major changes in US foreign policy that will have the US capitulate to some of ISIF's demands. That Eldon is what I believe ISIF's mandate is; change the way America insists on policing the world and cripple its economy while doing so."

"Holy shit Billy, that is quite the scenario you just laid out."

"I think Billy is dead on," Kimberley replied. She'd been listening carefully to every word Billy said. Her State Department instincts told her that Billy described things to a T. "Eldon, that's it, that is what ISIF wants, look, look at the first message we got from them."

Kimberley read it out loud, *"We seek justice for the unprovoked aggression and military action against the sovereign State of Iraq that led to the fall of our government, our country, and our beloved President Saddam Hussein. ISIF will now have justice. For close to twenty years we have planned and waited. The time has now come."*

"If you read between the lines it makes sense. They want justice for what they claim was unprovoked military aggression, so in return, ISIF wants the US military out of policing the world, for the collapse of Iraq, they want America to fall in return. That part about Saddam Hussein their beloved

President, well… they want President Trenten to be deposed in return. As for the twenty years they've been planning and waiting; they're saying they're willing to keep bombing us for another twenty years till the US finally gives in," Kimberley said turning to everyone as she spoke.

Kimberley, I think you're right. Billy, you saw through this like a hot knife through butter. Okay, so now we might have a motive and a method to their madness. How do we stop this?" Eldon asked.

"That's going to be the hard part," Billy answered.

"But Eldon, just like in Moscow and Grenada, the more this thing moves along, the more potential answers will come to you and Kimberley, that's how these things go," Felix piped in after listening to everything."

"God, I hope you're right Lix," Eldon replied. "So, we see how things play out in the coming days, there isn't anything we can do about this at the moment."

Kimberley by now had come around having heard the logic being brought back into the atmosphere. She was feeling much better and was so grateful to have Billy and Felix in her and Eldon's life.

"Well like, Scarlett O'Hara said in *Gone with the Wind; tomorrow I'll think of some way… after all, tomorrow is another day,*" Kimberley said.

MRSHLLA

***

CHAPTER

THIRTY

TXES

All the President's men and women gathered in the White House situation room. It was March 25th 7:50 AM on the east coast of the United States. ISIF was about to address the American President in ten minutes.

Eldon stood in front of a podium at (World International News Network) WINN's Cairo Bureau offices with ISIF's statement in his hand.

The world's news media had already pre-empted their regular broadcast to announce this upcoming 8:00 AM statement from ISIF. At this point, the world was tuned in to the news awaiting the announcement from ISIF.

"The Davis's, you say they're mixed up in this because they got the Finns to relocate that damn conference?" Trenten asked Mike Lance of DHS.

"Mr. President we can't be sure, but that is our best guess right now.

These terrorists must be pissed at the Davis's for not shying away from everything especially after their cultural exchange program went up in flames and still, they refused to cave in. They became even more defiant in the face of adversity.

We believe, that is Director Moss and I believe that would be the reason they've been chosen to be the filter for this ISIF group. This will be the first time the world has heard of ISIF. It appears they've remained hidden for almost two decades making themselves known with the first set of airport bombings here in the USA," Mike finished saying.

At 7:59 AM, the WINN news anchor switched over to the cameras covering Eldon at the podium.

The news anchor then gave a brief preamble, "We are awaiting exactly 8:00 AM Eastern Daylight Time in the USA.

We are about thirty seconds away. Most of the world will be listening to the words spoken by Mr. Eldon Davis." The news anchor's voice stopped, the camera zoomed in onto Eldon's face, the stage manager pointed at Eldon with a go sign, and Eldon read the statement:

Start of Statement. To the American President: Head of the Beast.

We are ISIF Tomorrow March 26 at 9:00 AM NY Time a major explosion will take place in an unnamed American City. ISIF does not negotiate. ISIF has spoken.

My name is Eldon Davis ISIF forces me to speak their messages to America. Any attempts by you or your assignees to contact my family or me will lead to more devastation in America. You do not contact me, ISIF contacts you. ISIF will speak again through the media. End of Statement.

"That's it! That's fucking it?" Trenten ranted. What the fuck, we're supposed to negotiate with that?"

His Cabinet members were silent for a moment. Then-Secretary of DHS spoke up again, "Mr. President, that's just their point sir, you heard Eldon Davis say ISIF does not negotiate.

"So we're just supposed to sit and wait?" Trenten replied

"No sir, we can still do anything we want to, that has not changed. The pertinent question to ask would be, what is the prudent thing to do? That Mr. President is why we are all gathered here in this room," Web Moss of the CIA said, almost lecturing Trenten.

"All right, all right, so what did we get from this statement. Who are these fuckers again..ISIF?" Trenton said.

"We are receiving the transcript now sir, yes, they call themselves ISIF, Mr. President," his NSA Director said.

Web Moss then continued with his initial analysis. "The thing is Mr. President, we have no way of responding. At this point, it's a one-way street. But one thing for certain. In case anyone thinks ISIF is using Mr. Davis as a token puppet or that this statement is not serious, well, think again.

When bombs explode in the homeland tomorrow morning, ISIF it will have verified his legitimacy.

It is intended to be notification by ISIF to us and the world that when Eldon Davis speaks it really is ISIF speaking.

They no doubt have threatened the Davis's with

some serious shit as well, probably threatened his family and to blow up his hotels. That'd be my guess, Mr. President," Web Moss added.

Mike Lance of DHS, then said, "what I want to know is how ISIF communicated their statement to be read by Eldon Davis, that's what I want to know."

"Well, Eldon Davis would know that. We have to ask him," Trenten responded.

"Yes, we can certainly ask him, but he won't tell us Mr. President, and he may have good reasons not to," replied Moss.

"How's that?" Trenten asked.

"Mr. President, he will tell us that ten or twenty or who knows, a hundred more cities across the US will explode, and he's not about to have thousands more Americans' blood on his hands; a pretty good reason I would say."

"So how the fuck would anyone know he told us?"

"Because Mr. President, if he told us, we'd no doubt act in one way or another leading to the disruption of ISIF's gameplan, which in turn would lead to cities exploding," replied Moss.

"Not if we get them fuckers before they get us!" Trenten fired back.

"And who exactly is them Mr. President?"

"Well fucking ISIF, who do you think?" Trenten was about to lose total control.

"And where is ISIF sir?"

"Fuck, they're everywhere in America…fuck!

fuck!" Trenten fumed.

Everyone sat in silence.

Round one was over.

Eldon's reading of the ISIF statement to the US President took all of the forty-four seconds. But it was probably the most critical forty-four seconds of his sixty-two years. He had carried this burden all night long as did Kimberley neither one getting any sleep through the night. It was just this morning after Kimberley left for the US Embassy that Eldon managed two hours sleep. But suddenly he felt wide awake with this burden having been lifted off his shoulders.

After his statement, the media surrounded Eldon, peppering him with questions. He remained quiet, saying not a word, made not even a gesture, no shoulder shrugging, no grimacing, no raising of the eyebrows, nothing. He stayed stoic.

Kimberley, Bill, and Felix were at the WINN offices as well, waiting for Eldon to make the statement. Felix and Billy acted as buffers for a push through the throngs of reporters firing questions at Eldon as he made his way back to the car. Kimberley was waiting for them, and as soon as they got in, Kimberley drove away.

On March 26th at 7:57 AM, Amir Kura, (Steve

Kirkman; his legal name change, after immigrating to America) was on his way to work as he had been every day, five days per week, for the past eight years. Steve was a plant maintenance mechanic and pipe fitter, at the Westside oil refinery in Corpus Christi Texas. Although his route this morning was the same as always, today things would be different. He made his way to UP Road, across from the Tule River, driving past the oil tanker unloading terminals. Amir held the remote control detonator in his right hand. A quarter of a mile before the plant's entry gate, at 8:00 AM CT and 9:00 AM EDT, Amir pressed the radio frequency sending button. One second later multiple explosions blasted through the refinery with erupting fireballs. Entry to the plant was impossible, he kept driving to a safe distance another half mile and pulled over to the side of Up Road as did the other workers driving to work that morning. Having parked his car, he got out and watched the refinery burn, blending in with his co-workers.

ISIF sleeper cell number 31 had carried out Zara's instructions.

President Trenten was notified six minutes later about the Corpus Christi explosions. By half past nine, local news channel helicopters aired live feeds across the US of the burning refinery.

ISIF had verified Eldon Davis's legitimacy as their spokesman.

◇◇◇

In the USA everything was going well, in fact, better than Zara had hoped for. Of the twenty-two

ISIF sleeper cells he activated, nineteen carried out their first round of orders; an eighty-six percent success rate. Now that the beast had been awakened, ISIF would let it sit in peace for a while, before making it squeal and run in circles. ISIF's main campaign to destroy America would begin just when signs of normalcy started returning.

After the oil refinery explosions, the train station bombings and two rounds of airport explosions, the country had come to a virtual standstill. Commerce had taken an enormous hit right across the county. Most supermarket shelves were now just half stocked. Parcel post deliveries had stopped in its tracks. UPS, FedEx, and all other air freight no longer moved. Auto parts deliveries were ground-based only. Without air traffic and air cargo, much of the American economy suffered. Shipping container movement from the seaports was still in operation as was trucking, but even that had suffered cutbacks.

For the next three weeks, ISIF remained dormant, a lull in the bombings, brought about a return to some normalcy. The country needed to start moving again to maintain the economic engine. After two weeks of no reported bombings, American airspace was reopened, passenger trains started rolling again, commuters began using the rail system, and trading resumed on the stock market. Some Americans who had taken refuge in Canada were returning home, but for as many that returned, twice as many were still heading to Canada. Canadian airspace had opened just a few days after it had closed. This allowed many Americans to return home through Canada, flying to Canada, renting a car and driving it back across the border dropping it off back home. A costly alternative but many chose that path.

With North American airspace now reopened again, a rapid return to regular life ensued.

"I'm afraid it's not over Web," Mike Lance of DHS said.

"No, I don't think it is either. We haven't heard a thing from ISIF for almost a month, I'm guessing we soon will," Web Moss replied.

"We've made every attempt to contact Kimberley and Eldon Davis, but neither one takes our calls, and they are prevented from going to our Embassy in Cairo, we haven't been able to talk with them. Anyone we send over to talk in person is refused," Moss the CIA Director added.

"Mike, we're still virtually in the dark."

"I know the NSA has scoured all internet traffic in and out of Egypt. The Jewel of the Pharaohs website has been looked at, but they haven't hit pay-dirt there either," Mike replied.

"Argyle has been watching everything in Cairo as well. The DND has repositioned three Argyle platforms over the US, New York, Chicago, and Los Angeles. Secretary Andrews tells me the DND is ramping up to produce two dozen more Argyle platforms and have them operational by the end of this week. I have no doubt that with a year, every city in America with a population greater than a hundred thousand will have Argyle surveillance 24/7," Web.

"Talk about big brother, hell we'll be way past anything George Orwell's 1984 foretold. Pretty soon, Mike, our government will start microchipping everyone, and artificial intelligence algorithms will hunt you down before you even think of stealing a car," Web replied.

"Yes, it will come to that one of these days, but for now I'd be satisfied to catch even just one of these sleeper cell bastards, just one," Mike said.

"I'm with you on that," Web replied. "You know Mike, back in 2003 when we went into Iraq, all because of WMD's and then found none, I figured back then that it will come back to bite us in the ass."

Mike Lance listened and thought for a minute or so. Then replied as if a lightbulb went off in his head.

"Web, this might be a longshot, but I think you may be on to something. I think that's where we should be concentrating our efforts, hear me out on this one."

"Shoot."

"These bombings are obviously sleeper cells, there is no doubt about it. And they would have had have been set up a long time ago."

Web Moss was listening carefully, he could see that Mike was on to something.

"So, let's assume this ISIF Jihadist organization is looking for retribution for the Iraq invasion of 2003," Mike paused, looking at Web.

"Yeah, go on," Web replied

"It would make sense to look for Iraqis, right?"

"Right."

"It would also make sense to look for Iraqis who currently have or, had access for the past say three years, to the various places that have been bombed right?" Mike added.

"Ok, you're right, so then we access all these

companies' employee files, airlines, oil refineries, rail companies, vulnerable target types of businesses and filter out anyone with Iraqi names who work there or have worked there over the past years," Web responded.

"Yes, now we're on the same wavelength, I'll get on it as well, we'll find them, and in case it's not Iraqi's we'll look for anyone with middle eastern names working at these facilities. If nothing else, it's a start. Christ Web, we should have been on this weeks ago! Fuck!"

The time had come to pass. ISIF was to begin its main campaign. Service-based industries, as well as manufacturing centers, were targeted. This time, however, medium-sized cities would suffer the most. ISIF planned to demonstrate that no place in the USA was untouchable. Towns in rural agricultural States such as Iowa, Nebraska, and Kansas would also be targeted. Some of the urban centers to have terror rain down upon them were: Omaha, Cedar Rapids, Wichita, Sioux City, Helena, Grand Rapids, Burlington, Rochester, Winston-Salem, Raleigh, San Jose, Portland, Eureka, Fairbanks, Honolulu, and fifteen more including major metropolitan areas.

It had been planned out and thought out by Faaz and the Council of Ten, for almost twenty years. This new wave to be unleashed upon America would have devastating effects across the nation. Faaz and the council estimated that it would bring about a sixty to eighty percent reduction in the GDP (Gross Domestic Product). Once again, the airports would be down, rail service would come to a halt, both passenger and cargo, and this time the trucking industry would also be hit. Anarchy would erupt in the streets, and soon the National Guard would not be enough to quell the violence. The Posse Comitatus Act of June 18, 1878, limiting the powers of the Administration in using the military to enforce domestic policy and curtail violence would be out the window. America would decline into a failed state. Most of the population will no longer have paychecks or jobs.

Faaz and the Council of Ten predicted that it would be at this juncture, perhaps one month after the new wave of bombings that the United States will have reached its tipping point. The President would be ready to ask how he could meet some of ISIF's demands before the nation disintegrated. America would have no one to bomb but itself.

ISIF would then make its demands known, bringing about a new world order displacing America from the top of the global economic food chain. The US dollar would have collapsed by that time, with the world's economy in flux.

Zara acted. On the first of May, after forty days of quiet across the US, the blasting could be heard again from coast to coast as well as Hawaii and Alaska.

Shopping malls, automobile plants, shipping ports, universities, airports, railway tracks, highway overpasses, hydroelectric dams, food distribution warehouses, chemical manufacturing plants and food production factories were targeted to name a few.

INN FORMATION

America came to a halt overnight. Nothing moved, soon, the nation was beginning to run out of food, and full-scale anarchy took over in the streets. It was as ISIF had predicted; the beast was now ready to listen.

Immediately after the news of the bombings reaching Cairo, Kimberley checked the King Tut page. There was only one message, like the one she deciphered before. This new message read: WAIT AGAIN.

Having received a message to wait again, Kimberley checked for new words every day, morning afternoon and night. An entire week had passed, and on the seventh day, the menu contained Zara's new words for Eldon to read. Kimberley deciphered the hieros as before, and the statement read:

To be read and aired on live Television at 6:00 PM New York Time May 7th

Begin Message

To the American People.

We are ISIF we do not negotiate. To bring an end to further ISIF action you will do the following.

The American President will step down. Clyde Trenten will be flown to Iraq and imprisoned to pay for the crimes of past American Presidents against the sovereign State of Iraq. He must be in Iraq by May 31st.

All American ground-based troops and Airforce personnel in the Middle Eastern countries shall immediately leave. The sovereign nations are; Saudi Arabia, Kuwait, Bahrain, Iraq, Oman, Qatar, United Arab Emirates, and Afghanistan. All military equipment remains behind, including aircraft. All US troops must be out by May 31st, to never again return. No American Military personnel shall ever set foot in the countries of Egypt, Lebanon or Syria.

The US Navy must immediately cease operations and leave the Gulf of Aden, the Red Sea, the Persian Gulf, the Gulf of Oman, and the Gulf of Arabia north of the 10th parallel. Also, the US Navy must never sail east of longitude fifteen and north of parallel 34 in the Mediterranean Sea. All US naval ships must vacate the stated regions by May 31st. Comply, and peace shall return. The new world order has begun. ISIF has spoken.

As Kimberley was deciphering the new message, Eldon Billy and Felix sat by waiting. They had all agreed with Billy's scenario on what ISIF wants, this new message may now detail those demands.

Kimberley finished.

"You were right on Billy," Kimberley said, "but let's have Eldon read it out loud to us, it's chilling."

Eldon took the message from Kimberley and started reading it, so everyone heard it as Eldon would read it to the United States and the world.

"Wow, wow!" Eldon said after he finished. He was left speechless as were Billy, Kimberley, and Felix. They all figured that the message would be something like this, but to actually hear it out loud, knowing that Eldon will read these words to America and the world was unthinkable.

"Eldon, do you think the US will comply with this?" Kimberley asked.

"Actually, I do. For the life of me, I cannot see another option. It may take them a few days, but other world leaders will also demand the US Administration to cave. This now has a global effect. I just cannot see any other way out. The US will have to buckle and do what ISIF wants. That at least will give America a chance to live and to maybe fight another day. By now the American people will demand that something is done to give their lives back.

Patrick Henry's *Give me liberty or give me death* isn't something most mothers and fathers are shouting in the streets of Peoria right now. They're more interested in feeding their children and bringing life back to some level of normalcy.

Americans are about to hear ISIF's demands loud and clear. Don't forget, there are millions of Americans calling for the removal of American soldiers from around the world and to stop meddling in other countries' affairs. This will be their calling to topple the Trenten administration. If they don't, America will be destroyed," Eldon added.

Eldon dropped himself on the couch, rubbing his forehead trying to think.

"Well, tomorrow morning at 1:00 AM, I'll be reading this statement at the WINN offices here in Cairo. Washington is seven hours behind us, so at 6:00 PM Washington time, Trenten will know he might be spending the rest of his life in an Iraqi prison. Holy crap, this is just so surreal," Eldon said, looking at everyone.

"After this new message is delivered and the world knows ISIF's demands. The pressure for the US to comply will come from every corner of the world, you watch. Sure, we had that great terrorism conference here back in March, but nobody was prepared for something like this," Kimberley said.

"This ISIF thing is an entirely new dynamic in terrorism, look at what it's done to America. I'm hoping this will lead to wiser thinking in the future, but something tells me that humanity is its own worst enemy. It seems we just cannot get along. Maybe this is our destiny, to hate, suffer, and wallow in our greed. If anything, good ever comes out of this, it better happen soon, or all will be lost for America," Kimberley said, expressing some thoughts for everyone to ponder.

"But right now, I'm going to call Cathy and talk for a while. Eldon, I'll let you know when I'm done talking with Cathy, I'm sure she'll want to hear your voice," Kimberley said as she excused herself.

"Yes, Cathy, it's been just awful for your father and me as well. I'm amazed you are holding up as well as you say you are, it must be tough for you with all that's gone on. I'm so glad nothing has happened in West Palm Beach," Kimberley said, talking to Cathy, trying to have as much of a normal conversation as possible. But normal was not a word in most American's vocabulary lately. Cathy, I'm going to figure out a way I can come home and spend a few days with you. I'm sure the NSA is now listening in on our conversations, which is fine by me. I'm sure by now they know how many chocolate bars I ate between the ages of eight and nine," Kimberley let out a little laugh. "But yes, sweetheart I'm going to request a clearance to come to see you in the next day or two."

"Oh mom, promise me you will but only if you will not be in danger," Cathy replied.

"How are Afraa and Talia coming along Cathy?"

"Much better than I would have expected. I think they will both be ready to receive prosthesis in another two or three weeks. Nawar is the one I'm most worried about, she's not handling this well at all. She wants to go back to Egypt with her girls. I think she misses Mr. Ahmed quite a lot. You know they are all very much used to having the father figure in their lives, and this has really thrown all of them for a loop," Cathy replied.

"Well, I assume they often talk on the phone, so Zara should be aware of the good news about his girls' recovery. Has Talia's jaw been healing as well as you'd like?"

"Yes, quite well, mom. She cannot open wide or anything like that, but she can now consume pureed foods, and she seems to be swallowing without pain, so that is excellent news. Another good sign is that the sisters are talking with each other and started to play some games together. They both like to draw," Cathy said.

"Well that's great news Cathy, I'm surprised you had enough medical supplies on hand to keep your practice open, isn't the hospital running out of supplies?" Kimberley asked.

"Well we were running really low for a while, but we got a shipment of what I needed come in from Canada via ground. *The Hospital for Sick Children* in Toronto sent us down a care package, we were so thankful to them," Cathy replied.

"Okay sweetheart, I'll let you know tomorrow about me flying back for a few days, I love you. I'll get your dad on the line here, hang on Cathy," Kimberley said, saying goodbye.

Kimberley called Eldon. As he came into the bedroom, Kimberley said, "I didn't mention anything about your upcoming statement later tonight, we can't, you know they're listening to us, but I did tell her that I plan to fly back to the States for a few days. Eldon even with the airspace being closed again, I will receive special clearance, you and I both know that, so I'm going!" She said before handing her husband the phone.

"Hi, sweetheart."

"Hi, dad," replied Cathy.

TXES

***

CHAPTER

THIRTY-ONE

DEDLYN

Unfortunately for the United States, the American way of life had taken a steep decline deteriorating with every passing day.

There remained pockets of relative normalcy in rural regions of the country, but city life throughout the US was not like it used to be. With several national carriers of the trucking industry being hit, consumer goods and food deliveries were down to a trickle.

Perishables were rotting at the distribution centers, with food processing plants shutting down due to lack of supplies.

The US Department of Agriculture forecasted a fifty percent drop in available foodstuffs, not due to lack of supply but due to the general crippling of the distribution network. The hard fact of the matter was that without food, survival was impossible and basic instincts take over. Survival of the fittest mentality was slowly starting to permeate throughout American society, and those with the biggest guns and most ammo were looking to become the kings of their jungles.

"Another month of this Mr. President is about all our country can handle," the Secretary of Homeland Security said.

President Trenten and his Cabinet, along with the leaders of the US House of Representatives and The Senate all gathered in the White House, awaiting ISIF's next message to America to be aired in the coming few minutes.

"Mr. President, our country is on the edge sir, we must find an end to this. The American people have been under martial law far too long.

The suspension of our citizens' liberties and habeas corpus hasn't helped in finding these terrorists. Do you have anything at all you or your administration can offer Americans?" Asked Cole Hallman the speaker of the house.

Trenten sat quietly and did not respond. In fact, he had no answer. Trenten hadn't been himself over the past month, and now with the recent full-scale attack by ISIF across America,

Trenten had become pretty much M.I.A. His leadership had faded into the cracks of the oval office. The fear for his personal safety overcame his ability to lead. The president's crucial cabinet members; Roger Andrews, Mike Lance, the CIA Director Web Moss, Drew McCoy, and Greg Armstrong all witnessed his decline. Clyde Trenten had become like a dog with his tail between its legs twenty-four seven.

"We're working on it, Mr. Speaker. We are all working on it. You must realize that the enemy this time is within, woven into the fabric of our society, it is systemic. We need more time, and that is what we are working on, to see how we can buy more time to root these terrorists out into the open. We believe Speaker Hallman, that once we catch a few, we'll catch them all. We just need more time," replied Mike Lance of DHS

"Let's just hear what they've got to say this time, that's why we're all here," added Lance.

Trenten still just sat, not wanting to be in the room.

The time had come. Eldon Davis was on screen.

Eldon made no introductions to himself, he read the statement as monotone as he possibly could and stoic as before.

Begin Message

To the American People.

We are ISIF we do not negotiate. To bring an end to further ISIF action you will do the following.

The American President will step down. Clyde Trenten will be flown to Iraq and imprisoned to pay for the crimes of past American Presidents against the sovereign State of Iraq. He must be in Iraq by May 31st.

All American ground-based troops and Airforce personnel in the Middle Eastern countries shall immediately leave. The sovereign nations are; Saudi Arabia, Kuwait, Bahrain, Iraq, Oman, Qatar, United Arab Emirates, and Afghanistan. All military equipment remains behind, including aircraft. All US troops must be out by May 31st to never again return.

No American Military personnel shall ever set foot in the countries of Egypt, Lebanon or Syria.

The US Navy must immediately cease operations and leave the Gulf of Aden, the Red Sea, the Persian Gulf, the Gulf of Oman, and the Gulf of Arabia north of the 10th parallel. Also, the US Navy must never sail east of longitude fifteen and north of parallel 34 in the Mediterranean Sea. All US naval ships must vacate the stated regions by May 31st. Comply, and peace shall return. The new world order has begun. ISIF has spoken.

Having read ISIF's message, Eldon stepped away from behind the podium and was off camera.

Shock and silence filled the room. No one had words to follow that message. American foreign policy was now being dictated to the US Congress and the President of the United States by the Jihadist terrorist group; ISIF. To make things even worse, it was broadcast across America and around the world.

"Replay the message, Pete," Roger Andrews the Secretary of Defense said. "I have to hear that one more time to make sure I heard that right."

Pete Jericho replayed the ISIF's message.

"Yup, I heard it right the first time!" Andrews remarked.

"All right, we all heard what we heard, Mr. President I suggest we adjourn this meeting, and we all think about things for the next day or two. I think we are all in a state of shock and disbelief. Brainstorming now will just lead to confusion. Let's all breathe deep and gather our wits before we start making futile suggestions. Let's reconvene in two days," Greg Armstrong finished saying, looking at Trenten to give his approval.

Mr. President? Greg waited for Trenten's approval, but he just sat in his chair like a mannequin.

Trenten still didn't respond, so ten seconds later Armstrong jumped on it, "Okay, that's a yes, come on people let's clear the room and give the President some space to think."

Web Moss, Mike Lance, Roger Andrews, Drew McCoy, Greg Armstrong, and Pete Jericho remained behind. Even Trenten left the room and headed back to the oval office.

"Did you see the reaction on President Trenten's face when Eldon Davis read that Clyde Trenten will be sent to Iraq and imprisoned? I thought he would faint, I really did. I looked at the guy, and he was visibly shaking. My God, we have to do something," Drew McCoy said.

"Yeah Drew, we all saw it. I saw it first on Airforce One when we were on our way to Colorado. He showed his true colors then. But this time he was even more terrified, I think he's about to lose it."

Drew McCoy's cell phone came to life. He recognized the ringtone to be from The US Ambassador to the United Nations. Before he answered he remarked to his fellow Cabinet colleagues, "well that didn't take long," raising his eyebrows, "it's the UN."

"Ambassador Sherman, I was expecting a call from you, but not this quick. I take it that the security council wants an emergency meeting?" US Secretary of State Drew McCoy said, greeting his Ambassador.

"Mr. Secretary, yes sir. The Secretary-General of the

United Nations has called for an emergency meeting of the security council. He wants it now Mr. Secretary, like I mean right now, tonight. He's called only the five permanent members to meet at the stroke of midnight. Mr. Secretary, I need you here for this. And if you could bring President Trenten with you…" McCoy cut in.

"Jim, I'll make it for midnight, but count President Trenten to sit this one out. Let's just say he's not feeling well," McCoy said.

"Well, then bring the Vice President, Mr. Secretary," Jim Sherman replied.

"No, I'm not doing that either, Jim. If I do that, there will be questions as to why the VP is there and not the President. Best they both stay put in Washington this time. You and I both know there will be follow up meetings in the next few days. Let's first get a feel for what Russia and China are thinking okay? McCoy replied.

"All right Mr. Secretary, I'll see you in New York."

Jim Sherman was one who had his ears to the ground. Over the past month, he'd heard sentiments leaking from the White House that Trenten wasn't handling the crisis well. His Cabinet had been shielding Trenten while managing all the country's needs. Presidential leadership was a rare commodity at 1600 Pennsylvania Avenue of late.

The five other men sitting with McCoy didn't need to know the other side of the conversation, it was clear what Drew was talking about.

"So, all hell's breaking out at the United Nations I take it," Web Moss commented.

"I should think that would be an understatement Web, I'm flying up to New York tonight. Let's reconvene tomorrow afternoon providing this doesn't last more than a day," McCoy replied.

"Before we all go our ways here, and do what we need to in our areas, I think I may see a way out of this mess, but I must tell you, not one of you is going to like it. It's the worst-case scenario, but we'd live to fight another day," Greg Armstrong said.

Everyone was starting to stand up to leave, but with Greg's out-of-the-blue statement they all looked at one another and sat back down.

"No, not now, Drew, go to the UN Security Council meeting, and depending on what happens there I will know better. You have to trust me on this, besides I wouldn't be a bit surprised if you all had this run through your heads at some point already in the past few days," Greg said, looking back at his colleagues.

"Christ Greg, you sure know how to keep us hanging. I'm sure we all have some ideas, how about we air them all when we meet tomorrow. This nation needs solutions. I think we agree at this point that it's not about to come from Trenten. We have us, and then we have us, and that's all we must solve this crisis. Let's not lose more fellow Americans. I've had enough bombings for one lifetime," Secretary of Defense Roger Andrews said.

"Amen to that!" They all replied.

◇◇◇

The permanent members of the United Nations Security Council are the five states who won world war II. The five members were granted permanent seats under the UN Charter of 1945. The five are The United States, Great Britain, Russia (now the Russian Federation) France and China. The five-member states are also known as the P5 or the Big 5, all nuclear weapons states.

The other ten nonpermanent members that serve two-year terms were not invited to this emergency meeting.

Drew McCoy and Jim Sherman represented the United States. Allies, France, and Great Britain were very sympathetic to the crisis in the US and willing to do whatever it took to bring an end to the American dilemma.

However, with the new bombings of last week and the gradual coming apart at the seams of the United States the situation had become a global concern. China, although not an ally as was France and Great Britain had its economy closely tied to the US. A collapse of the United States would result in the plunge of the Chinese economic machine. The hundreds of billions of dollars in trade that China enjoyed with the US had slowed to a crawl, and now China was seeking a solution to the crisis just as urgently as the US.

Some of the powers that be in Russia truth be told couldn't be any happier about everything. The Russian Federation was on the verge of becoming the foremost superpower with the envisioned new world order. The Russian economy was intimately entwined with the European countries especially regarding energy supply but had very little trade with the USA other than wheat, and soy, which they could always obtain from South America or Canada. But Russia would join the global effort this time, it had its reasons as it still does. Now was not the time to pounce.

"Secretary Sherman, this urgent meeting of the security council is needed, so we understand what the intentions of America are going forward," UN Secretary-General Oleg Haarken remarked.

" Allow me to describe the lay of the land if I may," Secretary-General Haarken said.

"Please do," Sherman replied.

"Let us all at this table understand that The United States of America has no conflict today with the government and country of Iraq. The two nations are at peace with one another and have been ever since Saddam Hussein was deposed in 2003; for almost twenty years.

The United States of America is being challenged today by Islamic Jihadists who feel that their country was taken from them. These Islamic Jihadists do not recognize the sovereign nation of Iraq and wish to cause chaos in both countries. Their actions to date have certainly accomplished that. Today, Iraqis in Iraq walk the streets, drive to work, pray in the mosques, and lay in their beds, fearing more American aggression towards them for something they had no part in. The situation is chaotic on both sides of the Atlantic. The Iraqi government wants to bring these Jihadis; whoever they may be to justice as much as America and the world do. We now have two countries on peaceful terms both fearing one another. It is a dynamic never before seen in world history, friendly nations; allies, with one another, fearing that any moment one might drop a bomb on the other."

Secretary-General Haarken paused and let that sink into the Ambassadors around the table.

"The one hundred and ninety-five countries of the world cannot all be made to suffer from the feud between the United States, and its enemy, whoever this ISIF group is. There must be a way found to bring this to an end, even if just a temporary end until it can be finalized, and the terrorists eradicated. They must be found. But gentlemen, let wisdom guide you in your decision to coming to a resolution. It is unthinkable for the United States of America to threaten some sort of nuclear attack or annihilation of a Muslim nation. And all because a group of radical Islamists decided to take revenge and then to have the United States, in turn, disintegrate into a complete failed state will not serve well America or the world," having said that, Secretary Haarken stopped and looked around the room.

McCoy and Sherman sat listening as did the other countries' representatives. No one had yet interrupted, it appeared that Haarken was presenting a good case so far.

McCoy then spoke before Secretary-General had a chance to continue. "Secretary Haarken and Ambassadors, The United States finds itself in a position where it must act to put an end to this. We do not wish to harm the world. We also understand that these Jihadists are willing to be martyrs and die for their cause and beliefs. We do not want for more Americans to die for what we believe in but make no mistake, we will fight to the end.

America has not yet reached its end and never will. We will go on and rise and prosper once again, mark my words. America believes in freedom and our

American way. But as you poignantly point out Secretary Haarken, if we both so firmly believe in who we are and how we live, to in the end only eliminate us both, then we must ask ourselves, did anybody win? No, perhaps the battle this time may be won by the Jihadists, but America will have final victory in the war," McCoy said.

The UN Secretary General then replied saying, "Ambassador Sherman and Secretary McCoy, we in the security council welcome your words of wisdom. Great Britain, The Russian Federation, France, and China have put forth a resolution for the five countries including the United States, to bond together and bring the USA back to economic viability, restore the American Dollar as the currency of the international market and bring world stability back in order. This will be a binding resolution to include the G20 nations of the world in restoring world order. The proposed new world order of ISIF will not stand. The governments of the world look to underwrite and guarantee the future stability of the United States in regaining its economic status. We believe once started the USA will recover quickly.

But of course, for this to happen, the United States of America must retreat and hope to find a solution, a final solution another day. Our resolution calls for the USA to comply with the demands of ISIF to buy time so that all five nations around this table can join forces in eradicating ISIF. The United States must take the lead and allow for this resolution to move forward for the good of the world," Secretary-General Haarken finished saying.

UN Ambassador Nigel Balfour of Great Britain then said, "Secretary McCoy, and Ambassador Sherman,

Great Britain stands by you on this. We are prepared to assist you as you supported us in world war two. Great Britain will never forget the leadership and sacrifice America made to fight the enemy. Great Britain owes much to America, and we are prepared to repay and sacrifice to restore your country and the world as it ought to be. Take this opportunity Secretary McCoy and bring your Congress to see the light in giving in a little to regain much later," Nigel Balfour pleaded.

Yuri Maltov of the Russian Federation then presented his country's stance, "Mr. Ambassador and Secretary, the Russian people also stand by America at this juncture. Speaking plainly Mr. Secretary it would be in the interest of Russia to gain power at the demise of America, this is no secret. Russia and America are not the allies that Great Britain and France are. But Russia must be wise in times like this. To see the demise of America and the rise of Terrorism is not in the best interest of the Russian people. Therefore, Russia stands with America and vows to join the world in restoring the balance of power economically and militarily. We realize that American military strength is as strong as it has ever been, regarding global reach. But we see that you suffer from cancer within, and no neighbor wishes to see another UN neighbor suffer from such a fate.

Russia has not forgotten how America was there for the new Russian Federation after the fall of the Soviet Union. America helped us into the world G8 enabling Russia in understanding free markets, capitalism, and world banking. America was there spending millions in securing the loose nuclear weapons helping to make the new Russian Federation a safer new State and then later to join in a blossoming collaboration in outer space. We too stand with America but not without a showing of their appreciation for The Russian Federation's hand in this combined effort. In exchange for the Russian Federation's cooperation in the restoration of the American global position, we look to have all sanctions currently imposed on Russia to be removed. Mr. Secretary by that we mean all sanctions, financial, trade, and technological sanctions be immediately lifted, and Russia will be happy to sign this resolution," Ambassador Maltov finished saying.

The Chinese Ambassador Hong Ming then briefly stated that it was in the best interest of China to see America prosper and urges the American Secretary to agree with the terms of the resolution the group put forth.

The French Ambassador then said, "Mr. Secretary, all the French have to do is look at the American graves in France, we are with you Mr. Secretary, but you must act now, and give this ISIF group what they want, for now, Mr. Secretary for now only. It will give you and us another time to fight. Please Mr. Secretary, let peace come now and we will work with you," said Francois Benoit.

"All right let us come back to you in due course, our nation will consider this resolution, thank you for your support. America will let you and the world know when we are ready." And with that Secretary McCoy and Ambassador Sherman left the UN security council and flew back to Washington.

Decisions had to be made, there were about three and a half weeks left.

◇◇◇

"Yes Mr. Ambassador, I'm asking you to arrange for an open window into American airspace for our company plane. I wish to fly to back to the States to see my daughter in Florida. I will be traveling alone, with my pilot Mr. Billy Simpson," Kimberley said to the US Ambassador to Egypt.

"Well, I can't see DHS refusing your request. I will put the call in to make the request and get back to you just as soon as I hear. I expect this will be escalated to the Secretary of Homeland Security; Mike Lance. He will be very interested in talking with Eldon Davis's wife I'm sure. You know they've wanted to talk to either one of you, but you've been untouchable. Is that about to change Mrs. Davis?" The Ambassador asked.

"Ambassador Borden, with all due respect sir, just get me and Mr. Simpson our clearance," Kimberley replied.

"I understand Mrs. Davis," Borden replied.

Kimberley and Billy left the American consulate and, returned to The Jewel of the Pharaohs.

"Well that went all right, now let's see how long that takes," Kimberley said.

Cairo traffic was just as horrendous as any other major metropolitan region and maybe worse. Kimberley was thankful that she was looking down at it from fifteen hundred feet above. Billy brought the Sikorsky chopper down onto the hotel's helipad and made her way back to her suite.

"Well, you'll never guess," Eldon said as she walked in.

"Not five minutes ago, Ambassador Borden called, your DHS clearance to enter US airspace has been granted. The Embassy is having it delivered here this afternoon, but there's more."

"More?" Kimberley asked.

"Yeah, clearance for me as well," Eldon added.

"That's no surprise, you know DHS and CIA really want to talk with you and not so much me if they had their choice," Kimberley replied. "They have no clue that I'm in this loop in receiving the messages. Right now, they think ISIF communicates directly with you," Kimberley added.

"Well, we don't know that for sure, but anyway, you know they'll be anxious to talk with you if they can't talk to me. They're going to want to question you Kimberley, are you sure you want to go through with this? It could be very stressful for you and Cathy, they may even hold you there, invoking national security reasons," Eldon said.

"Not if I tell them that you told me I have to be back within five days, and if I'm not they're not going to like that," Kimberley said.

"And you're willing to take that chance?"

"Yes, because I don't believe they are willing to take the chance of having more cities explode by holding me, yeah, I think I'll be okay, we are on the same team you know," Kimberley replied.

"Kimberley, I know we are, but you know what the CIA and DHS can be like," Eldon replied. "But you're right, if they wanted to hold you or keep you, they already could have just picked us up right here in Egypt. The first message from ISIF said we weren't to be touched, no doubt that kept them at bay. You'll be fine Kimberley, and they'll look at it as a lucky break to talk with you. You know they will."

"Well, I can't tell them anything Eldon, I'm not going to have more American's blood our hands."

"So, until the end of the month things should remain peaceful, I can't imagine what will happen after the 31st if the US does not comply," Kimberley said.

"Yes, I was going to talk to you about that, I'm glad you beat me to it. I'm talking about getting Cathy out of harm's way. Look, we have three and a half weeks. Cathy will be performing the last critical surgery on Talia in two. I know my daughter, she will not want to leave those two girls without having completed their critical operations. Talia still needs another two weeks before Cathy can go in for the final procedure. Tell her to be ready right after that to fly back to Egypt with the two girls and their mother. I want her out of harm's way, just in case."

"Eldon, do you really think it will be safer here than in the States? You know if there are to be mushroom clouds, those clouds won't be over the USA," Kimberley said.

"God only knows in which direction harm's way will meander in the coming weeks or months. It may turn out that the US might be a safer place to be, but I think humanity is not yet ready to wipe itself off the face of the earth. Right now, the way I see it, Kimberley, I think we'll be all safer here. You need to tell her in person, you know we can't talk about this on the phone," Eldon said with foreboding in his voice.

Kimberley walked up to her husband and hugged him, holding Eldon close to her, feeling his strength wishing this was all over with.

"Before I leave for the US, I want to call Mr. Ahmed over here and tell him in person that I will have an update on his daughters. Eldon, I'm not going to be long, I expect to be back within four- or five-days max," Kimberley added.

"Mr. Ahmed, peace be upon you," this is Kimberley Ashton-Davis.

"Peace be upon you Mrs. Ashton-Davis," Zara replied.

"Mr. Ahmed, come and see my husband and me here at the hotel. We have some news for you."

Zara was mindful of events that happen in chronological order and how those events might be perceived and picked up by prying eyes high in the sky. He assumed things were being watched all over the Mideast, but more so over Egypt. Zara needed to go to the Jewel of the Pharaohs but without being tracked. He was concerned with the possibility of eyes in the sky.

Zara left his house, walked to the bus stop, waited and took the next bus to the Cairo east center shopping mall. He got off the city bus and went inside the shopping mall, took his hat out of his coat pocket and put it on his head. He waited a few minutes and then staying close to a small group of people walked back outside of the mall to the bus stop and waited for the next bus which he took to the Jewel of the Pharaohs. The eye in the sky tracking ended at the shopping mall.

No linkage from Zara's house to the Jewel of the Pharaohs was tagged by Argyle.

DEDLYN

***

CHAPTER
THIRTY-TWO
RETRET

Web Moss, the CIA director, walked into his boss's office, and said, "Morning Greg, is Drew McCoy back yet from New York?"

"Hey Web, yeah, have a seat, I was just about to call him. I want to get together with him, Jericho, Lance, Andrews and maybe the V.P. but not sure about that yet," Greg Armstrong replied.

Just as the Secretary of the NSA was about to call McCoy, he walked into Armstrong's office.

"Drew, I was just about to call you!" Armstrong said.

Walking in, the Secretary of State said, "Secretary of Defense Andrews will be joining us in a minute or two. I had him come as well, we have urgent issues and little time. I'm glad you're here too Web. We're going to need all the brainpower we can get, but I don't want a shouting match by calling everyone in on this."

"Perfect Drew, perfect," Armstrong replied.

"Ah, good morning Mr. Secretary," Greg said as

Roger Andrews walked into the NSA Directors *quiet room* office about thirty seconds later.

Everyone stood to shake hands.

Pete Jericho and Mike Lance should be here momentarily as well," Greg said.

Five minutes later everyone had arrived, and the group's attention focused on Drew McCoy.

"Greg, you were about to say something yesterday… you have an idea on how to end this?" McCoy asked.

"Well, I might, but first I need to hear what happened at the UN."

"Okay, it's a Duzzie. I brought a few drafts of the proposed resolution, you can read it over later," McCoy said, as he handed out folders of the resolution.

"So, what have we got Drew?" Greg asked.

Drew started in, "this will take a while, gentlemen. UN Secretary-General; Oleg Haarken was well prepared. The five hours before I got to New York had given the four other members of the security council enough time for them to come to an agreement and present me with a proposed resolution for our review. Apparently, they already received approval from their countries' presidents and prime ministers, but even if they hadn't, I'm convinced everyone is on the same page," Drew paused, looked at the men and then started in again, virtually reciting word for word what the security council proposed.

"And that about wraps it up, they want us to capitulate for now," Drew finished saying, and taking a drink from his coffee cup while looking around group waiting for a response."

"What about President Clyde Trenten, did anyone bring up the fact that ISIF wants him in prison?" Asked Pete Jericho, the President's chief of staff.

"No, that wasn't brought up, but it also wasn't singled out in their proposal. I don't believe the security council could single it out because it's not something in their control. But I understand your question, Pete. For anyone, to demand that we just hand over our President, well fuck! I just don't see how that's going to happen," McCoy replied.

"I do," Greg Armstrong replied.

Everyone was taken aback with The National Security Advisor's quick comeback.

"Holy shit, Greg, what are you saying?" asked Mike Lance, of DHS.

"Here's what I'm saying. I'm willing to bet that most of you here, probably all of you guys have had this run through your mind already but it was so radical or surreal that you dismissed it," Greg said, making no bones about it.

Look, what this country needs right now is a President, a leader who has the fortitude of character conviction and that embodiment of patriotism which will rise to the occasion, step to the front lines of the battle, to face the enemy saving his people and country. That is what and who we need."

Greg had everyone's attention now.

"If we agree to go along with the UN resolution, our military will be out of the picture. We will actually have to retreat from certain regions. That leaves only one person; the one person in charge of the most powerful military machine the world has ever known, to be our one and only soldier who can lay down in the battle for his country today, so his country can win the war tomorrow," a few of the men started nodding.

Greg went on, "gentlemen, regarding our President…Secretary of Defense; General Andrews, what is the oath the President takes when he is sworn in as the commander in chief? Greg asked Andrews.

"I do solemnly swear (or affirm) that I will faithfully execute the Office of President of the United States, and will to the best of my ability, preserve, protect and defend the Constitution of the United States.

"Thank you, General Andrews," Greg responded.

"It is a Presidential responsibility and requirement for President Trenten to protect and defend the Constitution of the United States. Gentlemen, without our country we have no Constitution. The country is ready to collapse! Our military cannot act as the situation stands now. Only the President can step forward and defend this nation and its Constitution upon which it was built. To protect our country, he must present himself to ISIF so we can fight another day. We'll bring Trenten home when we win this war."

"Wow, that's a hell of a stretch Greg," Lance replied.

"No, it's not. I think the NSA Director makes perfect sense," Roger Andrews fired back.

"I've lived through the Vietnam war, Desert Shield, Desert Storm, and several tours in Afghanistan. I have seen more than my share of death and suffering. I am a warrior. But before I am a warrior, I am a man of peace. My duty as Secretary of Defense for these United States isn't to create war but to prevent war. That is what makes our country great. I am the Secretary of Defense, and not the Secretary of Offense," Roger Andrews declared and went on.

"Planning, strategy, and tactics today can lead to victory tomorrow. I agree that the prudent thing to do now is to retreat. But before I finish, let me point out that some of the greatest victories in military history came about with well thought out retreats. I am a student of history on the battlefield," Rogers pointed out.

"Gentlemen, you've all heard of the Battle of Hastings in 1066. You know of it, but I bet you didn't know that when William II of Normandy invaded England and fought King Harold who had his troops on top of Caldbec Hill, the Norman forces had no chance of breaking through. So after not having success, the Normans faked a retreat and started backing away. The English thinking the Normans were cowards and giving up, left their positions, and chased after them. Once on they got to the bottom, the Norman archers and cavalry mowed them down," Roger Andrews stopped to take a breath, he went on trying to make his point.

The battle of Carrhae, in 56 BC, another brilliant example of how a retreat can lead to victory. Licinius Crassus, led a Roman army into Persia, today we know it as Iran. His command of fifty thousand strong camped outside the town of Carrhae. The Parthian General challenged the Roman army with ten thousand warriors on horseback, but Crassus's fifty thousand seemed to overwhelm the ten thousand on horseback, and they retreated with the Romans following, only to have the Persians double back on them in two flanks and defeat them with a barrage of arrows." The Secretary paused. "I site those two long ago battles to demonstrate that well-planned retreats have led armies to victories for centuries, with many more retreats-won battles in modern wars. So, I say let's go with the UN resolution and suck these terrorists in with our retreat today, to spit them out tomorrow," Secretary Andrews concluded.

"So, Secretary Andrews is on board," McCoy affirmed.

"Let's do this in two parts, those on board with the military retreat, bringing our forces down, capitulating to their wishes. And then the second part will be about the President.

"Those in favor of the retreat...McCoy said.

All hands went up except for one, Mike Lance, Secretary of the Department of Homeland Security, he raised his hand only halfway.

"What's up Mike, tell us why you're hesitant," McCoy said.

"It's not that I'm against this idea, but I think we need to toss a few other options in the ring."

"Okay, toss away, that's the reason we are here," Armstrong responded.

"Us pulling out of the middle east altogether, out of all those countries, holy crap, what a huge effect that will have on the Gulf nations. The instability it will cause might be just as bad if not worse than what's happening to us," Lance said, paused and went on.

"I thought it might be feasible to round up all the Iraqis inside the US, and just hold them all, but then I realized that would, in fact, be impossible to do in the time we have left. Even if we tried, the word would get out the next day, and it would activate all the sleeper cells at once probably blowing everything to kingdom come, so that idea is out the window. I investigated that possibility and realized with over three hundred thousand Iraqis in the US, well, it's not possible in the time we have. These fucking terrorists… they've killed a lot of our people in the last couple of months, thousands, maybe tens of thousands. But then I realized that the latest count of Iraqis killed because of the Iraq war is almost half a million. I don't want these bastards ending up killing a half a million Americans to avenge every Iraqi dead, so although I'm hesitant, I'm in. I agree with the pullback of US troops and make the retreat to fight another day," Lance said.

"Well, let's all not forget that we can always just go back in after we round ISIF up," Web Moss said.

"Yeah, we can unless the Russians move in before we solve this shit show," added Drew.

"Russians moving in on our turf in those countries? No, that won't happen. We, by that I mean our military will make sure that it doesn't. Everything we leave behind is US property. We can keep an eye on what's moving in and out of those countries. If the Russkies try anything, we'll know about it, and we'll just tell them to stay the fuck away. They'll get the message. We're still the most powerful nation on earth," Secretary Andrews said.

"All right, so we've all agreed, as far as this group goes," Armstrong confirmed.

"Now to deal with the President's situation, standing, future, whatever you want to call it," Greg continued.

"The President needs to step up to the plate and show his bravery, and we'll get him back later. That's a sword he will have to be willing to fall on, for his country. It's the oath he took. None of this will work without him doing so, although I think if we pull our troops back first and show ISIF that we are willing to play ball, they may just change their minds on the POTUS, that's a long shot, but still…."

"Okay, and if Trenten decides he wants no part of it, refuses to give himself up, then what?" Asked Jericho.

"Then we have two options. First option; the President's removal from office for treason. Trenten's refusal to carry out the covenants of his Presidential oath to protect and defend the country and Constitution as commander in chief of the armed forces, that's the first option."

"But treason, doesn't that require one to conspire with the enemy? We can't charge him with that, he's not conspiring," said Mike Lance of DHS.

"Well you may have a point Mike, but if he refuses to defend the United States then it could be claimed that when he took the oath to defend the Constitution at his Inauguration as President, he did it under false pretenses, was fraudulent, deceitful, and led to his eventual betrayal of America, and thousands of dead Americans. Yeah, it might be a stretch, but it does have wings.

"Wow, yeah, that might work!" Jericho responded.

"And the second option is the exercising of the twenty-fifth amendment, which gives the Cabinet of the United States (that's us) together with the powers vested in the Vice President, to declare the President "unable to discharge the powers and duties of his office" and have him removed. At which point we can just hand him over to ISIF and hope we can get him out of their hands later," Greg Armstrong finished.

"Oh God, that's fucking terrible!" commented Pete Jericho. "I'm not a big fan of the loudmouth, well not so loud lately, but even I'm not keen on doing that!"

"Well, it's either that or having thousands more Americans dead only to see our nation crumble even further."

"All right, so. we are all in agreement?" Armstrong and McCoy wanted to push this along and get a full agreement from everyone before they presented the group's solution to the entire Cabinet.

"Raise hands," Greg said.

All hands went up this time.

"Okay, no time to waste, let's get all the members of the Cabinet together. We should have the Speaker of the House, the majority and minority leaders of the Congress and of course the Vice President," it's showtime.

"I'll make the calls," Pete Jericho, President Trenten's chief of staff said.

Their meeting was over.

◇◇◇

President Clyde Trenten found himself all alone in the oval office. He hadn't been feeling like his old self over the past two weeks, and he knew it. Something wasn't right with him. Trenten needed to get the cobwebs out. He'd fade in, and out of this funk, he seemed to be finding himself in every day. Lately, he'd look in the mirror and almost not know who he was any longer. It wasn't that he couldn't recognize himself, it was more of a *what-ever-happened-to-you-Clyde* kind of feeling.

He decided to go for a walk in the White House. Trenten walked the halls, trying to get a fix on himself and the world. The world as he knew it used to revolve around him at one time, lately nothing's been spinning around him, not even his Cabinet members. He was indeed out of the loop. Trenten kept walking and stopped at the portrait of President John Fitzgerald Kennedy. It was an oil painting, by Aaron Shikler, one he painted in 1970, long after his death on November 22^{nd,} 1963, but it captured the essence of the man.

Trenten stood and looked at the painting. President Kennedy, standing, his head bent down in deep thought, his arms crossed, with the weight of the world on his shoulders. The Cuban missile crisis, the potential end of the world, nuclear war hours away. President Kennedy a PT Boat captain, World War II, 1943, a war hero.

Clyde Trenten stood asking himself, *could he ever measure up to President Kennedy? A war hero, a man who saved America, stood in the face of terror; the cold war, Russian nukes, could he ever do it?"*

Trenten moved on and stopped in front of another president's portrait. An oil on canvas by Herbert

Abrams, of George Herbert Walker Bush. Trenten stood looking at the painting as it almost came to life.

He thought *President Bush, World War II fighter pilot, American hero. What did Trenten ever do in his life to be a hero he asked himself. Sadly, he had to admit that the answer was; nothing.*

That night Trenten tossed and turned in bed, keeping his wife awake all night. He couldn't sleep, he finally got up and out of bed. He walked back down into the hallway where the Presidential oils on canvas portraits were displayed. He approached the painting of President Kennedy and standing in front of President Kennedy said out loud, "Mr. President, I will make you proud sir," and saluted President Kennedy. He then walked and stood in front of President George Herbert Walker Bush's portrait and once again said out loud, "Mr. President I will make you proud sir," and saluted President Bush!

President Trenten then went back upstairs. He showered, shaved, got dressed and came back down to the oval office. He took his seat behind his desk, picked up the phone and called Pete Jericho.

"Mr. President, sir, how can I help you?" Pete answered, glancing at his bedside digital clock, it showed 2:29 AM. He was taken entirely by surprise.

"Pete, call my Cabinet, I want everyone here within an hour and a half, tell them to come in their pajamas if they need to, but they are to be in the situation room, no later than 4:00 AM.

"Yes Mr. President," Jericho said.

"Holy shit!" Jericho said to himself, "this was totally out of left field."

Jericho proceeded to call everyone, the entire Cabinet. They were all gathered by 3:55 AM in the situation room awaiting the arrival of the President.

Trenten walked in looking very Presidential.

"Thank you all for coming on such short notice. I don't believe this has ever happened in the history of the White House, some of my Cabinet members are sitting here in their pajamas!" Everyone let out a little chuckle.

"We all know why we are here, the country is in crisis and time is running out," Trenten paused and looked around the table at his Cabinet members who there to serve him! Him of all people on the face of the earth, they would all do what he told them to. He continued.

"You are the finest group of people I have ever worked with in my lifetime in serving our nation. Our country is in a crisis. Together we will weather this storm, but while we do, I am not about to let even one more American child, mother, father, brother, sister, man or woman, boy or girl, lose their lives because of some fanatic group, hell-bent on bringing this country down. We are America, we may have to bend in the wind this time, but we will spring back after this storm has been weathered," Trenten paused, then looked around the room.

There was nothing but silence. After a few seconds had passed, Pete Jericho couldn't believe his ears and started clapping slowly at first, then quickly, and everyone joined in.

The clapping stopped, and the President continued.

"That last message read by Mr. Davis from ISIF;

we will comply. We will comply but just for now. I will go to Iraq. Secretary Andrews, you will give the order to start pulling our troops out of the middle east.

Our Navy is to sail to the stated coordinates in the communiqué from ISIF. Our submarines; those that can remain on station to carry on normal operations will do so, and the rest of the sub fleet will be repositioned to counter the relocation of our surface naval forces."

"Yes Mr. President," Roger Andrews replied.

Trenten stopped talking for a bit, waited then continued in again.

"Secretary, McCoy, I want a full briefing on what transpired at the UN. Secretary Armstrong and Director Moss be in my office to provide an update on NSA and CIA developments. Secretary Lance be prepared to review where the nation stands on the efforts in locating ISIF explosives. I want to see all four of you in my office at 10:00 AM.

"Yes Mr. President, they all replied.

"People, that is all for now. We will have peace going forward in the USA, and final victory will be ours when we round these fanatics up once and for all.

Thank you for coming, now go back to your families, and God bless America.

Pete Jericho and the five other Cabinet members who had met in Greg Armstrong's office stayed behind.

The six men could not believe what had just taken place. They were in a word, stunned!

"Well holy shit, I sure as hell didn't see that

coming!" McCoy said.

"It's like he's an entirely different person. Did you catch that? Not even one word of profanity! Trenten must have had an epiphany, or maybe he saw Jesus...Jesus! Armstrong replied to McCoy's statement.

"Well you know I saw this happen on Airforce One. He went into his shell, scared shitless after he was rushed by secret service onto the plane in Miami, clammed right up like a scared rabbit, and then suddenly on the turn of a dime, he was Vlad the Impaler," Jericho said.

"All right, so it looks like we will have some breathing room for a while longer. I have no doubt that in just a few more weeks or perhaps a month or two we will get these ISIF guys.

Then again, something might even break later today or tomorrow or anytime.

We live in strange times, my friends. I'm just glad we have the team we do. And it's looking like we have a real President now," Mike Lance of DHS said.

I hope you're right Mike. But look, this thing about Trenten falling on his sword to buy us time, I don't know where he got the courage to step up, but it looks like he did somehow. Let's all make sure these ISIF bastards don't lay a hand on him till the last possible day, May 31st," Roger Andrews said.

"Agreed?"

"Agreed," they all responded.

Pete Jericho looked at his watch, "well it's 4:29 AM, hell, almost time for me to wake up! Guess I'll just mosey on down to my office since I'm already here," everyone chuckled as they all left the situation room.

RETRET

***

CHAPTER
THIRTY-THREE
QESCHNS

Sitting in the lobby Jewel of the Pharaoh's Resort and Spa waiting for Eldon and Kimberley, Zara felt a certain strangeness overcoming him. Here he was; in the house that Eldon and Kimberley built. A hotel, not just a house, but a magnificent building that housed people from the world over. And yet, it was he who was summoned by the two people whom he controlled through the language of the Pharaohs. That language represented by his beloved hieroglyphs surrounded him in virtually every direction he looked was suddenly making him feel the strangeness.

There were hieros on the walls, on the support columns, hieros carved into the façade of the front desk, even on the tables and chairs. An eerie feeling set in. Zara felt as if the hieroglyphs were about to close in suffocating him of his last breath. His heart rate increased, and he started to sweat.

Thankfully, a few moments later, Eldon and Kimberley arrived, snapping Zara out of his strange feeling.

"Ah, peace be upon you Mr. and Mrs. Davis, do you have news of my daughters?

"Peace be upon you Mr. Ahmed," Eldon said.

"Mr. Ahmed both Talia and Zara are recovering very nicely. Even Dr. Davis has been surprised by their progress," Eldon replied.

"Yes, Mr. Ahmed and I will have more news for you in a few days. I will be flying to Florida to see my daughter, and I will visit with Nawar and your girls. Afraa's eye muscles will regain their normal functionality as she grows. She is being fitted with a prosthesis in another two weeks. The other good news is Talia will have her third operation in two weeks' time as well, and after that, your family can come back home to your loving arms," Kimberley said, smiling at Zara.

"I will notify you after I return in four days Mr. Ahmed at which time, I will have more details on everything concerning your girls. As you know American airspace is currently closed to commercial air traffic. With everything that has been going on with this ISIF group, and somehow our involvement in being this group's messenger, I've received special clearance to see my daughter in Florida," Kimberley added.

"Mr. Ahmed," Eldon then addressed Zara. "Circumstances in these strange times we live in can be challenging to comprehend, perhaps they're in the hands of God himself. What I'm referring to is that your wife and two daughters are in the USA. For most everyone on this planet, the US is not reachable, American airspace is closed to the world, and yet my wife and I find ourselves in this unique position what enables us to fly back and forth. I've heard from my daughter how fraught your wife is, having to be away from you and your guidance. She misses you very much, but we will bring her and your two daughters back into your loving arms, as my wife just told you. Peace be upon you Mr. Ahmed, we will call you when my wife returns from America," Eldon finished saying and shaking hands with Zara.

After saying goodbye to Eldon and Kimberley, Zara couldn't wait to get out of the hotel. The choking atmosphere had returned. As Zara made his way towards the front door, he realized his colossal mistake. Zara had forgotten to include in his instructions to Kimberley not to leave Egypt. For Zara to now send an ISIF coded message telling Eldon and Kimberley to stay put, would surely cast suspicion onto Zara. No one knew that Eldon and Kimberley were about to fly to America, only Zara. He eerily sensed the hieroglyphs on the lobby walls suddenly chasing him out of Eldon's hotel.

"Billy… Eldon, we will be ready in an hour, we'll meet you on the helipad," Eldon said.

"You're coming too?" Billy asked.

"Yeah, just in the last minute, I decided to come as well, nothing's going to happened in the next few weeks anyway and I want to get a feel for what's happening back home, yeah, I know it's not going to be good, but I want to know for myself," Eldon responded.

"Okay Eldon, I'll be waiting in the chopper, see you in an hour."

After taking off from Cairo International Airport,

ten minutes into the flight Billy called Eldon and Kimberley to the cockpit.

"What's up Billy?" Eldon asked.

"Ah, looks like we're going to have the US Airforce accompany us all the way to Florida guys," Billy said.

"What?" Kimberley remarked.

"Yeah, I was just contacted by Lieutenant Bolton, call sign Crossbow, F-22 Raptor pilot of 31st fighter wing out of Aviano Airbase in Italy. We will have F-22 fighter escort all the way back to the USA, fuel stops and all! I guess, they don't want us to get lost on the way over to the States," Billy said.

"You should see a pair of Raptors coming up on both sides of us in the next minute or so, yup, there they are, Billy said," looking to his left and right with Eldon and Kimberley over his shoulders.

Lieutenant Bolton in his F-22 waved to Billy, Billy waved back, then gave the thumbs up. Bolton saluted Billy and had his F-22 pilots drop back out of Billy's view. Lieutenant Bolton was aware of how intimidating being escorted by fighter jets could be to civilian aircraft. There was no need to crowd Billy's airspace.

"Well you know our government is going to want to talk to us," Eldon said.

"You can bet on it hon, we're not going to escape that!"

"No, now that we're out of Egypt and will be in American jurisdiction, don't forget martial law is in effect, we are all at their mercy," Kimberley replied.

"Yes, we are," Billy said, but I really do think we can all relax. Our government and the people of the United States need the two of you. Right now, as it stands, Eldon is the one they're interested in most because you're the one who speaks for ISIF Eldon, but I'm sure they'll want to question you as well Kimberley."

"Yeah, we're all on the same side, I think," Kimberley said.

"Okay Billy, we'll catch you later, is it looking like a smooth flight ahead?" Eldon asked.

"May get bumpy closer to the Canaries, there's a storm brewing off the African coast, I'll try keeping it smooth for you," Billy replied.

Eldon and Kimberley left Billy to fly and chat with the escorting fighter pilots. Billy was former naval aviator F-14 Tomcat pilot. Billy would want to know about the Raptors, Eldon figured.

Kimberley and Eldon settled in.

"We're going to have to tell them about the website Kimberley, and I think we should now that things have escalated to this point."

"Yes, I was thinking about that as well. The thing about all this is that that's all we know." Kimberley replied.

"We haven't a clue as to who these people are or how the website gets updated and by whom to change the King Tut menus, Eldon we really don't know anything."

"Yes, but the NSA will find out how the menus are updated, you can bet your life on it. You can be sure they've scoured our website for anything they could find, but obviously, they haven't yet caught on about the hieroglyphics and they probably won't. So, we need to tell them. That will also show them we have come home to help in any way we can."

"Do you think ISIF knows we're on our way to the US?" Kimberley asked.

"That I don't know, I don't think so," replied Eldon.

Billy touched down at West Palm International Airport.

An entire fleet of government black SUV's was there to greet their plane.

Upon deplaning, they were greeted by the Director of the FBI; Mindy Beaton.

Introductions were made and immediately afterward Billy, Eldon, and Kimberley were driven to FBI regional offices in West Palm Beach. Although the FBI was civil and courteous, it was very apparent that the atmosphere was martial law. Civil liberties weren't what they used to be, and the three of them knew that treading lightly will go in their favor. This was not a time to resist. On the other hand, Eldon, Kimberley, and Billy had nothing to hide. They had come to the US to see Cathy and to help their country in any way that they could.

At the regional FBI offices, the three of them were then introduced to CIA Director Web Moss, DHS Secretary Mike Lance and Secretary of State

Drew McCoy.

Billy was excused and asked to make himself comfortable in another part of the building.

Eldon and Kimberley were asked to sit around a table with the four government officials.

"Secretary McCoy, it's unfortunate we have to meet under such circumstances, but it is nice to see you again," Kimberley said.

"Likewise, Mrs. Ashton-Davis, we do go back a long way," McCoy answered.

Kimberley and Drew were colleagues twenty-three years ago working together at the US consulate in the Bahamas, where Kimberley was Drew McCoy's boss, but that was many years ago.

"It's too bad our paths need to cross at such a time in history," McCoy added.

"Yes, it is Mr. McCoy, but perhaps my husband and I can shed some light on the situation, perhaps the information we provide today can somehow help in bringing this to an end," replied Kimberley

CIA Director then said, "Kimberley and Eldon, I along with my colleagues around this table would like to keep this as uncomplicated as possible. We all recognized that both of you have been under tremendous amounts of stress, as has our nation. Without having to make this uncomfortable for either one of you, I ask you to do the following," Web Moss said very directly to Kimberley and Eldon.

"What we need for you both to do, is simply tell us everything, and I do mean everything you can about what you know about this ISIF group, go ahead, either one of you who'd like to go first," Web finished.

"Okay, I will start, my husband can fill in after. The way my husband and I heard about ISIF the very first time was when I received a manila envelope at the hotel, delivered by a local courier, bicycle courier I believe, addressed to me marked urgent. I brought the contents of the envelope with me, and here it is." Kimberley gave the contents to Web Moss.

"Go on Mrs. Davis," Web said.

Web read the note and reviewed the blank page with the hieroglyphs and passed it around the table.

Kimberley paused, and said, "please, everyone take a minute to read it and look at the parsing I've made, it will help for me to explain the rest."

Kimberley reached for Eldon's hand taking it, looking her fingers together with his as she started in again after everyone around the table had read and looked at the note and hieroglyphs.

"So, you see lady and gentlemen, they communicate with us through Egyptian hieroglyphs, it's quite simple once you know to which alphabetic letter each symbol pairs up with. The hieroglyphs on the King Tut menu, it turns out can be translated by anyone. The letters corresponding to the individual hieroglyphics are the letters already paired long ago on a hieroglyphic chart. But unless you looked and actually wrote down the letters, you would have no idea that an actual message was hidden on the frame of the menu. It's not something that would occur to anyone, I think it's called hiding in plain sight," Kimberley said.

She looked around the table for signs of facial expressions. Both she and Eldon detected some element of surprise and maybe a *how'd-we-ever-miss-this* look on their faces.

"That's all there is to it, the two messages communicated to us, and that I read on the television were deciphered by my wife, as you see, and I read them as instructed to do so," Eldon replied.

"But now that the situation has gotten to this point, both my wife and I knew we had to act in some way to let you know how they communicated to us. Now I don't believe they know we've left Egypt, if they did, they might not be too happy about that. We have what, three weeks before the next ISIF wave comes?" Eldon said, looking around the table.

"Now Kimberley and I want to point something out to all of you. If you could please access The Jewel of the Pharaohs' website on your cell phones, I can show you something of interest, we only caught on to this a day or two ago," Eldon said, watching everyone take out their cell phones and entering the resort's name and then landing on the Jewel of the Pharaohs website.

Kimberley glanced at Eldon as everyone was now following Eldon's instructions. Kimberley thought, "hmm this is going much smoother than she expected it to go, so far the hammer hadn't come down on either her or Eldon and now it looked that they were taking control over this meeting." She hoped it would continue like this.

Eldon then asked, "okay, we're all there?"

Everyone nodded, Web Moss then said, "go ahead Mr. Davis, we're all with you."

"All right, first go to the Restaurants category, select King Tut, and you will see the hieroglyphs all the way around the edge of the menu. So that is how they communicate with Kimberley and me, but here's the part you all will be most interested in. This will be the section we know nothing about, but it sure as hell points to a huge possibility," Eldon said.

"Go to the top menu bar and click on Banquets. Now you will be able to scroll through a hundred different banquet menus, all framed inside of Egyptian hieroglyphics. But none of it makes sense, the hieroglyphs do not translate into meaningful text, when paired up with the letters that I have matching each symbol, well it's just *gobble-dee-gook* lady and gentlemen, *just gobble-dee-gook,*" Eldon finished.

"But my husband thinks there might be something more to it. I initially dismissed it as just proper documentation tracking to keep things in order, but I think Eldon was onto something and I missed it. We think there may be some sort of code in the document numbering at the bottom of each menu that may act as a source code unlocking the messages in the hieroglyphs. We certainly couldn't figure it out. But we know you at NSA Secretary McCoy and Director Moss, your supercomputers may be able to break the code if those indeed are codes and not just documentation indexing," Kimberley said.

"My wife and I thought about contacting our I.T. department, but like their message to us clearly said, if we did that, more death and devastation would come to Americans to our family and the both of us would be killed, so we waited, but the wait can no longer go on. We hope that ISIF has no idea we are in the USA. It is quite likely that the instructions to the sleeper cells are contained in the hieroglyphs, on the banquet menus. For that matter, all the thousands of other hieroglyphs you see on our website, there must be thousands throughout our resort, and anyone one group of hieroglyphs could contain a message activating a sleeper cell, we just don't know, Eldon finished saying.

"Is there anything else Mr. Davis, Mrs. Davis?" Mindy Beaton asked.

"No, that's it, that is everything we can think of, Kimberley replied with Eldon holding Kimberley's hand nodding his head in agreement."

"All right, you have been a tremendous help. Mr. and Mrs. Davis, don't forget, we may be under martial law in these United States, but we are on the same team. Director Web, Secretary McCoy, and Lance including myself, we all understand the stress you two must be under, it does not escape us. We would have liked to have heard from you sooner, but we understand your reasons. We are glad you decided to fly to see us. You can rest assured we will get on this right away. In fact, our people are working on it as we speak, I'm sure you understand how that is possible," Director Beaton said.

"And Mrs. Davis, we have been keeping an eye on your daughter ever since your husband aired the first ISIF message. The FBI has been keeping a 24/7 guard on Dr. Davis, we wanted no harm to come to her, we understand the dangers and implications involved. The stakes are too high for us to let anything fall between the cracks. Now go and visit with your daughter. You are scheduled to fly back in three days is it?" Director Beaton asked.

"Well that was the plan, but Eldon and I discussed this, and we both feel it would be best for us to return almost immediately, we don't feel we should risk ISIF knowing we were out of the country, they surely would suspect us having talked to you," Kimberley responded.

"I think that would be wise, for you to return to Cairo after your visit with you daughter Dr. Davis," Web Moss said.

"You all might be aware that our daughter has been treating two little Egyptian girls who were severely injured, limbs lost and major trauma head wounds in the Giza bombings. My husband and I recovered the two girls at the bomb scene and were able to chopper them into Cairo General just in time for their lives to be saved. We picked up three other bomb surviving children, one being Robbie Fox, the thirteen-year-old boy from Ft. Lauderdale. He is doing well and back at home. The two Egyptian girls' father back in Cairo is very much looking forward to having his girls return home. We are very thankful to Governor Warner for asking the State Department and Department of Homeland Security in granting special medical access visas to the two girls and their mother. We are grateful, Secretary Lance and Secretary McCoy for expediting the paperwork," Kimberley said.

"If that is all, then we will be on our way to visit with our daughter," Eldon said.

"That will be all for now," Mindy Beaton replied. "We know where to find you if we have a need to but have a good flight back to Egypt, and we'll have our people on this."

"Your flight back to Egypt will be Airforce escorted as well, just so you know. We want no harm to come to you or your pilot, Commander Simpson. We value Mr. Simpson's service to our county, there are not many in the military who've earned the congressional medal of honor, and we salute Mr. Simpson for his service," Web Moss said.

"You will have an FBI detail escorting you wherever you might drive while in the US. Please be aware of that. Also, your daughter Dr. Davis, while this crisis lasts," Mindy Beaton added before Kimberley, Eldon, and Billy left.

"Eldon's car was already parked at the private jet hangar. The three of them drove to Eldon and Kimberley's home on Jupiter Island. The FBI followed.

QESCHNS

***

CHAPTER
THIRTY-FOUR
KODBRAK

Cathy was already there when Kimberley, Eldon, and Billy arrived. Cathy hugged her mother and father and then hugged Billy.

"Mom, dad, it's so good to see you! I was going crazy here not knowing what is going on with you! Dad! You've been all over the news, and the TV hasn't stopped showing your face for the past month every day! Billy, how are you doing? I'm so glad you're there for my mom and dad, I think they'd be lost without you," Cathy said.

"No, Cathy, I think it's the other way around," Billy replied.

"Well, it's just good to be back home, even if for only a day," Kimberley said.

"Only a day!" Cathy exclaimed shockingly.

"Yes, sweetheart, both your father and I, we wanted to see you so badly and spend a few days with you, but having met with the powers that be here, it's been decided it's best we go back right away. We'll be leaving immediately after we visit with you, Nawar, Talia, and Afraa. Mr. Ahmed will want to hear how his girls are doing right from Eldon and me after having seen them in person," Kimberley replied, and then hugged Cathy.

"Well the girls are doing pretty good, here have a look, I've got a few x-ray films in my briefcase," Cathay replied.

Cathy went to fetch her briefcase, brought it to the backyard gazebo overlooking the Intracoastal Waterway, and sat down beside Kimberley.

Eldon and Billy went to get themselves a couple of beers.

Cathy placed her briefcase onto her lap and started to open the hinge locks when the briefcase slipped off her lap falling onto the gazebo floor. The x-ray films and other sheets spilled out onto the gazebo deck. Cathy immediately bent down began gathering them when Kimberley looked over to Cathy's open briefcase.

"Cathy, what are these?" Kimberley asked as Cathy was busily gathering x-ray films.

"What is what mom?" Cathy asked.

"These, hon, these things, where'd you get these from, what are they?"

"Oh, remember I told you over the phone that Talia and Afraa both liked to draw?

"Yeah, I remember, you mean they draw Egyptian hieroglyphs?"

"Yeah, they do, tons of them, that's how they spend their days, coloring them just like the real ones in King Tut's tomb," Cathy said.

"Oh, and that's not all, they have hidden

messages in them, Mom. The one you're holding says, I love you Dr. Davis, but to read the message, you have to know the code, it's their secret way of talking. The girls make a game of it each day, trying to figure out each other's messages. They put the code on the bottom in numbers, they told me their daddy taught them how to play the game," Cathy said.

"Eldon, Eldon!" Kimberley screamed! "Eldon! Oh my God, Eldon! It's Zara, Eldon. It's Zara!"

Cathy was already bending down almost slipping off the couch reaching for the x-rays. When Kimberley suddenly started shouting at the top of her voice like she'd lost her mind, Cathy lost her balance and found herself flat on the deck looking up at Kimberley. She started running towards the house for Eldon holding the girls' drawings like she'd gone mad.

Both Eldon and Billy came running hearing Kimberley screaming.

"Eldon look! Look!

Kimberley could hardly talk. She was overwhelmed, showing Eldon and Billy the drawings while they stood in the backyard.

Cathy ran up to join them.

"Cathy, tell your father what you just said to me about those drawings the girls made, Kimberley said, her voice trembling.

Cathy was dumbfounded, she couldn't imagine what was going on, but she repeated her words to Eldon and Billy.

Eldon then said, "best we go back to the gazebo and not talk about this in the house, you never know."

Eldon took the sheets of hieroglyphic symbols and parsed them out himself, but it made no sense.

"The code Eldon, the code, it's on the bottom like you said it would be," Oh Eldon, what are we going to do?

"We go see the girls, that's what we do and tell them we'd love to play the game with them.

Kimberley and Eldon explained it all to Cathy. Now it was all clear.

It was just four in the afternoon, plenty of time to see the two girls.

Talia and Afraa would not know who Kimberley and Eldon were. Cathy would have to handle this gingerly to have Talia and Afraa warm up to them both, and quickly.

They arrived at the hospital, but Cathy thought it would be best if only Kimberley came in with her to see the girls. Two strangers at one time might be a bit too much.

Talia and Afraa shared the same hospital room. When Cathy and Kimberley walked in, both girls were sitting up in their beds, which had been moved together so they could share things between them, like pencils, paper, books, and the like.

"Hi girls, how are you this afternoon?" Cathy asked.

"We are good," Dr. Davis Afraa answered, as she paused drawing.

"Afraa, Talia, I'd like you to meet someone very special, this is my mom; Kimberley," Cathy said, holding onto Kimberley's hand. "I told her about the two of you, and how wonderful you are, and how well you are both doing. My mom came here to see you and ask if she can help you."

"It's very nice to meet you both Talia and Afraa, you are both so beautiful, even more, beautiful than Dr. Davis said," Kimberley said.

"Nice to meet you too Ms. Kimberley," Talia said. "My sister and me we love Dr. Davis, my mom too, we all love Dr. Davis she is so kind to us," Afraa said.

"You know Mom, Talia and Afraa are really good at drawing, look at these beautiful pictures they draw of the Egyptian hieroglyphs, aren't they just gorgeous!" Cathy said,

"Oh, how beautiful, and both of you can draw like this?" Kimberley asked.

Both girls nodded, Talia managing a little bit of a smile while nodding her head. Afraa had a big smile on her face.

"But that's not all mom. Afraa, tell my Mom why you draw the pictures, I bet she has no idea!"

"Afraa started to giggle, and then said, well…we draw them to send secret messages Ms. Kimberley!"

Kimberley gasped, looking at Cathy and then looked at both Talia and Afraa, exclaiming, "secret messages!"

"Yes, and sometimes we don't even put down the secret code to see if we can figure it out not using the secret code!" Afraa said.

Then Talia, whose mouth was still wired, and was only able to open wide enough to put a feeding tube into it, so she could eat pureed meals, said, "yes, here is something we drew today, Ms. Kimberley but this time I will put a code in so Afraa can read my message," Talia said.

Kimberley's heart was in her throat at this point. Before she could get a word out, Talia said, "here look, I'll show you, and then Talia showed Kimberley how it all works.

Kimberley held it together but wanted to run out of the room directly into Eldon's arms, to tell him she's got it. She's got it! But she didn't, she wasn't about to alarm the girls.

"That is so clever sweetheart, who taught you how to do that?" Kimberley asked.

"Oh, daddy did, he showed Afraa and me how to talk in secret. Daddy does it all the time, he has books and books about talking in secret with the language of the Pharaohs," Talia said, trying to smile at Kimberley. "It's a lot of fun, especially if you don't have the secret code because then it might take a long time to figure it out, or maybe never ever ever! Talia finished saying, speaking while opening her mouth just enough enabling her to form words, maybe a half an inch.

Then Afraa said, "yeah, and sometimes you can write a code that really isn't a code, but it looks like one, that confuses people, it's a lot of fun!

"Oh girls, it was so nice to meet you, and thank you so much for showing me your beautiful drawings. Maybe we can see each other again, I would like that very much," Kimberley said as she bid farewell.

"My God, Mom, what are you going to do?" Cathy asked, now that she knew everything.

INN FORMATION

"First thing, I'm telling your father, second we're going to see if this works on the menus in Banquets, that's what I'm going to do," Kimberley answered as they both rushed down the hall, heading back to see Eldon who was waiting in Cathy's hospital office.

Eldon, quick come with me, we must go outside, now! Kimberley almost screamed at Eldon.

She couldn't tell Eldon in Cathy's office thinking the FBI may have already bugged her hospital office.

"We've got it, Eldon, we've got it.

Kimberley pulled out her cell phone and accessed the Jewel of the Pharaohs website and then clicked onto the banquets category menus.

She looked on the first few menus, they all had document codes at the bottom of each menu.

Kimberley followed the instructions given by Talia.

You take the sequence of numbers; the first number tells you how many numbers to count to the right.

The first number was the number four. Kimberley counted starting with number four to the right four spots, and that was the number six.

Then she took looked at the normal hieroglyph to Alphabet pair, but now the sixth hieroglyph in line was the letter A, not the letter E as it normally is. All other letters in the Alphabet shifted over six hieroglyphs as well, so the letter B was now represented by the seventh hieroglyph that usually was the letter F. Kimberley wrote the letters down following the sequence around the frame of the first banquet menu. Then she wrote down the matching letters.

myamiayrprtalgatsmrch211215pm, she went to the next menu and wrote gndrnwfndlnd145pm

Having done that, she then parsed it out.

myami/ayr/prt/al/gats/mrch/21/1215/pm and the second menu gndr/nwfndlnd/145/pm

Miami airport all gates March 21 12:15 PM, and the second menu, Gander Newfoundland 1:45 PM.

There was more information and more to be translated, but this was enough. This was it! Zara was behind this all!

"My God, look, it's got to be Zara! It's all here, and damn clever too! Oh my God, Eldon, what do we do? Do we go back to the FBI and CIA? Do we tell them right now?" Kimberley asked, looking at Eldon with total desperation in her eyes.

"No, we go back to Cairo today," we can tell the CIA tomorrow after we arrive," I want us to handle this first, then the CIA can have Zara," Eldon replied.

"Yes, we did Mr. President. Kimberley and Eldon Davis were very cooperative and extremely helpful. They've provided Secretary Lance, and Director Moss and McCoy with information we are now running through our computers at NSA," FBI Director Beaton said.

"Good, good, and the Davis's where are they now Director Beaton?

"On their way back to Cairo, with fighter jet escort all the way," Mr. President. The sooner they return, the less chance ISIF knows of them even having left Cairo for two days," replied Beaton.

"But you're on top of things, right?" Trenten asked.

"I assure you, Mr. President, we're all on it."

"All right let me know as soon as you know something, we only have about three weeks left," Trenten concluded.

KODBRAK

***

CHAPTER
THIRTY-FIVE
INFORMSHN

"Billy, remember that weird thing Zara did at the hospital, whispering into our ears, that we will not be forgotten?" Eldon asked.

"Yeah, that was strange, so this is what it was all about, that we would all be in his plan, that S.O.B!" Billy responded.

"Yeah, it sure looks like that to me. Zara had us pegged as easy marks, because we had gotten so close to him, having saved his girls, that we'd never in a million years suspect him to be involved in something like this. To deceive someone at such a level as he did.

"But he didn't say that to Kimberley," Billy remarked.

"You're right he didn't, but I think, it's a male-female kind of thing with Muslims. For him to move in on Kimberley like he did with you and me, would have been much too close and intimate," Eldon replied.

"Yeah, that might be it."

INN FORMATION

Darkness had fallen upon Cairo, another moonless night. Eldon, Kimberley, Billy, and Felix met and planned out the next few hours, they hoped it would all be done in two. Eldon would call Zara over to the Jewel of the Pharaohs with news of his daughters.

While Zara was gone, Billy and Felix would enter Zara Ahmed's home. Billy was adept when it came to security alarm disabling. Besides, coming back home would be the last thing Zara would want to do if he was to find out he'd been made. Both Billy and Felix now knew how the hieroglyphics were decoded and how to read the source codes. They all had burner phones for this operation tonight. No ownership attached to the phones, it would take time to track to the owner. The phones could be traced to the location but not to the owner, and everyone conversed from the open street.

"Mr. Ahmed, Eldon Davis, "Peace be upon you Mr. Ahmed, we are back earlier than I thought we'd be. I'm sure you can understand, it was imperative for us to return as quickly as possible, but we did have a nice visit with our daughter, and I'm glad to say I have good news for you. Please come over so I can discuss this with you in person," Eldon said, with as pleasant of a voice that he could muster.

Zara thought *it was now almost 7:00 PM, it would take him an hour and a half to get there by bus. Okay, that was still a decent time to be out.*

"Yes Mr. Davis, I will be there in approximately two hours at the most, I will call you from the hotel lobby when I arrive."

"That'll be fine Mr. Ahmed, see you then," Eldon

said.

Felix and Billy were already down the street from Zara's house, watching for him to walk out or drive out. Kimberley had gotten Zara's home address from Cathy's hospital records on the two girls and Nawar.

Kimberley called Felix on her burner phone, "Okay he should be on his way any minute."

"Got it," Felix replied on his.

"Any minute Billy."

Zara walked out and headed for the bus stop just before the corner of his street not more than fifty yards from his house.

"Yeah, this guy is avoiding the eye in the sky Felix, just like we did, only he's taking a bus, probably to another station, going inside and coming out again, to break the link from his house to the Jewel of the Pharaohs, it's not foolproof but it is a good throw-off move. Just like the way we picked up this rental car in the underground parking, well this does the same thing, but still not foolproof. Those CIA guys know way too much already about you and me Felix, but it never hurts to make them earn their pay," Billy said.

The bus came, and Zara got on. As the bus pulled away, Billy said, "okay, time to move."

Billy and Felix got out of their rental and walked casually up the street and directly to Zara's house. It was already dark in Cairo, just after 6:00 PM and now it was almost 7:30. It was perfect, Zara's home was bordered on all three sides with stone walls acting like fences. The space between the stone walls and the sides of the house wasn't more than maybe three feet, the width of a doorway perhaps. Felix tried a window, no luck, another window, no luck and then he was going to try another window around the back but before he even tried, he saw that it was open!

"Billy, around here, this one is open, no alarm system, nothing!" Felix remarked in a whisper. They were in!

The house was modest inside but well appointed as far as they could tell. Zara had left the lights on. Billy figured Zara left them on to show that the house was not empty and someone was home. Looks like he took some safety measures but apparently not a whole lot when it came to his personal security. Some people were like that. It wasn't uncommon for professional accountants to never balance their own checkbooks, but were meticulous with their clients' needs. Maybe Zara was one of those kinds of nuts, who knew, the main thing was, they were in.

It didn't take very long, Billy made his way to Zara's library and started looking around. There were tons of books about Egypt everywhere he looked. Felix said, "holy shit, look at all these books on Egypt and hieroglyphs, it seems like everything in here is about that.

Billy started looking closer at things and picked up some books, all the books had titles of some sort or another on the front, either in English or Arabic. He then reached for a binder, a three-ring binder, one that holds at least five hundred pages Billy estimated.

The cover of the binder had hieroglyphs on it, nothing unusual about that, everything seemed to have hieros on it. But the binder was different, it was the only binder in the entire room. Billy opened the cover, to see the first page had hieros. There were three rows, but no code on the bottom. He then flipped the pages. Every subsequent page of hieroglyphs contained a series of numbers on the bottom.

Billy quickly flipped back to the first page. He took out his legend prepared by Kimberley which contained the default alpha characters that matched the hieros and Billy started writing down the letters. It read; The rise of ISIF and the fall of America.

"Holy shit Felix, this might be everything we are looking for; the smoking gun, the golden egg, whatever you want to call it."

Now knowing how to unlock the source code, Billy and Felix started translating a few pages.

Billy picked the twentieth page in. He opened the binder, snapped open the rings, removed a page handing it to Felix for him to translate.

Billy started writing down the letters, halfway through he already knew they had what they came for and a hell of a lot more.

Billy's page translated to; Cell 301 Houston Texas, Muhamed Abbat, Cory Longwood, Houston Gas, and Electric. USA 2004. Billy read it and couldn't believe it, the whole damn thing was here.

"It's all here Felix, he kept a diary of everything it looks like," Billy said.

"Yeah, same here Billy, this one talks about some council of ten in Baghdad, and it appears he's listed the names of the council members. Holy shit Billy, we have this guy.

"Let's get the hell out of here, and call Eldon and Kimberley, tell them to hold Zara, we have the goods, and more than we ever could hope for."

On their way back to the hotel, Billy commented to Felix, "Yeah, for all the secrecy this guy puts into his hieroglyphs, he sure is lax about other things like security at his house or even leaving this binder so accessible."

"Billy, this guy believes in hiding things in the open. Eldon and Kimberley were saying something about that remember? No, security at his house, no gate. I think the laxer lifestyle he lived, the less suspicion he brought upon himself. This binder of pictures would be of no use to anyone. Egyptian hieroglyphs in Egypt are like evergreen trees in Alaska Billy, they're everywhere, nobody would want to steal this, but we have," Felix replied.

"Man, this guy is such a Jekyll and Hyde, but we got him, Felix."

"Hi, we have it, we have it all, hold him when he gets there. Don't let him out of your sight," Felix said.

"Well, he's not here yet," Eldon replied on his burner phone.

"We might be back before he arrives, he took a city bus,"

"Okay," Eldon replied and ended the call.

"Kimberley I'm calling our director of security, Mr. Hamed, I want him up here with a taser when Zara arrives.

"Mr. Hamed, good evening."

"Good evening Mr. Davis, how can I help you sir?" security director asked.

"Mr. Hamed, please come to my suite and bring a taser with you."

"Yes sir Mr. Davis, right away sir," Hamed replied.

This was a first for Hamed, being called to Mr. and Mrs. Davis's suite, but to make sure he brought a taser with him, this was nothing like he'd ever expected.

A few minutes later, Zara arrived and called up to Eldon and Kimberley's suite to say he'd come.

"Peace be upon you Mr. Davis, I have arrived."

"And peace be upon you Mr. Ahmed, come on up Mr. Ahmed, my wife and I are looking forward to speaking with you, it will be much more comfortable in our suite than in the lobby I'm sure, our suite is 901. Yes, it is on the 9th floor, turn right when you exit the elevator, and it is at the very end of the hallway.

"Thank you, Mr. Davis, I'll be right up."

Zara walked through the hotel lobby and felt the hieroglyphs closing in on him again. It was the strangest feeling he'd ever had. Coming to this hotel lately did not sit well with Zara, he couldn't put his finger on what it was, but he could feel his heart rate increasing, and he became nervous. Well maybe hearing good news about Talia and Afraa will snap him out of this.

He knocked on suite 901, Eldon opened the door and invited Zara in.

Zara noticed right away that something was not right. Mrs. Davis was not smiling to see him, even though apparently they had good news for him. Mr. Davis did not reach out to shake his hand. Before Zara could utter a word, security director Hamed, came up from behind after Zara walked in and tased Zara on the back of his neck, Zara fell to the floor. Director Hamed handcuffed Zara behind his back, immobilizing him, and removed his cell phone. Eldon and Hamed then picked Zara up and placed him on a chair.

Just as they had Zara now sitting on a chair, but still dazed. Billy and Felix arrived and knocked on the door. Kimberley let them in.

Billy was holding onto Zara's diary.

Zara, still recovering from the taser, tried focusing on Billy and what he held in his hand. Zara's brain finally kicked into gear and realized it was his diary.

Zara seeing Billy holding his diary cried out, "ISIF will burn America!"

Zara had everything in his diary. It contained a complete record of the rise of ISIF, Faaz's creation of ISIF, the Council of Ten with their names along with the sleeper cells throughout the USA, detailing their Iraqi given names, their legally changed new anglicized names. Additional information on each member such as the month and year they immigrated to the USA. It detailed their addresses, their employers, the jobs they held, and their assigned sleeper cells numbers. But most importantly, listing where the preloaded C4 to be detonated was located throughout the USA. Everything was there. Zara could only hope that his source code would protect all the information.

What Zara did not know, was that his own flesh and blood had given up the source code. His girls had given away his secret, in the spirit of friendship.

"I don't think so Mr. Ahmed, if anything, America has burned enough, and the time has come for us to put out the fire.

"Mr. Ahmed, before we call the American authorities to come to get you. My wife and I would like for you to know that you are a very disgusting human being. Perhaps your upbringing has blinded you in understanding the truth about your country's former leader. But the final decision to do what you did, was up to you. You decided to be who you are; a murderer. No matter what you think Mr. Ahmed, Saddam Hussein was a butcher. Have you never heard of him being referred to as The Butcher of Baghdad? You must have, the entire world knew of him as The Butcher of Baghdad.

You hate America so much that you've killed thousands of innocent people all because of your love for that dead butcher. Your hero, Saddam, killed hundreds of thousands, half a million of his very own citizens. Perhaps America was wrong in looking for WMD's in Iraq because there were none in the end, but America was more than righteous in liberating your country from the tyrant that he was. With the fall of Saddam's government, not one Iraqi ever had to fear of being dragged away in the middle of the night for having said something that didn't sit well with Saddam Hussein. Thousands of your countrymen, hauled away to have their tongues cut out, their eyes gouged out or to be hanged in public. Bodies hanging from lamp posts left to decay for days on end throughout Baghdad. That man is your hero Mr. Ahmed, that man?" Eldon asked.

Then Kimberley walked up beside her husband, wrapped her left arm under his, holding onto Eldon's hand, stood looking at the man whose daughters' lives Eldon and Kimberley saved, and to whom Cathy gave her loving care.

"You deceived my husband, you deceived my daughter, you deceived Billy Simpson, you deceived me, and you've brought a lifetime of shame upon your wife, and your two daughters."

She leaned forward and slapped Zara on the side of his face that sent him flying off the chair.

"No, don't bother picking that piece of garbage off the floor," Eldon said as security director Hamed was about to put Zara back on the chair.

Kimberley looked down on Zara as he lay on his side, with his arms tied behind his back.

Then, looking down at him said, "You Zara Ahmed, along with your precious Saddam Hussein can rot in hell along with the likes of Pol Pot, who murdered three million of his own people, running them over with bulldozers, feeding them to crocodiles, burning them alive. You can join him in hell along with Aldoph Hitler and Joseph Stalin who sent his own people, forty million of them to the gulags. Yes, join him in and all other despots in hell. The world has had enough of your kind. Soon you will be in the custody of the American government. The head of the beast will deal with you directly," Kimberley finished saying to Zara.

"Kimberley, CIA, DHS or US Ambassador

Borden here in Cairo," Eldon asked.

"Call Mike Lance, Secretary of Homeland Security, that's what this is all about, protecting our homeland," Kimberley answered.

"I agree with that! Eldon said."

Eldon called the Department of Homeland Security back in the US and was put through to Secretary Mike Lance.

"Mr. Secretary, thank you for taking my call. Mr. Lance, my wife and I have the ISIF leader in handcuffs and immobilized. We are holding him for you, here at the Jewel of the Pharaohs Resort in Cairo."

"Yes, Mr. Secretary, you heard me right, we have him, Zara Ahmed of Baghdad Iraq, the whole thing is very complicated, but then these things usually are," Eldon replied.

"Please have either your people or the CIA station chief pick him up. Right now would be a good time, we'd like this piece of garbage out of our hotel.

When your people arrive, hotel security will show them the way to our suite. My wife and I are also in possession of ISIF documentation that needs to be guarded with the lives of our nation, Mr. Secretary." Eldon said.

"Mr. Davis, this is unbelievable. You have captured the ISIF leader?" Lance couldn't believe his ears.

"Just like I said, Secretary Lance, and I believe the ISIF documentation will reveal each and every sleeper cell in the USA, where they live and who they are, along with everything you need to disarm all the pre-staged explosives."

"Yes, Secretary Lance, that's right. We have the motherload sir, send your people now Mr. Secretary, and God bless America," Eldon said, ending the call.

Billy flew the Learjet 85 in low over Bermuda. Eldon and Kimberley looked out the window with St. Georges coming into view. The crystalline turquoise blue surrounding waters and the pink sand beaches was a scene straight out of heaven itself. Kimberley and Eldon's heavenly home soon to be.

"Look hon, there, on that piece of land sticking out into the ocean, that's where I want our house," Eldon said.

"Oh Eldon, I would love that, it's time for you and me to start enjoying our lives Eldon," Kimberley said, leaning into Eldon and kissing him as Billy circled again over Eldon and Kimberley's favorite place on earth.

"Kimberley, starting today I promise no more, terrorists, no more Russian mafia, no more FSB and KGB, no more murderers in our lives. That is all behind us forever. You know how I want to kick it all off?" Eldon asked, with a mile-wide smile on his face.

"How my darling?"

"You and I are going to enjoy spending our first day back in Bermuda as tourists. We'll take a buggy ride through town, we'll ride mopeds along the south shore, we'll walk the beach on Horseshoe Bay. We'll ride our moped motorbikes down to the Pub on the Square in St. Georges. We'll sit on the patio and order grouper fish sandwiches for lunch and drink a

Bermuda Dark and Stormy, or maybe two or three. Eldon declared, kissing Kimberley on her lips.

"That sounds absolutely wonderful Eldon, and by the way, I do have to admit, that I prefer it dark and stormy, just for your *Inn formation*"

INFORMSHN

The End.

FRANK JULIUS BOOKS

BLOOD DICE

(Historical Fiction – Crime Suspense Thriller)

MOSAIC LIFE TILES

(Autobiographic Anthology Series 1)

THE RED JEWEL

(Historical Fiction – Crime Suspense Thriller)

INN FORMATION

(Historical Fiction – Crime Suspense Thriller)

MOSAIC LIFE SQUARES

(Autobiographic Anthology Series 2)

COMING SUMMER 2019

About the Author

Frank Julius is the author of *Blood Dice and The Red Jewel.* His new novel, *Inn Formation* is the third in his trilogy centered on the international resort hotel and casino industry. His autobiography, *Mosaic Life Tiles* is the first in a planned series of short stories.

He is a veteran of the hotel business having started his career as a bellhop and then progressing to corporate level multi property financial controllership responsibilities. With an international background covering North America, the Caribbean, parts of Europe, and Russia he exposes the industry's dark side in his imaginative works of historical fiction.

Frank Julius immigrated to Canada as a political refugee from Communist Hungary in 1956. He is an avid motorcycle enthusiast and nature photographer. He now lives in the cottage country region of Ontario.

***

INN FORMATION

FRANK JULIUS BOOKS

READER REVIEWS

AND

COMMENTS

WELCOMED

AT

WWW.FRANKJULIUS.COM